continued . . .

Also by Stephanie Tyler

The Eternal Wolf Clan Series
Dire Warning
(A Penguin Special)
Dire Needs
Dire Wants
Dire Desires

Lonely Is the Night
(A Penguin Special)

The Section 8 Series
Surrender

UNBREAKABLE

A Section 8 Novel

Stephanie Tyler

A SIGNET ECLIPSE BOOK

SIGNET ECLIPSE
Published by the Penguin Group
Penguin Group (USA) LLC, 375 Hudson Street,
New York, New York 10014

USA | Canada | UK | Ireland | Australia | New Zealand | India | South Africa | China
penguin.com
A Penguin Random House Company

First published by Signet Eclipse, an imprint of New American Library,
a division of Penguin Group (USA) LLC

First Printing, November 2013

ISBN 978-0-451-41350-5

Printed in the United States of America
10 9 8 7 6 5 4 3 2

This time, it's for T and E.

"With you, I know I'm home."
—"Home" by ZZ Ward

Prologue

The man secured to the metal chair in the middle of the cinder block room still fought.

That was more disconcerting than anything. The Gunner she knew would've been chill, sitting calmly, watching and waiting. This man was wild. Untamed.

Or maybe these men are one and the same. Maybe you only saw what you wanted to.

He didn't even look the same. His hair was dark, no sign of the bright blond that seemed so natural with his coloring. The dark hair made him look far more dangerous. She'd dyed her hair back to its natural blonde color from the dark brown Gunner had picked for her. It was some kind of odd role reversal. And it looked oddly right on him.

"I didn't know your hair was dark," Avery said, because she couldn't think of anything else.

"Now you do." His lips curled derisively and she wondered which was the real Gunner—

that's how good the man in front of her was. She was doubting the one she'd met at the tattoo shop months earlier, the one who'd taken her in, helped her and her brother. The one who'd risked everything, revealed himself to save all of them.

Jem had been circling Gunner for a day and a half, alternating between talking and yelling and punching. Torturing. Using depravation and exhaustion to make him vulnerable. And Gunner simply took it. All of it. Used it to fuel his rage.

The chair creaked with the pressure he put on it as he rocked back and forth, struggled to get out of the bonds. At one point, Jem kicked it over and Gunner managed to slam himself and the chair back into the upright position.

She thought her heart might actually break. She'd murmured, "Please bring him back," so many times over the past months it had worn a groove in her brain.

Now that he was right in front of her, she was still saying it.

It would've been easier if Gunner ignored her, but he was able to meet her eyes so easily. They were flat. Dull. And they looked at her with complete contempt.

"What has he done to you?" she couldn't help but ask.

He gave her a grin that was more like a leer. Spat blood in a straight line through his teeth and refused to tear his gaze from hers. "He didn't do anything. This is me, Avery. I told you—go to Key and stay the hell away."

Jem brought her in here because he knew that would make it worse for Gunner. Avery agreed, knowing how hard it would be on all of them. Knowing Gunner might never forgive them.

Jem could live with that. Could she?

Chapter One

Six months earlier

Avery was dancing on the bar.

She wasn't sure how she'd gotten pulled up there, but had to admit she didn't care. When she looked over, Grace was dancing up there too, along with several other women shaking their asses to the local rock band intent on tearing the house down. The loud vibrations from the bass and drums, the sexy screech of the lead singer thrummed through her body and seemed to go straight through to her soul. It was loud enough to drown out everything . . . except her feelings for Gunner.

Those feelings made every note amplify, and God, it felt good to just have *fun*. There was a time for mourning, and that wouldn't end soon, but they all needed this. Her brother, Dare, was smiling as he watched Grace—Avery had known they were perfect for each other from the first time she'd seen them together. Jem and Key, brothers and Avery's friends, were keeping an eye on them but chatting up some women in the corner at the same time.

And Gunner was . . .

She glanced around for him, found him standing almost right in front of her, watching her. They locked eyes for a long moment while she danced. Just for him.

He'd been watching her like that the whole night. Circling her, but always staying just out of reach.

This bar was down the alleyway from his tattoo shop, one of the first places she'd gone when she'd arrived in New Orleans. And somewhere along the way, maybe even from the first day she'd slammed into his shop, she'd fallen for Gunner. The tattoo he'd given her had cemented it, pink and white flowers trailing along her side, grazing a breast and a hip. It was so graceful. Perfect. He'd marked her and in front of Jem and Key. And things might've progressed naturally between them if not for the turn the mission had taken.

The mission that would always haunt them.

She pushed that out of her mind. Tonight, she wasn't the daughter of a mercenary who ran a legendary group called Section 8. Tonight, she wasn't a fierce warrior who'd decided that she would resurrect the group with the help of her brother, Gunner and the others.

No, here in this bar, she was drinking and dancing. She was a woman who wanted a man to finally decide the timing was right. If she'd learned nothing from the past months, it was that whoever dubbed patience a virtue was a goddamned liar.

The band segued into a new song—still a wild one with a slower, sexier beat. If she jumped down, Gunner would catch her. She was about to test her theory when a guy popped up next to her, grabbed her hands and began dancing with her.

At first, it was all friendly and fun, and then he was tugging on her too roughly, pulling her close, and when she glanced at Gunner, his expression had grown tight.

"Buddy, hands off," she said, because the last thing they needed was trouble.

But the guy was past the point of reason. He was sloppy, drooly, unattractively drunk and although she could handle him on her own—and easily—she decided that playing damsel in distress would still allow her to remain dancing on the bar.

Gunner raised a brow at her and she gave a quick nod. In seconds, his tattooed arms shot up and grabbed the guy off the bar as if he weighed nothing. At first, he flailed and cursed. When he saw who he was up against, he stilled. Which was smart. Gunner was six feet five inches with spiky blond hair and covered with tattoos. A big guy with an expression that read *you're going to get hurt if you don't cut the shit*.

"Hey, get the fuck off my friend," a male voice yelled above the music.

Gunner turned in time to stop a fist from exploding into his face. Still holding on to the drunk guy by the front of his shirt, he shoved the other guy's arm down and yanked it behind his back.

"This can't be good," Grace said in her ear loudly. Because the music hadn't stopped. If anything, it seemed to ramp up in anticipation of the impending, inevitable fight. "Where's Dare?"

Avery pointed to where her brother had jumped into the fray with a gleeful yell, diving headfirst into several men the bouncers were trying to pull apart. Some of the fighting included breaking beer bottles, and suddenly someone was thrown at the bar. At them.

Before she could do anything, Grace was grabbed to safety by Jem and Avery was whooshed off the bar into strong arms and found herself held against Gunner's chest. For a moment, their faces were inches apart and it would be so easy to kiss him. Actually, the perfect place—her refuge from the storm.

Yes, maybe have another shot of whiskey, Avery.

And then Gunner carried her and placed her in the safety of a corner near the back hallway next to Grace and flew into the melee.

"They're all enjoying this." Grace pointed first to where Dare was fighting with a couple of biker types. And smiling.

"For the love of all that's good and holy," she muttered when she saw Jem throw someone over the pool table. Key caught the guy and tossed him back to Jem.

Avery and Grace shoved away anyone who came too close to them, both trying to keep an eye on the men. Avery automatically scanned the crowd for weapons, like knives or broken beer bottles. Because if you were going to brawl, it should be about fists.

"I hope this place doesn't get raided," Grace said.

"Considering we're with the owner, I'm guessing we're okay," Avery pointed out.

"Considering the owner just hung a man by his pants on a hook, maybe not?" Grace asked, and Avery looked to where the drunk guy who'd manhandled her literally hung by his belt loops on the coatrack nailed to the wall. "Is this what college would've been like?"

"I guess we've got some making up to do." She noted that the bouncers had called in reinforcements. Gunner was talking to one of them who looked as if he could pick the pool table up with one hand, and he was shrugging sheepishly, looking like a little kid who'd gotten caught but was having too much fun to care.

"Closing time!" the bartender yelled, and Avery heard the sounds of sirens in the distance. A normal sound for this bar at this time of night. It was nearing two in the morning and Grace took her hand and led her out the back door and around the outside alley toward the front.

"Mama, come. Let me read you."

Avery glanced over at the woman who'd set up shop outside the bar, promising the drunk boys and girls who stumbled out lifetimes of happiness and love and babies. "No thanks."

"You don't want to know your future? To see what's coming?" the palm reader persisted.

Would knowing what she knew now have made Avery do anything differently up to this point? She could confidently answer no. She shook her head and let Grace lead her down the alley, both giggling giddily. Drunk, but fun drunk. Anyone who saw them might think they were two single college girls. They'd be so very wrong, but Avery liked the idea of being normal every once in a while.

Avery turned and found Gunner following them, but he was also staring down at his cell phone and holding it a little too tightly. When he realized she was looking, he shoved it in his pocket and shrugged.

She was more than happy to shrug it off too, especially when Jem came up to her, saying, "Sometimes all you need's a good old-fashioned bar fight," and Key whooped his approval. She got the distinct feeling they were disappointed that it ended so soon, that if they had their way, they'd start another one just for the hell of it.

Key threw an arm around her shoulders and she grinned at him, knew he was doing it to get a rise out of Gunner.

She'd kissed Key at that bar months ago; she'd been drunk, and he'd been too, and although they'd been good kisses during moments of boldness, exacerbated by being free of her old life and by lots of Dutch courage, she'd ended up going home to Gunner.

Ever since, Gunner had been subtly trying to push her into Key's arms while acting jealous when she spent any time with Key. An interesting paradox, but one that told her what she needed to know.

Gunner wanted her.

She also knew that Key didn't. Not really. Because that same night they'd kissed, Key had murmured another woman's name in her ear. She'd dismissed it at the time because it had mingled in with the other Cajun French he'd been whispering, but now that she'd been around the dialect for a while, she knew for sure.

Emmeline. Whether she was a high school sweetheart or a long-lost love, the woman who broke his heart, she didn't know and she'd never asked.

When she'd talked to him about this, Key had said, "I've known where your heart belongs. Knew it from the night he gave you the tattoo.

"I was mad because I figured he'd break your heart," Key explained then, and now he glanced back at Gunner and then winked at her.

She swore she heard Gunner's growl behind her, and that made her smile.

They tumbled into Gunner's place, through the back door that led to the kitchen. Dare and Jem were cooking eggs and bacon and she sat at the table and ate and laughed. The mood tonight was exactly the note she'd wanted tonight to end on.

A far cry from two weeks earlier, when they'd been somber and moping and exhausted. Shell-shocked, really, because they'd rescued Grace from her stepfather, and they'd rescued her and Dare's father as well, only to have him die before they could get him help.

The bright spot was that the man responsible for hurting the families of Section 8 and the operatives themselves had been killed on that island. She knew Gunner and Dare were ultimately responsible, but neither man was talking about what had happened in the room where Richard Powell was killed by his own men.

Now they were all worried about Gunner. He'd stopped taking tattoo appointments, stopped drawing. They'd been lucky to get him to go out at all—he'd been growing more and more closed off, although no one could blame him after what he'd been through.

She couldn't do much because she had promised everyone their space, including him. And he wasn't exactly asking her for advice. Finally, in a moment of what she deemed pure brilliance, she convinced everyone to go away, take a vacation and, most important, make some decisions about the future of the new Section 8.

A couple of months ago, she'd been all alone. Now she had a half brother, a soon-to-be sister-in-law and three other men in her life, all of whom would combine to become a mercenary group based on the original Section 8. Her father had been one of the original members, and he'd been killed for his efforts. She was a legacy, along with Dare.

Would it be all or nothing? She hadn't been certain when the others left, but she'd had to make sure Gunner was really, truly okay.

So far, that wasn't the case.

She'd wanted to take a room in a hotel, give him some space, and although he wasn't exactly himself, he refused to let her leave. And he still used all the security equipment.

She figured that was simply a hard habit to break. That he was still protecting her, worried about blowback. But Rip—aka Richard Powell—worked alone and his men, who'd actually been the ones to kill him, had scattered to the wind. They were afraid for their own lives.

Tonight was the last night before Dare and Grace left for the Seychelles, before Key left for parts unknown and Jem went to Texas, although nobody knew what he'd lost in Texas, and he wasn't telling.

After she'd said good night to everybody, bid them safe trips, knowing it would be the last time she saw them for a while, she sat on her own bed and debated.

Tomorrow, the place would be emptied of everyone but her and Gunner.

Now she padded down the stairs to Gunner's room. His was the only one on the second floor—Key and Jem slept in the panic room on the shop level with all the cameras, because they felt most comfortable there. Gunner's floor held the same sort of security setup.

Dare and Grace were already pretending to be on their honeymoon on the third floor, down the hall from Avery's room, and everyone granted them their space.

She'd been sleeping with headphones on.

Now, shivering more from anticipation than the cold, she stood in front of Gunner's door, wearing just a T-shirt that skimmed her thighs, the neckline stretched comfortably enough to fall off one shoulder. It was actually his T-shirt she'd grabbed one day and never given back.

She knocked lightly and he opened the door quickly, like he was expecting her.

Duh, because the cameras probably picked you up the second you left your room.

"What's wrong?" he demanded. He held his gun in his hand and she touched his wrist and pushed it so the gun faced the floor.

"Nothing."

"Oh." He stared at her. "You're sure?"

"Never more sure," she murmured. She took a step closer, stared up his body. Put her free hand out to trace the swirl of tattoos along his neck and he let her. Stood stock-still, frozen, watching her face.

Her hands traveled along his arms, starting from his shoulders and moving downward and then back up, the muscles bunching and flexing under her touch.

Still nothing from him but the stare. She really hoped he didn't want to talk about this—about anything—because she did not come here for conversation tonight.

Finally, she stood on tiptoes, slid a hand around the back of his neck and brought her lips to his. She closed her eyes and melted against him, the heat of his body calling to her like a beacon.

It took her maybe ten seconds to realize he wasn't kissing her back.

*   *   *

Gunner had tried to back away, but he'd found himself mesmerized by her touches, by the smooth expanse of tan skin that showed around the old white V-neck T-shirt of his she wore. When she wrapped her arms around his shoulders and kissed him, the instinct to pick her up and carry her to his bed and *fuck everything else* nearly won out.

God, she was sweet. He wanted to sink into her and not pull out for days. Weeks. Forfuckingever.

But none of that was in the cards.

Your whole life is a lie.

He ripped his mouth away. She looked stunned. Stepped back, touched her swollen lips with her fingers. Stared at him like she didn't recognize him.

Had she sensed something? Did she know?

He hoped not. There was so much more to his past than Avery or the others knew. Finding out he was Richard Powell's son had only scratched the surface of a very tarnished past, one he'd wanted to stay buried.

"Sorry," she whispered, backed away and he didn't go after her, not even when she turned and ran. He stood like stone, steeling himself for what was coming next.

When he heard her race up the stairs and lock her door, he knew what he had to do. The rest of the crew would leave in a few hours. He lay on his bed for most of that time, listening. Waiting. When he heard the last of them leave, watched the cabs pull away for the airport, he knew he was nearly ready.

It was only then that he used the blade to lightly go over the tattoo already embedded in his skin. Recut and press the herbs into the welling blood to keep the charm active. Most would tell him he only had to rub the herbs, not do the cuts. But Josephine—*his Josie*—had made him promise to do it like this. Said it was more effective.

He'd keep that promise to her until the day he died. Could hear her chiding in his ear, *"That's it, chère . . . perfect."*

Perfect.

She would hate that he'd mourned her for so long that he'd left a string of broken hearts in his wake, trying to forget.

She'd be angry, but she'd understand, and that was the bitch of it all.

He muttered her name like a prayer. Remembered the most important words he'd ever learned.

"From this moment on, all your lies are your life."

He'd been lying for as long as he could remember.

The first thing he remembered was being woken in the middle of the night. *He's twelve. He should be asking what's wrong, should be scared, but*

*it had happened so many times before, he's just mov-
ing. Sleeping on his feet. By the time he wakes, he's
in a moving car with the bag he'd carefully packed
hidden, shoes shoved on, and they'll be in a car heading toward a train or a plane that's also going somewhere.*

*Doesn't matter, because he won't have a choice.
That somewhere won't matter. At least it never had
before.*

*But this time, as the helo hovers over the landing
strip on the small island, his stomach's tight, muscles
tense.*

This time, everything's different.

The bag he always kept packed was bigger
now, held more sophisticated things, but a go
bag was always the same, made the same feelings surface. There was a silence that wouldn't
go away. No matter what he did, no matter how
many good things he accomplished, it would always be there.

His voice mail still blinked, the message from
the private number as yet unplayed. He knew
what it would say, who it was from. He'd already
gotten a call the day after they'd returned from
the island, the day after he'd killed his father.

The threat was so fucking real, and what was
worse, he'd been waiting for it every single minute of every single day for more than ten years.
Once he'd been on his father's island again, he
knew there was no going back.

He'd been caught on surveillance tape while there. His life would never be the same.

Now he picked up the phone and redialed the number he still knew by heart. All the messages that had been left for him daily had said exactly the same thing.

Welcome back from the dead.

Drew Landon picked up on the second ring. "Cutting it close, James."

"Under the wire's always been my specialty."

"You disappeared after you fucked up my job a second time," Landon told him. "Imagine my disappointment."

"What do you want?"

"Work off your debt. If you're as good as you used to be, you'll work maybe five years."

So fucking reasonable. "And if I don't?"

"I can send every criminal you ever helped after you. Ever family member of every trafficker you ever took down will have your picture. And pictures of your team members. The deal I'm proposing isn't so bad now, is it?"

"Haven't you done enough?"

"I haven't even started. But I'm a man of my word. Your friends will be safe. I trust you've been making arrangements while you've been ignoring my messages. The next step would've been a visit to your shop."

Your friends will be safe.

Why should he trust Landon now? Just because

he didn't have a choice was the only answer he could come up with. "You didn't keep Josie safe."

"I never promised that. But I had nothing to do with Josie's death, James. If I did, don't you think I'd admit it? I'm outright threatening your team—obviously, I'm far from terrified of you."

Maybe Landon had never been, but now he should be. Gunner would make damned well and sure of that.

Not that it had ever been the same. Not for long, anyway.

He slung the go bag over his shoulder and grabbed the file folder that held the contracts for the sale of the tattoo shop and the other properties. Dare and company had a month to vacate, and he had a job to do. One he never should've tried to get away from.

He promised himself he'd never try to again.

Avery hadn't wanted to leave her room, not after Gunner's rejection hours before. He'd just pulled away and stared at her. She'd never forget the look on his face, although she couldn't quite place it.

Could she have misjudged this so badly? Or was he that freaked out by what had happened?

God, she felt stupid. Humiliated. And maybe she'd ruined any chance of him working for S8.

Would you really want to work with him if you couldn't have him?

She wasn't exactly in the headspace to answer that question. Maybe after coffee, which she smelled brewing. Maybe it was a peace offering.

It was just after seven in the morning. Sleeping in—or much at all—wasn't happening these days. She was about to cut around the corner to the kitchen when she saw the note propped up on his favorite tattooing chair, her name written on it.

She went over to it, noting how quiet the shop seemed. She ripped the envelope open and found a note in his handwriting telling her that the shop and the surrounding building and garage had been sold. And that she needed to vacate within a month's time.

She wavered between hurt and anger. The anger won out at first. She slammed one of his tattoo guns against the wall, watching it break in half.

You have a month to vacate.

Well, thanks for that. She'd take about a minute.

Although it didn't work like that, because after the initial anger wore off, she realized that leaving Gunner would be like wrenching her heart from her body. Was it that easy for him?

She couldn't bear to think that it was.

He had to have been planning this. His rejection of her last night made sense in light of that. She read through the note again, focusing on his last lines.

I can't be a part of S8. I can't be who you want me to be. Key's a good guy. He's good for you.

"He's kidding me, right?" she asked out loud. He'd left her, the shop. The team. He'd waited until it had been just her here. The lease, the note, it was all for her.

And that's why he rejected you last night. That's why he'd been acting so oddly. This had been in the works for weeks. Maybe from the second they'd stepped foot back in Louisiana.

She wondered if it was because there had been blowback she didn't know about, stemming from the murder of Richard Powell, an ex-CIA spy who nearly ruined all of their lives. But she knew Jem was still monitoring the situation. They all were. If something big had come up, vacation or no vacation, they would have gotten in touch.

Which meant Gunner chose to walk out of her life, wanted to get away from Section 8, and from her. This was a major statement and one she wasn't taking too well.

And then she went into every single nook and cranny of the place, looking for clues. He'd left a lot of his stuff behind, presumably for the new owner to simply throw out.

She knew she'd neatly pack up his clothes. His books. The framed pictures of his tattoos. She'd put them all in storage for when he came back. But for right now, she sat in the quiet of Gunner's shop, unable to stop thinking on the strange, sometimes miraculous and equally heartbreaking turns her life had taken in under a year's time.

It started out with Avery and Dare trying to save themselves from a man named Richard Powell and ended up with them finding a new group who felt like family.

Section 8 had been assembled in the eighties, comprised of seven men and one woman who'd gotten dishonorably discharged from the military for many different reasons. Typically, for not being leadable enough, and one of those men was Avery and Dare's father, Darius O'Rourke. S8 was charged with doing black ops missions for a handler they'd never met, and after one mission gone wrong, the original S8 was disbanded. But when their handler called them back together, disaster stuck and the original team, save for Darius and Adele, were killed.

After Darius and Adele discovered their mysterious handler was Richard Powell, they helped his stepdaughter, Grace, escape from his island. Powell in turn hunted down anyone and everyone who was ever associated with S8 and tried to kill them.

Unfortunately for Powell, he'd underestimated Darius's children and Grace herself. Together with Dare, Grace, Jem, Key and Gunner, they'd taken down Powell.

Or rather, Gunner had. The fact that Gunner's

father was Richard Powell, who was also Grace's stepfather and the man behind Section 8, was a twist none of them had seen coming. So Avery and Dare were legacies. The rest were guilty, as it were, by association with S8. And so the new Section 8 was born. At least until Avery took the practical measure of reminding them what they'd all been through, and how a future in such a group would not be easy. She was telling military men this, and Grace, a survivor in her own right, but it needed to be said. Coming off the high of a completed mission, coupled with the low of Darius's death and learning Gunner's secret, things were complicated, to say the least.

Six months, Avery told all of them when they'd gotten back to Gunner's shop after burying her and Dare's father, Darius. Six months to decide if they were truly in or out of the new S8.

She'd thought more than once about asking Dare what really had happened on the island when Powell was killed by his own men, but she'd stopped herself. It was more Gunner's story than Dare's, and she would wait for him to make the reveal.

She had a feeling she'd be waiting a long time, at this rate, anyway. She was haunted that she missed Gunner's leaving, possibly by mere minutes. Gunner had been pulling away faster than any of them had been able to reel him in. And now he was running.

When Avery first met Gunner, she'd been running too, first from the police and then from the men Richard Powell sent to kill her.

Richard Powell, who'd been responsible for the deaths of both her mother and her father.

Richard Powell, the biological father of the man she'd fallen in love with.

Trying to reconcile Gunner to that monster who'd made sure she'd only met her father long enough to hold his hand while he died . . . it was impossible.

Grace was adopted by Richard Powell, but Gunner was his blood.

God, what a complicated mess, hampered by the fact that she was more worried about Gunner and what all of this had done to him. She knew he was nothing like Powell. She had a feeling he wasn't as sure, and it was breaking her heart.

They'd grown close in a very short period of time. Danger and proximity often did that to people, but what happened between them was more than that. She'd never felt this way about any man before him. And she felt closer to understanding many of her mother's decisions because of that.

Everything was in limbo, with all of them deciding whether they were ready to take this on. And they all needed time to tie up loose ends, get their heads together. Because once they started working, downtime wasn't going to be as free.

If they decided to be a part of the new Section 8. She'd known there might be hesitancy, but she hadn't figured any of them would quit outright. Not like this.

Dare had taken Grace to the Seychelles. Key hadn't mentioned where he was going, but knew he'd stay in touch with his brother, Jem, who was spending time in Texas.

She didn't bother to ask why. With Jem, it wasn't so much why, but rather *why not?*

Jem, who'd been the most reluctant to leave her behind. "Worried about you, kid," he'd told her a couple of nights ago.

"Who're you calling kid?"

He'd laughed, then handed her a phone.

"What's this?"

"A phone."

"Jem, I have a phone."

"Not like this, you don't. You call me, any fucking time. Got it?"

"You're worried."

"Very." He'd glanced toward Gunner, who'd been on the computer, not talking to any of them, not joining in their conversation. There, but not there, the way he'd been the entire month. "Something's up."

"Well, yeah, after what he's been through . . ."

"Something's. Up." He'd stared at her. "You call me. Dig?"

"Dig," she'd said, although barely able to with

a straight face. Now she was never so grateful for what she'd dubbed the bat phone in her entire life. She'd hold on to it like a lifeline and pray that Gunner would come to his senses. Because it was never too late.

Chapter Two

For the past three weeks, Avery had walked around in a daze. Every time she saw a tall, blond man from the back, she fought the urge to run up and hug him. Or punch him.

It was never him, anyway. And while she hadn't called any of the others about Gunner's disappearance, she'd finally worked up the courage to visit someone who might be able to give her insight.

Being able and being willing were two very different things and she'd been bracing for a rejection on the entire walk over, which was why she hesitated outside the restaurant. It was quiet—the dinner rush hadn't started yet, and she knew she had to take advantage of that.

The first time Gunner brought her here, she'd been a fugitive, sent by Dare to secure Gunner's help. She hadn't been back since, because there hadn't been time for restaurants when she'd been fighting for her life.

Now she saw the waitress she was looking for. Billie Jean was one of Gunner's three ex-wives, although Avery didn't know where in the lineup she fell. Billie Jean spotted her and ambled over, cracking her gum.

She was pretty. Loud, from what Avery remembered. And she'd looked at Gunner that night as though she still loved him.

Avery could finally relate to her.

"We're not serving for another half hour," Billie Jean told her. The tight black shirt across her chest spelled the name of the restaurant in bold white letters. Her hair was piled onto her head, some of the loose curls falling down. She was maybe a couple of years older than Avery.

"I'll wait," Avery said.

"Suit yourself." Billie Jean turned to walk away and Avery couldn't make her voice work to stop her. But then Billie Jean couldn't resist asking, "Where's Gunner? You chase him away?"

Billie Jean tried to look tough and unconcerned as she spoke, and failed miserably on both counts.

"I don't know," Avery said, slumped into the booth and waited for the woman she'd once threatened to laugh, to say she'd gotten what was coming to her.

Instead, she slid in across from Avery. "He got to you."

"I guess you know the feeling."

"*Chère*, you have no idea." She called over her shoulder, "Lenny, bring us two beers."

"Whatta I look like, a waitress?" Lenny asked.

"You will when I rip your balls off," she said in a falsely sweet tone before turning her attention back to Avery. "He was into you."

"Nice of you to say, Billie Jean."

"Call me Billie. And he drew you," she said, as if Avery was supposed to know what that meant. "That night you were here, he drew your picture on the menu."

Avery recalled that. She'd been wearing a cap pulled low, because she hadn't wanted to be recognized. Hours later, Gunner had helped cut and dye her hair.

And hours after that, you were kissing Key. "He drew my picture a lot."

But he'd never let her keep any. She'd see them drawn among various tattoos he was sketching, or mixed into other scratches of pictures on the paper he always had with him. She figured drawing was his nervous habit, although he never seemed nervous to her at all.

Billie shook her head. "You really don't know a lot about him, do you?"

"No."

The woman had been expecting a challenge, not the deflated answer she'd received. It softened her features for the moment. When Lenny put the beers down, still grumbling, Billie clinked the neck of her bottle against Avery's, like a fragile peace offering before both women took healthy swigs.

Finally, Billie said, "Look, Gunner never drew me. Not his other two ex-wives either. Never gave an explanation, but hey, he's not with any of us."

"And he's not *with me* either."

"You sure?"

"He never even kissed me." She left out the part about her humiliating attempt.

The look on Billie's face told the story. "He loves you, *chère*. Make no mistake of that."

"Where would he go?"

Billie's face twisted. "When Gunner goes, he just goes. I think he had a secret life I didn't know about—one that was always more important than me."

"Are all his exes here?"

"Three of us are. Well, the first is too, but she's passed on."

"The first?"

The ghost of a smile twisted Billie's lips. "You didn't know. We're not supposed to. He never talked about her. It's one of those stories that starts as a rumor and gets passed around, although the details are really sketchy and change depending on who's doing the telling. But the common thread was that she was the one true love of his life. We all thought we'd be the next, but . . ." She spread her fingers on the table in front of her and stared down at the wedding band. "I still wear it. I think it brings me good luck, as crazy as that sounds."

"It doesn't sound crazy at all," Avery whispered. "Will you tell me about the first one? Everything and anything you know?"

Billie sighed, pointed to the beers. "You're going to need more of these."

Four hours, several beers and a full dinner later, Avery said good-bye to Billie and decided to walk back to the apartment she'd rented in this quarter to clear her head. She only had a couple of days left before the new owner took possession of Gunner's place, and she still had some packing up to do there. But she hadn't been able to bring herself to sleep there since the day he'd left. Too many ghosts.

Her conversation with Billie spun through her mind as she clipped along the darkened streets, the revelers just starting to come out for the night.

She'd forgotten it was a Saturday. Date night, she thought bitterly, as men and women—and men and men—walked by her, hand in hand. She stuffed her own hands into the pockets of her jeans and tried to picture a younger Gunner, running around New Orleans.

The rumors were plentiful, the gist too similar

to be denied despite a few disparities. Gunner had been married young—most mentioned nineteen—and he'd come home one night and found his young wife had been murdered while he'd been gone.

"Some people say it happened here, in Louisiana," Billie had said. "But I don't think that's true at all. How could he come back here and no one recognize him?"

Because people change, Avery thought, but she hadn't said it out loud. Thought about the tattoos covering him. That protective armor would've taken years, was still a work in progress. But a nineteen-year-old could turn into a warrior with the right training. Gunner had certainly had more than his share.

And more than his share of tragedy. She'd thought having Richard Powell as a father was the worst thing that could've happened to him. Now she realized that might've only been the beginning, because Billie had also shared the information that the police had liked Gunner for the killing. Billie refused to believe that—Avery couldn't either, but she was still furious that he would leave instead of confiding in her.

"Dammit, Gunner," she bit out. A random couple turned to look at her and she couldn't help smiling back at them, especially liking when they scurried off.

She was more than halfway home when she

had a suspicion she was being followed. With a block to go, she was sure of it. She wound around the streets several more times, popping in and out of shops, going out back doors and finally sliding into her building past a man headed out with luggage who held the door for her.

Perfect. She hit the stairs instead of the elevator, went inside and breathed a sigh of relief when the buzz of the alarm greeted her. She turned it off as she locked up behind her. She leaned against the wall for a brief moment, listening to see if she heard footsteps.

Nothing.

"You are extra paranoid tonight," she chided herself. She ran her hands through her hair, stopping to massage her temples. She'd pay for those few drinks tonight. Time for ibuprofen and sleep.

She stripped her shirt off on the way to the bathroom. She'd spilled hot sauce on it. She kicked off her shoes too, and stopped, because a shiver went through her body.

She turned around quickly, but no one was there. Because no one could be there. The place was locked down tight. It was all the stories from Billie. The superstitions she'd talked about too. The lore and the bayous were enough to make anyone a little loopy.

She shimmied out of her jeans, went into the bathroom, the tile cool under her feet. She leaned over the bathroom sink to splash cold water on her face. She held on to the sides of the sink after she did so, letting the water run off her face, down her neck. She splashed the water a few more times, grabbed the towel and blotted herself dry.

When she looked into her reflection in the mirror, Gunner was standing behind her.

Gunner.

Here.

Gunner.

Following you.

Her mind raced, but anger was the strongest emotion. She grappled for something to hit him with, but he was fast. Strong. He'd pinned her body to his, even as she struggled.

"That was you behind me."

"You need to learn better E&E." God, his voice sounded deeper, the drawl thicker, sliding across her skin like a caress.

She had it bad, dammit. And she didn't want to. "I don't need to learn anything from you."

His laugh vibrated through her. She'd spent the past weeks wavering between hating him and missing him, and now that she had him, she didn't know what the hell to do with him.

He was obviously more prepared, seemed to know exactly what to do with her. At least, what he wanted to do. His hand was on her breast and she was conscious of being half naked in front of him in a way she had never been.

Her nipple hardened under his simple touch and he knew, because he rubbed his palm against it lightly while she tried to pretend it didn't affect her. "Let me go."

"Just remember, this is what you wanted," he murmured, moved his hand from her breast to her tattoo. "Am I wrong?"

She couldn't breathe. His hands were like ribbons of fire on her skin. She closed her eyes because the room was spinning. Gunner's arms weren't enough to steady her or stop that. She wanted to ask, *What do you want?* but she didn't, not when he carried her into the bedroom and placed her on the mattress.

He proceeded to tie her arms above her head and to the headboard while she watched, unsure of what he would do next.

He stared down at her before he pulled his KA-BAR knife out of his pocket, ran the cold edge of it over her skin and then slit the front of her bra open.

"Oh, fuck," she breathed. His lips quirked a little, and he did the same to her underwear. And she was naked in front of him, completely, utterly stripped in a way she'd never been before.

His eyes just took her in and there was nothing she could do but let him. She wanted to ask him why he'd pushed her away when she'd kissed him, but she didn't.

And then his mouth was on hers and she

couldn't think any longer. His tongue played along the seam of her lips before he became more demanding. When she opened her mouth to him, his tongue licked hers. It was sensual. Hot. Exactly the way she'd imagined it would be. It made up for him standing like stone when she'd kissed him.

God, she'd missed him. And all of this she'd missed out on while she'd been living in his place, eating his food, sharing his weapons. She hadn't known exactly what she'd wanted, besides this man. But she'd assumed him unattainable.

She'd assumed so wrong, if his kiss was any indication of his feelings. And she wanted to touch him so badly, strained her wrists against the T-shirt ties. But he pulled back, shook his head and then his mouth was on her breast, tugging at her nipple. His hand on her bottom, his fingers stroking the wetness between her legs, and she was rubbing against him instead of pushing him away, cursing him, telling him that he'd ruined her.

He'd given her no quarter. She was bared to him and all she could do was whimper at the strokes of his fingers. She stopped thinking and just let it happen. If this was all the time she'd have with Gunner, she'd make it her best memory. Burn it into her brain.

"Spread your legs for me," he murmured. She did, and his hand moved between her thighs, stroking her. Between the beer and Gunner himself, she was completely drunk. Her body soared. She would open for him, do anything he asked of her. Because he'd come back. For her.

She was sure of it.

But he was angry too. Knew she'd been asking questions. Or maybe he was angry that he'd recanted and come back to see her.

She would let him lead. Do what he asked.

His finger brushed her bare cleft and she moaned, trapped between his body and the mattress. There was no place to go. No place she'd rather be.

"I want to fuck you nine ways from Sunday," he growled.

"Only nine?"

"You're pushing your luck, Avery."

She was actually hoping, praying, it had finally run out if it meant Gunner making love to her.

"Like that, baby?" He circled her clit, light pressure and then heavier until she was moving her hips to his rhythm. She could come from that alone. She leaned up and bit his shoulder a little and he shuddered above her. She heard him groan her name and she smiled against his skin.

"Need to taste you," he told her, and she nodded as his head dipped between her legs, put her thighs on his shoulders and ordered, "Watch me."

Oh, God, oh God . . . he licked her cleft, his gaze

daring her to look away. She didn't, couldn't. He was in total control, something she'd never thought she'd want in any way, shape or form.

She wanted. He licked her slowly, maddeningly so. Grabbed her hips and stopped her when she tried to get him to increase the pressure. But he was intent on torturing her, his blue eyes grabbing hold of her, the orgasm building so slowly in her womb that she swore she couldn't take it.

"Gunner . . . please . . ."

She could tell he was smiling, and then he plunged his tongue into her, burying himself in her sex. He tongued her sex, stopping to press her clit hard. She nearly jumped off the bed, clutched the air and then fisted her hands as she tugged at the binding around her wrists.

He wasn't stopping. Held her hips, buried his mouth against her sex and took her more thoroughly than any man ever had.

Her body arched, skin goose-bumped as she tried to make the sensations last. But her belly tightened, her womb constricting, and the orgasm hit her like a freight train. She didn't break his gaze as she climaxed against his mouth, and he didn't stop licking her, even when she grew too sensitive and tried to pull away.

She was climbing toward another orgasm. She stopped resisting, let her body do what it wanted to. Its natural inclination was to climax again, far more quickly than she'd ever thought possible. He played with her nipples as he continued to pleasure her, his tongue deep in her, his fingers alternately flicking and squeezing the sensitive peaks. She watched the pink nipples roll in his tanned fingers, his hands so big they covered her breasts . . . his eyes watching her from between her legs as he gently brought her down from the second orgasm that made her cry out his name in a frantic chant.

"Taste so freakin' sweet, Avery . . . knew you would," he murmured against her neck as he entered her. "Could stay between your legs all damned night, just tasting you."

Gunner kissed his way up her rib cage, tracing the ink with his tongue. Marking her again.

Every kiss was a good-bye. She was helpless to pull away. Because if this was all she'd ever have of him, she wouldn't regret it.

She didn't ask him why he didn't just stay away, why he was making this harder on both of them. She'd regret the words instantly and they'd change nothing.

All she could do was offer herself to him, drag him back to her reality, one kiss at a time. And then, he began shedding his clothes, and she watched intently. She'd seen Gunner strip down when they were prepping for the battle against his father.

But having him in bed, where she could take

time to explore his ink was a whole different matter. She noted that he was only partially tattooed on his chest, but his back didn't seem to have any skin untouched. He'd also started a piece on his right hip that wrapped around his thigh. Intricate symbols in grayscale.

She wanted to ask the hows and whys behind each tattoo. Instead, she planned on making it her mission to touch or kiss all of them when he freed her hands.

I'm going to make you remember me forever.

He rolled on the condom quickly. Her thighs remained spread and they were already trembling, but she wanted this, wanted him so badly she didn't care. Wanted to make him come as hard as she had, and would again if the tightening in her womb was any indication.

His cock was big, pierced with a bar that went through the head of it. "How's that going to feel?" she asked.

"You tell me." His fingers and tongue had already made her slick and open for him. He eased himself inside her, his girth making her gasp. But although he went slow, he never stopped sliding forward, filling her. Making her squirm against him.

"You like that?" he asked.

"Yes."

He moved his hips and she felt his cock bury deep inside her. He pulled back, let the piercing tease her folds, the metal hot and hard against her. When he plunged inside her again, she wrapped her legs around him and held him there, contracting around him.

The angle he used hit her in all the right places, and her body simply blossomed for him. There was no other way to say it. "Please, don't stop," she told him.

"No . . . intention . . ." he grunted as she held on for the ride.

Her legs wrapped around his waist, locking around his back. This pushed him farther inside her, filling her womb, making her quiver with pleasure. He rocked them both with a rhythm that drove her crazy. She wanted faster and harder, and he seemed intent on making her work for it.

He released her arms from their bindings but then pinned her hands over her head on the mattress instead, held them there with one hand by her wrists and didn't break eye contact with her. That was maybe the sexiest thing ever, because he didn't hide the enjoyment on his face.

His body was slick with sweat. She smelled like him, didn't want to ever wash that off. She held him tightly, her toes curling, her sex contracting so hard she wasn't sure when the orgasm would stop.

"Gunner!" she cried out as she came, climaxing hard enough for her to see stars, her body shuddering through both their orgasms. Because he came when she did, his body stiffening as he growled out a groan and stilled, the two of them locked together in pleasure.

Gunner's stomach growled. Avery was half dozing and he didn't bother asking her what she wanted, just ordered one of everything from the nearest place that delivered and was waiting by the buzzer to head down and grab it from the delivery guy half an hour later.

But then he didn't want to wake her. He figured if the smell of the food wafting over her didn't do it, nothing would. So he ate and alternated between watching her and the street below the hotel. The French Quarter hadn't changed much—damage from the hurricane hadn't touched here, leaving it eerily a "before" to most of the city's "after."

He hadn't been sure what he'd find left of the bayou when he'd returned; he'd been overseas when Katrina hit. He remembered watching helplessly with the rest of his team as the levees broke and the devastation that followed. He'd always consider Louisiana to be his home, since he'd first found peace here.

He'd left that peace behind each and every time he left the state. This time had been no exception.

"Hey, are you eating without me?" Avery

asked in a sleepy voice. She looked tousled and flushed in that way only good sex could make you look. And it was a good look on her.

"I saved you some. You looked too comfortable to wake."

She looked like she wanted to say something, but she didn't. He handed her some of the plates of the late-night snack food so she didn't need to get out of bed and she ate happily.

And still, she hadn't asked him a single question about where he'd been, why he'd left. Unlike the Avery he knew, and that sat uneasily in his gut.

After several minutes of silence, he felt her hand on his arm. She was tracing some of his tattoos. "You told me once that tattoos can be like a résumé."

"Should be," he corrected. "A lot of them are just people doing it for the wrong reasons."

"So what are the right reasons?"

"They're supposed to be a map of your life. Where you've been, where you're going," he explained.

"So all of yours are personal?"

"Yeah. Very." He waited for the interrogation to begin, but instead, she simply continued to trace down his arm with her finger and then, after a long moment of staring at them like she was trying to memorize them, she turned back to her food.

*   *   *

Avery was still drunk—partially on Gunner—
and everything was all jumbled in her mind. All
the questions she wanted to ask mixed with the
fact that she wanted him to stay, needed him to
stay.

She stared at him while he watched the city
out the window.

Had he come home to his wife dead? Was he
accused of murdering her? Who set him up? And
why?

Billie knew none of the answers and she'd admitted that she'd never had the courage to bring
it up to Gunner. She'd wanted to make him feel
safe, which meant not bringing up the past, and
Avery understood that.

It made Avery think about her mother, who'd
also loved a dangerous man. Darius had brought
nothing but pain and eventually grave danger to
both her mom and Avery herself.

But if she regretted it, she never actually came
out and said that. She'd smile, probably without
realizing she did so, whenever someone mentioned that New Orleans made people do crazy
things.

It certainly had made Avery do crazy things,
and looking back over the past several months,
she could honestly say she had no regrets, especially none trying to find Gunner.

"You've been okay?" he asked. That certainly

made more sense than her questions about his tattoos. At least he must've thought so, and she steeled herself from saying anything stupid like "not without you" and instead forced out "Keeping busy."

He nodded, a small frown furrowing between his brows. She didn't mention the sale or the fact that she'd packed his clothes and put them in storage. Didn't ask where he'd been or what he'd been doing.

Because she'd been the one to practically order everyone to take their time off and make a decision. You couldn't pull off a team like S8 half-assed. And she was going to honor Darius and Adele if it killed her.

Grace agreed. Avery knew she'd have the support of the woman who she was sure would be her sister-in-law at any moment. Grace credited Darius and Adele with saving her life. But Avery knew what the men in the group had been through, especially Dare and Key.

She knew Jem would be the first one back. This was his kind of gig.

Is it yours? She never even had to ask herself twice, but she'd taken the time off anyway. She'd kept up on what was happening around the globe, pleased with herself at being able to pick out things she'd have skimmed over without a second glance a year ago. She was in tune with the mercenary culture, could pick up subtle clues. She even found a publication that advertised the need for highly skilled bodyguards.

She knew all about the black ops groups that used the moniker private contractor. And she did all of that in the month that Gunner was gone, because otherwise she'd simply sit around all day in her underwear, eating cookies and being depressed.

She still sat around in her underwear eating cookies and being depressed, mind you. But at least she was being productive at the same time.

But she'd always had a thought in the back of her mind, when she'd sent everyone away, that if just one of them didn't return, this wouldn't work out. Together, they fit like the perfect pieces of a puzzle.

And you're keeping the fact that Gunner ran from you a secret.

She lost many a night's sleep over that, but something in her gut told her he'd be back. He just needed time, she'd reason. He had to deal with seeing his father again, having them all know what an evil man he'd been born to.

That had to be weighing on him, even though the Gunner she knew was a total one eighty from Richard Powell.

He made love to her again. When it was over, she didn't ask him to stay. She wouldn't beg, not for that, at least, although his touches did have her begging.

When she woke, she was alone, wrapped in Gunner's scent—dark, spicy. All man.

Was it going to be like this, Gunner coming and going between jobs? Or would he never come back?

Had she misjudged things that badly?

Leaving Avery behind at the hotel wasn't the hardest thing he'd ever had to do, but it ranked high on the list of things that ripped his goddamned heart out of his chest. It was nearly dawn and the streets were clearing of the nighttime players who would yield to the day soon.

The night was where he'd always been most comfortable. That's when he and his mom used to travel, when he would do Landon's jobs, when the Navy utilized the SEALs most. He hitched a ride to the airport so he wouldn't leave a trace of himself in a cab, and with a hat pulled down low on his head and a bag tossed over his shoulder, he looked like any random hitchhiker.

The man in the big old truck dropped him at the edge of the airport, and when Gunner stepped into the terminal, he felt the change go through his body.

He boarded the plane under the name James Smith with the ticket purchased for him. First class. Only the best.

He gave a small snort and felt the flight attendant's eyes on him. He looked up and accepted the beer he'd asked for. She'd written her phone number on the napkin.

Any other time, he would've found time to start getting to know her on this flight. But now he couldn't pull his thoughts from Avery.

His life story was full of holes, and that was the way he liked it, the only way to ensure his safety, from both the law and people who wanted him dead.

It was the only way to keep those people who wanted to get close to him away too. Whoever knew the full story was in grave danger.

He thought about Grace, how he'd been put out to pasture at Landon's to make room for her. He was so grateful to her, and so sickened at what she'd had to go through.

If you'd been there, you could've made things better for her. He would've found a way, somehow. Maybe they could've escaped together and avoided all this shit.

He hadn't wanted to discuss any of this with Grace, though. At first, he was too much in shock at what had happened and then he didn't want to burden anyone with it.

He was exposed because of Section 8. And now, because of him, he'd be as equal a danger to them as Richard Powell ever could've been, if not worse.

Arriving on that island was a death sentence. Traveling the world with his mother had, at times, been uncomfortable and even terrifying, no kind of life for a young child, but she'd loved him. He was sure of that.

He'd burned her file when Landon had given it to him when he'd turned seventeen. It was his birthday present, along with a new semiautomatic made especially to calibrate with Gunner's hands and eyesight. Custom, Landon had told him proudly.

Gunner sketched along the back of the magazine, in a small space of white along the side of an ad. He'd liberated the pen from the security guard, along with his cash, just to prove that he could still do shit like that.

It had been a long time since he'd stolen. A long time since he'd had to. But last month, he'd closed down his bank accounts, routed the money to Mike and Andy, the two men who'd helped him more than he could ever repay with no explanation, and just like that, Gunner had been gone.

It was that easy. Too easy. The past three weeks had been spent preparing for the job he'd finish tonight. A quick turnaround, but he'd thrown himself into it. Had little choice in the matter. And since he'd been unable to completely break from Avery, hadn't found the strength to cut off all ties, he'd come back. He wasn't sure yet if that had made things better or worse.

He'd take twenty-four hours to mourn. Then it would be time to move on.

Chapter Three

He watched her through the front window of the restaurant. Billie Jean was talking to customers, hand on her hip, laughing and lecturing. Earlier, she'd been meeting with Avery. He'd have given anything to have listened in on that conversation, but he had no doubt as to the topic.

The fact that both women had been sharing information . . . well, that could be very good or very, very bad.

He'd taken several pictures of them together on his cell phone, labeled them *James's women*. He took a few more of Billie now and then tucked his phone back into his jeans.

He had two more to track down, but decided to spend extra time here with these two. They were the most interesting and this town was where James seemed to have the most ties that he hadn't been able to cut, no matter how many enticements to do so he'd been given.

Maybe he just hadn't been given the right kind

of enticements recently. Because now that James was back in his grasp, he wasn't making the same mistake in letting him go again. Not ever.

The night was warm, the water Caribbean clear, and Gunner sluiced noiselessly until he reached shore. The water rose to erase his footprints along the packed sand behind him like magic, and under the full moon, he walked straight into his future.

He liked working alone. No one to count on him, no one to disappoint. Maybe no man was an island, but he'd gotten himself pretty damned close once before, and he'd get there again in no time.

He had no choice.

She let you go. Didn't even protest when you got out of bed and left. And he knew she'd been watching.

He knew the memory would remain like a fresh scar, reopening every time he brushed up against it.

Three weeks to plan this job, to lose himself in the minutiae of something that was, in fact, like riding a bike. He recalled every single time he'd done this before, including the last big fuckup.

Before that, he'd never fucked up this part of the job. This part had always been perfect and he was determined to keep it that way.

He unzipped the top of his black wet suit and

let it hang behind him. His body dried quickly in the night air, but he refused to shiver, held his body ruthlessly in check.

Landon said he'd find Gunner, that he should just continue walking the beach. Gunner did for ten minutes before he knew Landon was close by. Another half a minute and he spotted the man standing alone in what looked like the middle of nowhere.

Then again, he'd always been able to sense evil.

Some men were born with that presence. Others cultivated it and fooled most people by substituting confidence in its place.

"You'll never be better than me." Landon's final words before putting him into the car with the men who would beat him nearly to death.

He was sure Landon had spotted him first, though, and that pissed him off.

They were a quarter of a mile from the nearest houses that dotted the beaches here—most of them vacation homes, expensive, rarely used. This was one of the many perfect places to live for anyone who didn't want scrutiny from neighbors or the law.

"You're living here now?" Gunner asked.

"I'm on vacation," Drew Landon told him. Landon was the son of a small-time smuggler who'd taken over his father's business and grown it to epic proportions. He was ruthless and brilliant.

He was a killer, although he made others do his dirty work.

"It's done?"

"You have to ask?" Gunner handed him the small bag he'd swum with fastened to his waist.

"Yes."

Gunner looked at his watch. "Three, two, o—"

By the time he'd finished one, the explosion rang out across the ocean. Plumes of smoke rose above the water, although it was impossible to see the burning wreckage of the yacht from here.

Landon nodded, satisfied. "Not sorry to see the asshole go."

"You'll leave them alone."

It was a statement, not a question, and it made Landon bristle. "Is this about *them* or you?"

"I made the decision, but there's no reason they should pay for that."

"They killed Powell."

Gunner stared Landon down. "I killed my father. Make no mistake about that."

"You're a cold fuck, James. Always were."

"That's what you like best about me."

"I was hoping you hadn't gone soft." Landon stared at the burning boat in the distance. "You didn't even give them a chance to get on the life rafts."

The luxury yacht was named *El Coyote*, which made Gunner's job of wiring the boat to blow, with its four passengers trapped inside, not as chilling. Human traffickers didn't deserve an easy death. "Didn't think they deserved that."

Landon stared at him like he was trying to figure something out. When he didn't, he looked inside the bag Gunner had handed him and rifled through its contents with a nod.

"Welcome back. This one was to get you warmed up."

"Done. What's next?" But Gunner knew the drill—jobs interspersed with bouts of drinking, fucking and trying to forget. He'd done it for so long it was like riding a bike. The sick part was that it felt natural. And that's what scared him the most. The facade of Gunner, the karma he'd adopted had felt good—right, even—but it never felt natural. It was always a game of pretend.

This is you trying to convince yourself that you're bad, Josie chided in his ear. She wasn't with him all the time like that, just when he thought about going over to the dark side. And this was about as dark as it got.

He *was* bad. Look at where he came from.

"Some people are lucky enough to be born into their destiny—you were one of them. Stop trying to throw it all away." His father's final words to him before dropping him off at Landon's place.

Gunner had never asked why before. At first, it was because he hadn't been allowed to and then because it hadn't really mattered. It would only make him feel worse, and his goal was not to feel at all.

But this time, he needed to know. He was in it for good. "Why did I kill him?"

"Would you feel better if I said it was because he was a bad man dealing in human trafficking?"

Gunner stared him down. When they'd first met, Gunner was five foot nine and lanky. Within a year, he'd grown taller than Landon. Broader, stronger, at least physically.

It was at that point he'd learned the most important lesson of all. Physical strength was no match for mental strength.

"Fine," Landon relented. "He screwed me. And if I let that go with a simple warning, I'll get walked on. You know this business."

Gunner did. A *don't fuck with me* message was the only way. "I want to know the reasons behind every job."

"I don't have a partner for a reason."

"You've got one now," Gunner told him. "If we're getting into bed, I'm getting in all the goddamned way."

Landon reached out and touched Gunner's bare chest. He fixed the necklace after laying his palm over Gunner's heart. "I've been waiting for this for a long time. You'd better not be screwing with me."

"I've been waiting too." Waiting for the other shoe to drop, waiting for everything to be taken away from him. The time was here. And Landon hadn't answered his question about S8. "They won't come after me. I made sure of it."

"You'll do what I say. Just because I tell you why doesn't mean you get to say no." Landon smiled a little. "I'll leave your precious Section 8 alone as long as they do the same."

Could Gunner assure him of that? No. But he'd do everything in his power to make sure he and Landon remained off the grid. Even Powell didn't know much about Landon beyond his last name. The man was a legend, a ghost in a Keyser Soze kind of way. Ever changing.

The fact that Gunner had lived after seeing his face and leaving his payroll made him something of a legend in these circles too. A lot of people thought that James Connor-Powell didn't exist.

Gunner didn't let them ever think differently.

"Keep in mind, if you go missing again, I'll hunt you down. And you'd better pray I find you captured and not running."

"Understood."

"I know you hate me, James, but this is who you are. This is your legacy. Embrace it, the way your parents did. You do realize that the only time you get into trouble is when you fight what's natural to you, right? When you try to break away from your roots, innocent people die."

Gunner looked down to see the blood running

down his hand. He'd probably cut it along the hull of the ship, had been lucky not to attract sharks to him.

He glanced up at Landon. Any *more* sharks, at least.

He looked back down, watched the blood drip off his fingers onto the sand.

Blood and sand.

That's all it would be from now on. Blood and sand.

Chapter Four

Being inside Gunner's shop was like taking a bullet every time Avery walked inside. It hurt worse knowing this would be the last time.

Back at the hotel, her suitcase was packed, her ticket booked to some island resort where she could drink and sun and lose herself. Follow her own advice to the others.

Her flight left in two hours and there was no turning back. No reason to, especially now, she thought from where she stood in the center of the room, close to the table where Gunner had tattooed her.

She'd thought about calling Grace. Grace, of all people, knew what Gunner must've grown up with. Gunner's father had taken her in, adopted her and then attempted to destroy her, just because he wanted to see if she could survive.

But she'd tried to talk to him and Gunner hadn't wanted to listen. If Grace couldn't have convinced him to stay, to save him from his past,

Avery probably shouldn't have thought she could've been the one to do it either.

But she had. Still did.

And you let him go. Again.

"It was for the best," she said firmly, her hand rubbing the soft leather of his favorite tattoo chair. "It was the right thing to do."

But a small voice inside her kept telling her she was very wrong.

She loved it here. The closer she'd gotten to Gunner, the more she understood just how much of himself he'd poured into this place. It was apparent in everything, the photos of his art, framed. The meticulous attention to detail in order to make the place look sleek and modern and still inviting. A place that could combine his love of tattooing with a place where he felt comfortable and secure.

It made her sad at just how wired the place was. She hadn't thought anything of it before, because she'd needed the security measures. She'd thought it was simply a part of his job as a mercenary to have such a wicked system in place.

But all of this ran so much deeper.

She let her fingers trail over the steel breakfast table that somehow never seemed cold or imposing, but rather, masculine, always filled with food. A place to gather.

Gunner had truly left a home—his home—

behind. And there was only one reason she could think of that would make a man like Gunner, who wasn't scared of anyone, do that.

Someone hadn't just threatened Gunner—they'd threatened S8, and maybe her specifically.

She thought about what Billie said about knowing Gunner was in love with her. If she chose to believe that, she'd know that he would go to the absolute ends of the earth to protect the people he loved.

She hoped it was the truth. Because the alternative, that Gunner had run from her, rejected her because he didn't want anything to do with S8 or worse—her—was an unbearable thought.

It looked so empty with his things in storage, but she wouldn't let just anyone touch them, never mind throw them out.

One last look. She'd allow herself that before she left.

He can re-create this somewhere else, she reassured herself. She'd thought about taking a picture, but the reminder would hurt too much. It was the way things had been, not the way they were.

But a not so small part of her had been hoping he'd walk through the front door, telling her he'd made a mistake. That he'd reconsidered.

A knock on the door literally made her start. She turned toward it, had pulled the shade up from the glass to throw more light in, the way he'd liked it. She saw the man from down the street who owned the flower shop.

You're a moron, she told herself, and waved to Alfred.

"For you, doll-face," he said with a twinkle in his eyes when she opened the door. "I haven't seen Gunner around in a while, but I knew I was right about you two being right for each other."

He motioned to the flowers as he said that last part—could they really be from Gunner? "Thanks, Alfred."

"No problem. The delivery guy left these behind. Didn't want to leave them overnight."

He deposited the beautiful orchid plant in her hands. "Good night, *Jolie Blonde*."

She'd gotten rid of the dark hair this morning, gone back to her original blonde color but decided she'd keep it short. It suited her, framed her face.

Of course, the last time she'd looked in the mirror, she'd looked so haunted she'd been forced to turn away from her own reflection. She locked the door with one hand, the other balancing the glass vase, and then walked toward the middle of the shop.

And then she froze. She was inside what could be called one of the safest structures, built to withstand bombs and bullets. From the outside.

But the vase she held in her hands . . . there was nothing in this building that could protect her from that.

She'd accepted the flowers because she knew the man. None of this made sense.

She wasn't trained in explosives, not until Key had given her the down-and-dirty crash course. She knew things to watch out for—tripwires and the like—knew how to check her room after having been out. They were all vulnerable with Gunner gone, no matter how much he'd wanted the opposite to be true.

The locks had been changed and security-updated. She hadn't thought a flower delivery would kill her. She stared inside the glass, muted by cellophane wrapping, and she froze in place. Half fear, half survival.

She was alone, holding a bomb that would blow up the second she put it down.

Holding a bomb that was set to blow in ten minutes no matter what, with a note that wasn't inside an envelope, allowing her easily to read what was written in Gunner's own handwriting.

Never forget.

Chapter Five

Smoke rose from the fire on the half-decimated yacht and covered the beach, thanks to the strong crosswinds. It got in his eyes and throat, and even after Landon left him there, telling him he was *a crazy son of a bitch*, Gunner stayed.

He inhaled deeply and he was right back in that place again, disoriented, in pain . . . If he concentrated hard enough, he could hear the chanting.

He wanted to give up, but he wasn't built like that, even though he was dying. Everything was hazy when he opened his eyes. The first thing he saw were dark eyes, dark hair. He tried to focus on the face to see if he recognized it, reached out to make contact.

He hadn't realized he had a woman's arm in a death grip. She was a stranger, and she didn't struggle, looked unconcerned and somehow concerned for him at the same time.

"Am I dead?" he asked in a raw voice because he really couldn't tell. He was floating, suspended weight-

lessly, suspected that if he was alive, he'd be in excruciating pain.

The dark-haired woman blinked. Smiled. "You're very much alive, chère."

"Stay with me."

"I will. Even if you don't know I'm here," she assured him as his mind clouded and the heavy smoke drifted back over him.

"Are they trying to kill me?"

"They're healing you. Protecting you," she murmured. The buzzing sound began again, etching what would turn out to be his first tattoo into his biceps.

"Who left you to die?" she asked when he woke again, even as she laid a cloth across his forehead and chest. The scent soothed him, the sound of her voice more so.

"It was my only way out."

"You didn't answer my question."

"There are things you're better off not knowing." He glanced at his biceps. "You tattooed me?"

"It's an old custom to ward off evil. It's a charm. We have to press it with charms to keep the spell working, like we did before it healed. It's called a gad—a guard. It's a Voodoo charm that protects against harmful spirits. Some people say you can rub the herbs over the healing tattoo, but the right way calls for it to mingle with your blood. And you, my friend, need all the protection you can get."

The knife remained poised over his arm. He'd never let anyone with a knife get this close to him, but she mesmerized him. "Go ahead."

Fascinated, he watched as she used the tip of the blade to cut him so gently he didn't feel it. He watched the thin line of blood emerge from the ink, watched her graceful fingers press the herbs along the cuts and murmur what sounded like a small prayer of thanks.

"Why are you doing this?" he asked.

"Because you needed help. That's what we do here."

"Not in my world."

"You're not in that world anymore," she reminded him.

The reality was, he'd never escaped it. The call he'd been waiting for for over a year came on a Thursday at twelve fifty-three p.m.

He'd packed, told Josie he was going to visit a friend from the Navy who was having a rough time. And for the first time since they'd met, he'd been forced to lie right to her face.

She believed him because he was a damned good liar. The last words he'd ever said to her had been full of lies.

And the job . . . that goddamned job . . .

It should've worked out like this one. Perfect. Instead, it backfired terribly and would haunt him forever.

The blood on his hands was her blood. He could feel her in his arms, tried to choke out her name but couldn't.

Gunner was still holding Josie when Mike and Andy came in. He wouldn't let go, not until Mike forced him back so he could check on his daughter.

Gunner couldn't look either of them in the eye.

"She was dead when I got here," he said, his entire body numb with grief. "There was nothing I could do."

"She's been gone for at least twenty-four hours," Andy said. "Where the hell were you, James?"

"In hell," he echoed. "I went back to hell."

And Josie had paid the price.

Six minutes. Avery wasn't sure she was really breathing. She was flushed, sweaty, her hands holding tight to the glass, trying not to slip on the cellophane.

She didn't know a lot about flowers, beyond the ones Gunner had etched onto her body, a riot of pink and white flowers that trailed along her rib cage, licked her breast. Magnolias were the state flower of Louisiana, although she hadn't known that at the time she'd lain down on his table and allowed him the intimacy of etching something permanent into her skin.

At the time, they were simply beautiful.

He marked you. Pushed you away but marked you to make sure you couldn't be with anyone else without being reminded of him. And then . . .

And then this.

"We can't trust him. He's been gone too long," Jem had said, just a week earlier. "He's not the same man."

Then again, Avery wasn't the same woman either.

She desperately tried to picture Gunner doing this, sending her these beautiful, graceful white orchids and planting a bomb at the same time. Orchids died and rebloomed, but she knew it took time and patience. There was a lot of waiting and hoping. The message was sadistic.

Unless Gunner hadn't been the one to plant the bomb.

"You're really willing to give him the benefit of the doubt," she whispered to herself angrily. She swallowed hard. Sweat dripped into her eyes and she blinked it away because she couldn't do anything else.

But the way he'd touched her the other night . . .

The room was lined with Gunner's sketches, the first things she'd noticed besides the man himself when she'd first burst in here on Dare's behalf. She would take it all with her, all the portraits and the photographs, the tattoo guns, any last memories of the man she'd have.

Suddenly, strong hands were dragging Gunner off the beach, away from the choking thickness that lodged in his throat. He was shoved into a seat, an oxygen mask placed over his mouth, and told to *fucking breathe.*

Drew Landon was standing over him.

My hero, he mouthed, and Landon shot him the finger.

"I'm not letting you commit suicide."

"That's not what I was doing," Gunner muttered. Landon held up his wrists and showed him where he'd been cutting into his own wrists. The cuts were hard to see because of the tattoos there, and Landon was cleaning and bandaging him, something Gunner thought was possibly the oddest thing ever.

Or maybe this is all a smoke inhalation-induced dream.

Landon was muttering as he cleaned Gunner up.

Gunner in turn pulled the mask off. "You let me go. Why bring me back? There are plenty of men who can do what I do."

"You're wrong. You were the best. I think you still are. Your father might've thrown you away, but I never did."

"Not until I fucked up."

"You broke a rule, and you paid for it."

"And then you paid your men to try to beat me to fucking death. So I paid, Landon."

Landon furrowed his brow, as though he wasn't sure he wanted to say what he was thinking. But finally, he said, "You can't play dead forever unless you really are."

Gunner shook his head and refused to think about that piece of his past. Because going there would bring him over the edge and he was already barely hanging on. He still didn't know if he believed Landon had anything to do with

Josie's death, but he blamed the man just the same. Landon knew that and shrugged it off as easily as he did everything evil that tried to touch him.

One year, one month and four days was all Gunner had gotten with Josie. He'd disappeared and stayed dead for over ten years, until Avery showed up at his door.

She'd walked in and he'd known she was dangerous from the second she'd kicked the asses of two drug dealers on the street in front of the tattoo shop.

"I'm not playing dead to anyone but the people I want kept out of this."

"You've said your final good-bye to your female friend then?" Landon asked.

She let you go. Didn't even protest when you got out of bed and left. And he knew she'd been watching. "What the fuck—you're having me followed?"

"I don't need to, James. I know you better than you know yourself. You've finally given in."

"How do you know that?"

"Because you're here. I didn't have to track you down."

"And you would've," he muttered.

"Because I need you, yes." Landon shrugged. "You fucked up after I gave you a second chance and then you ran. You thought I'd just let that go?"

"I don't think for you. I have no fucking idea what makes you do what you do."

"That's not true, James, and you know it."

"I didn't fuck that mission up," Gunner said tightly, wondering why he bothered. "I don't care what you believe, but I would never take a chance like that."

"Then why run?"

"A lot of fucking reasons. You killed Josie and set me up to take the fall. If her father hadn't covered for me . . ."

Landon shook his head. "I told you that I had nothing to do with that. Nothing."

"And you didn't order the shit beat out of me?"

"No." Landon sighed, reached out and put a hand on Gunner's shoulder. "You disappointed me. I got rid of you. When the opportunity for you to redeem yourself came up, I gave you the second chance I knew you wanted. You fucked that up. I promised I'd find you and I keep those promises. Always."

Landon's hand lingered on his shoulder, then moved slowly down his biceps. Gunner willed himself to stand there under the touch.

"I like the new look."

"I didn't do it for you."

Landon smiled. "You didn't miss anything about working for me?"

Landon was better to Gunner than Powell had

been. Didn't hit him. Treated him like an adult. Taught him things.

Lured him in, let him think he was doing things for the greater good.

"I'm not like your father," was what Landon used to say, and Gunner wanted to believe that so badly that he talked himself into it.

"I never smuggled humans who didn't want to be smuggled. I don't play with life like that."

Gunner knew that—Landon had lost his mother and sister to human traffickers, which fueled his obsession with stopping as many of them as he could. It's what made believing he was doing the right thing so easy at times for Gunner.

Landon did, however, move people around like chess pieces on his own personal board, and Gunner reminded him of that. "You take out people to further your business."

"That's what business is all about," Landon said. "Stay with me tonight."

"Landon."

"Guest room, James. I don't want anything more from you that you're not willing to give."

"Well, that's a first," he muttered.

"I don't want to break you, Gunner," Landon told him, using that name for the first time ever. "I don't think anyone ever could."

He wouldn't tell Landon that one person could, that maybe she already had.

Gunner pushed himself up from the table.

"Call me James," he said before he walked out of the sliding glass door and back into the smoke.

Three minutes. Avery desperately tried to remain calm and was failing. Her hands shook and it was getting harder to hold on to the vase. None of this made sense.

Memories flashed in her mind, almost too quickly for her to hang on to any of them— Gunner, holding her while she'd cried. Gunner tattooing her. Gunner, in her bed . . .

She avoided talking about anything that could be construed as asking him to stay. Instead, she asked, "Why tattoos?"

"Tattoos are like a résumé," he explained. "They're where you've been, where you want to go. In some cultures, they tell everything about you, if you've been to prison. If you've killed."

He went quiet then, and she asked, "What do yours say?"

"More than you want to know."

But she *did* want to know. She thought on those final hours, about how Gunner had remained under her, how he hadn't struggled or moved. How she'd been the one to finally roll off.

He hadn't wanted to let her go. And she'd forced his hand, let him slide out of bed and dress and leave as casually as if he'd be back that night for dinner.

Now, two weeks later, she had more regrets than she could stand. And obviously, so did he.

She could believe the flowers were from him. But the bomb . . .

She wouldn't stand here waiting for death. She was going to grab that bitch by the balls.

She raised her arms above her head, felt her body shift into gear as adrenaline raced. And then she read the note one last time before throwing the flowers into the air and letting go.

Chapter Six

Avery was shaking so hard her teeth chattered. The only thing that kept her from falling apart completely and immediately was the thought of Billie Jean and her text, sent right before the knock on the door from the flower delivery.

Someone's been here asking questions about you.

She raced out the door of the panic room that led into the garage, took the alley away from the street and headed to find Billie Jean.

She only hoped she was wrong about not being the only target, that she wasn't too late. The fact that whoever did this to her tried to make her think Gunner did this to her made her angrier.

The door was locked. She banged on it, tried to see inside but it was dark.

"We're not open."

She whirled around to find Lenny getting out of his car.

"Please, I think Billie Jean's in trouble."

"She's not supposed to come in until seven," Lenny told her. She wanted to shake him, almost grabbed the keys from his hands as he jangled them, looking for the right one.

"Please. Someone tried to kill me. I think Billie's in real trouble."

She pushed past Lenny into the darkened bar, listened, heard a moan. Weapon drawn, she motioned for Lenny to stay outside as she cleared the room.

A light that escaped from the partially open kitchen door allowed her to see that there was no one in the main dining area.

She looked behind the bar. Nothing.

She peered into the kitchen. Saw the blood on the floor by the industrial stove. She kicked the door open, ready to take anyone out.

The only one there was Billie, lying on her side on the floor.

"Billie, I'm here. Lenny, call the ambulance and police now!" she yelled, and Lenny came rushing in.

"Shit," he said, grabbed the cordless phone from its holder and began dialing as she opened the door to the alley. It was well lit and empty.

She closed and locked the door behind her and grabbed clean towels. She put some under

Billie's head, used the others to press the wound in her belly.

Billie's eyes fluttered open and she laughed weakly. "Guess this ring's not such good luck after all."

"You're still breathing, so I'd say it is." Avery looked around. Where was the goddamned ambulance? "Billie Jean, help's coming. You stay with me."

"Trying." She gave a short laugh. "Funny, but I thought it'd be you who'd do me in when I first met you."

"You're going to be fine," Avery told her.

"You're not," Billie rasped, clutched Avery's wrist. "Avery, something terrible's going to happen to you."

"It already did. I got away," she quickly reassured the woman.

"Avery, there was a guy in here the other night asking about you. He wasn't Cajun but he lives here. Has for years. I got the feeling he might know Gunner."

Billie Jean's mother had been psychic, and although Billie Jean told Avery she didn't have skills anywhere close, she got strong feelings at times. It was how she'd known Gunner was in love with Avery. It was how she'd known Gunner loved her but wasn't in love with her. "You concentrate on yourself."

"Not . . . okay," Billie persisted.

"You will be," Avery reassured her.

"Man . . . looking for you."

"Is he the one who did this?"

"Not sure. He left . . . then someone came up . . . from behind. It was dark." Billie closed her eyes then, her breathing labored.

The ambulance came ten long minutes later, although the fire and police were already there, helping Billie, talking to Lenny and Avery. By that time, other staff had started to arrive and one of the other waitresses went with Billie in the ambulance.

She'd whispered to Lenny to say she was staff, and no one seemed to question that. Not yet, anyway. She owed Lenny, but he probably thought she just didn't want trouble. He didn't realize Avery was somehow the trouble.

Before he wandered off, because the man was in a daze, she asked, "Did anyone come in here over the past couple of days asking about me? Or asking Billie about me?"

He didn't want to answer, she knew, but he finally wrote something down and handed it to her. "I didn't see him talking to Billie at all. This was about a week ago he came to me. You didn't hear shit from me, hear?"

"I hear." She turned and found herself with a face full of Jem's chest. He grabbed her, pulled her tight to him and she hugged him back. He kept her face tucked against him and she felt the change in the air as he brought her outside the restaurant, away from the chaos.

And then he pulled her away and asked, "What the hell, Avery? I heard the explosions when I was halfway to the shop. I wanted to surprise you and got the surprise of my goddamned life." He looked shaken and she knew from experience how hard that was to do. He took her by the shoulders and stared at her. "Are you okay?"

"It's not my blood. It's Billie Jean's—one of Gunner's ex-wives."

"And the shop?"

"Gunner sent me flowers."

"Flowers don't do that kind of damage."

"There was a bomb." If she said more, she'd break down. She pressed her lips together and let Jem lead her away.

Once in the privacy of the truck, she told him what Billie and Lenny told her, about the man asking questions about her.

"So we're taking a trip into the bayou." Jem sounded resigned. "First, you need a shower and new clothes."

She didn't argue. "If we can get into the panic room—"

"Forget it. Place is still crawling with cops and arson investigators. And the bomb squad."

"I wonder what the new owner will do," she murmured, and Jem pulled the truck over.

"New owner? Start from the beginning. Where's Gunner?"

"He's gone."

"When?"

Twenty-four hours ago. "Three weeks ago," she admitted, because it wasn't a complete lie. "He left without saying anything. Left me the sale papers."

Jem gritted his teeth but put the truck back into drive again, not asking any more questions. An hour later, she was showered and changed into a shirt and cargo pants Jem had in his bag.

"Why do these fit me?" she asked.

He looked slightly embarrassed. "I figured, two women on the team . . . I always carry extra gear so . . ."

She hugged him.

"Hey, no crying or hugging on the team," he protested when she let him go, but he smiled.

"So, did you call Key and tell him any of this?"

"No. I figured you were pretty adamant about us making up our own minds. I've already done it. Just tied up some loose ends and was headed back here to look at places to rent." He paused. "But they're all going to be pissed if we don't tell them."

"I know. But not yet. They wouldn't get here in time to hunt these guys in the bayou, and I'm not waiting. Plus . . . this might color their decision to come back."

Jem, out of all of them, was the most open to keeping secrets and working on an alternative program. He would tell her it was because of his CIA training, but she had a feeling that was Jem's way from the cradle.

"I've got weapons." He paused. "You realize this could be a trap."

She'd considered that. But the man who attacked Billie might not be the one looking for Avery. There were too many people in play. "You don't know Gunner's other ex-wives, do you?"

"No."

"We have to ask Billie when she's out of surgery."

Jem was staring out the window. "Do you remember who the new owner was?"

"I took pictures of the sale papers." She handed him her phone as he opened his laptop. He typed something on the computer and frowned. "This guy's clean. And no doubt pissed."

"Good. Maybe he'll back out of the deal."

She paused a beat, then asked, "Jem—how did you know?"

"I've been there," Jem said. "I could see the signs. I stayed close, waiting for you to need me."

"Thanks."

"That's what we do for one another, right?"

She could only nod.

"We'll get him back, Avery."

"Does Dare know any of this?"

"I didn't want to disturb him or Grace. It's just you and me, kid."

"Then let's figure out a way to get Gunner back."

Soon, the jobs would blend until he could barely see straight. When Landon called him back into the house after he'd walked off, he'd braced himself for the inevitable, but he'd gotten the keys to a safe-deposit box where his cash was kept and his keys.

"The guesthouse is yours, James," Landon said. "Welcome home. You've earned it."

Did Landon have any idea how those words would eat away at him? He was going to say no, but the amount of time he'd be spending in the house would be nil if these last jobs were any indication of that. Easier not to fight. Instead, he took the keys and turned to leave.

"And, James? You've got a full plate for the next several weeks. Make sure you get enough sleep."

Sleep. Yeah, like that would ever happen. He nodded and went on his way, bag slung across his body, and walked across the lawn barefoot, boots in his hand. The grass was sharp here, cut into his feet as he strode, the lights on the guesthouse blazing. Landon had been waiting for him.

Gunner had no doubt he'd find a fully stocked kitchen and a hot meal in the oven.

He'd done the same for Gunner when he was sixteen and had no fucking clue what was going on.

He put a hand up to wave to one of the guards who was walking toward him, but the guy moved fast, put a hand out to stop him as he crossed the property. Another came up from the side and he tried to remember if either of these men was one of those who'd had a hand in beating him.

As much as Landon denied it, there was no denying he'd almost died the night he'd left this property all those years before.

"Where're you going?" the man in front of him said.

"My fucking room." He held up the key. "Check it with Landon."

"Oh, we will. Don't much like disloyalty here."

Gunner tried to step around him, but the asshole moved and blocked him. Gunner went left; so did Asshole. The second guy scoffed and Gunner noticed a couple of the other guards had come out of the woodwork.

"Hear you're some kind of hotshot," the asshole said. "Hear you're, like, some kind of expert."

"And I hear that you're going to get your ass kicked through the side of this building if you don't move it out of my way," Gunner told him calmly, as though he were reading a weather report. The anger that built inside him had had zero outlet, not until this moment. The guy in front of him had no idea what he was in for, and for his own sake, Gunner prayed he'd reconsider his decision to poke the lion with the stick and simply move.

But he didn't. Gunner cut his eyes right and saw that Landon had come out of the house, his shirt half on. He strolled across the lawn, crossed his arms and waited.

He wanted to watch this shit. Should've known. Landon loved these little grudge matches between his men. Good for morale. Kept the good ones from getting too cocky, showed the others what they had to learn.

Gunner was tired of tests. He dropped his bag, yanked his shirt over his head and threw it onto the ground.

The asshole grinned and did the same and Gunner remained still while the guy circled him, until he tried to go behind him. Gunner turned with him, still calm, keeping his face expressionless.

"Who's putting money on this one?" Landon called.

Bills were thrown into two piles as the men who'd gathered to watch widened their circle to give the men more room.

"Hasn't been a good fight here in at least a

year," one of the men said. "Not until you kicked that last jack-off's head in."

The man across from him smiled. Gunner bet he'd had a minimum of time in the service, just enough to think he was some kind of badass. And when he lunged for Gunner, Gunner was ready. Grabbed the guy in a headlock and slammed him to the ground, then landed on him, his weight causing the breath to whoosh from the guy's body.

He didn't remember specifics. He knew he beat the shit out of the guy, not caring that he wasn't supposed to fight. Because nothing was illegal on Landon's property, in his world. Nothing fucking mattered and Gunner punched the man who'd tipped him over the edge.

He snapped back to it when he heard yelling and clapping. This was a bloodthirsty sport, the men like caged animals barely let out to play. Landon had everyone so tightly wound that any downtime brought out the worst in them.

Gunner had fought like this when he was sixteen, the first week he'd been on the island. Two of Landon's men had cornered him and Gunner fucking shredded them. He might not have been the size he was now, but he'd never been a lightweight.

A born fighter, Landon had called him. He'd raised Gunner's hand over his head that night, the winner and champion of that particular fight.

Two nights later, four men jumped him. They'd gotten the same exact treatment. It had taken a month of men trying to kill him before they'd given up.

Now he blinked at the man on the ground in front of him. He saw the guy's chest rise and fall, and although Gunner had worked him over, he hadn't done any irreparable damage.

There's still a part of you that's always in control.

He grabbed his bag and his shirt and strolled across the grass.

"You forgot your winnings, James," Landon called.

"Keep it," he said without turning around.

In the privacy of the guesthouse—and it was private because he'd checked for cameras and bugs because Landon knew he didn't handle that shit well—he stripped down and showered, washed the dirt and grass and blood off him. His injuries were minimal, but he couldn't afford to look hurt. Not in front of this crew, which was meaner and rowdier than any Landon had ever employed.

He'd need an ally when he spent time on the property. Or maybe Landon would keep him so busy he wouldn't be on the property again.

He stared at himself in the mirror for a few minutes, ran his hand through his wet hair. Then he plugged in the electric clippers, slid it through his hair and said good-bye to Gunner. Watched the blond hair fall all around him until his head was bald. The dark hair would grow in fast, but for now, this suited him. He hadn't seen the tattoos along his scalp in years. Tribal designs floated across the left side of his skull. There was an eagle on the right that wrapped around the back. He'd wear a skullcap until his hair grew in and covered them again.

Instead of being cathartic, the haircut instead reminded him of the first night he'd met Avery, when he'd helped to disguise her. At the time, he hadn't known his father was the one who'd tried to kill her. No one had wanted to mention Powell, because they knew he'd know him. But they'd never suspected the biological connection.

Avery's blonde hair had immediately reminded him of Josie, and he told himself that's all it was—the hair. But when he'd helped her cut and dye it, the attraction hadn't gone with it. He'd wanted her more. And there wasn't really any resemblance between the women, except in their take-no-shit-from-him attitudes.

After watching her kiss Key at the bar, he'd broken two of his favorite tattoo guns and promised that when she walked back in, he was going to fucking kiss her silly. By the time she'd come back into his place, he'd calmed considerably and convinced himself it was the worst idea ever.

It still was.

He walked out of the bathroom and caught sight of the envelope on the bed. Fucker let himself in here and did that, a job that involved killing people left like a mint on his pillow, just because he could.

The outside of the envelope read *I thought you could use an outlet for your aggression.*

Gunner ripped it open and found his plane tickets that had him leaving in the morning, plus the new job. He read the missive, then lit it on fire. He continued holding the papers in his hand until the flames rose and they burned down to nothing between his fingers.

Chapter Seven

"This is a bad idea," Jem told her, five hours later as they traveled through the backwoods of the bayou in an old pickup truck he'd acquired.

Avery didn't ask from where. "So why agree to it?"

"Never met a bad idea I didn't like," he retorted with a grin. He sobered immediately when he said, "You know how goddamned lucky you are to be sitting here right now?"

"I know," she said quietly. "Billie Jean's out of surgery, but she's still critical. I don't know the names of the other exes to contact them."

"I've got a few searches going on that," he said. But that wouldn't help to warn those women anytime soon. "Suppose this guy who came in to ask about you is the one who tried to kill you?"

"Then at least we'll know," she countered.

"And if he's not, we're still screwed. But we'll hunt his ass down."

The great thing about Jem was he was crazy enough to try what most people wouldn't. His logic was different from other people's and he took risks because he could.

Jem truly lived. And that's all Avery wanted to learn to do. She'd already learned the lesson that life was too short.

The bayou was all narrow paths and missteps. Some of the paths were meant to purposely throw strangers off. It was easy to get lost here.

She and Jem both quieted when they reached the bridge that took them past Grace's old house and then farther along the old swamps, through roads that didn't seem as though they should be drivable at all. And they were barely so. It was only Jem's skill that kept them from rutting out or going into the bayou itself.

After another half an hour, Jem turned the headlights down. "We're close."

"And you know that how?" she asked.

"Bayou numbers are hard to find. You've got to just count from the start of the road, and sometimes that doesn't even make sense. But I know this house." He'd pulled over, cut the engine and pointed now to one they could barely see through the mist and the cypress trees that provided protection and coverage.

"How?"

"Old girlfriend used to live there. I snuck into her window more times than I could count, until her daddy caught me." He pointed. "Window's still there, but the tree's been pruned away from it."

"What if this guy's the father of the old girlfriend?"

"He owes me an ass full of buckshot. Let's move." He was out of the car, moving around the back of the house in a wide enough arc to not get spotted. She followed closely, her own weapon drawn. Her adrenaline raced again, although her entire body suffered from the fatigue of the day's earlier events.

It was so dark out here. She didn't dare look away from Jem for fear of losing him. He walked carefully, exaggerating each step. He'd warned her of the possibility of tripwires.

She was slightly more worried about snakes.

When she got close enough to be able to see the outline of the porch clearly through the low-lying fog, she paused. Took another couple of steps and realized she'd lost track of Jem. She couldn't call for him, so instead kept going forward.

Minutes later, someone wrapped a strong arm around her neck. Her arms were pinned in place before she could do anything. The grip was python-strong. She wanted to call out for Jem, but a rag was stuffed into her mouth. A pinch on her neck and everything went black.

When she woke, she stared drowsily at the man standing in front of her. He was massive—at least six foot six and broad as a door.

He didn't look happy to see her awake in the least.

She swallowed around the gag and he said, "I'll give you a sip of water. Don't make a god-damned sound. We've got your friend here, so there's no one coming to save you."

She nodded. Let him take the gag out and took a sip of water and then gulped it while he held the bottle. Whatever he'd shot her up with was wearing off and she hoped there was nothing in the water. But she couldn't have stopped herself from drinking it.

After a few minutes and more water, her head cleared considerably. "Who are you?"

He laughed, but there was no mirth there. "You come sneaking around my house with guns and you want to know who I am? Who the fuck are you?"

He leaned into her and his military roots were definitely showing. Just being around Key, Dare and Gunner gave her insight into what to look for. "I heard you were looking for me earlier—at Dove's bar."

His brows rose. He muttered something to himself and then stared at the ceiling. When he looked back at her, he said, "You've been asking questions you shouldn't be asking."

"So have you. And you hurt one of my friends," she snapped back.

"I haven't hurt anyone. Yet."

"You don't know who you're fucking with," Jem said, and she turned to see him several feet from her. He'd obviously just woken up and his eyes were dark with anger.

"I think it's a guy who's all tied up and should be shutting his mouth," another broad man said. He was shorter than the guy in front of her, but no less intimidating. Obviously, not to Jem, the way he goaded the man.

"Nice anchor, Popeye."

Popeye. Navy. Gunner. Okay. She blew out a breath. Maybe this could still be okay.

Maybe. "You know Gunner."

"Why are you asking questions about him?"

Oddly protective. And Avery suddenly knew who these men had lost.

"The story's true, isn't it? Your daughter was married to . . . James."

"Why does this interest you?"

There were so many things she could say, professional things. What came out was "I love him."

The men looked at her. Jem groaned and then suddenly he was free and slamming one of the men to the desk, pointing a gun at the other one. "Untie her."

"Do it, Mike," the man on the desk grunted. Mike moved forward and undid the bindings on her wrists and then her ankles. Jem didn't take the gun off the guy on the table, told Mike,

"Move to the corner and sit your ass down. I'm asking questions now."

Avery stood and Jem motioned for her to grab a weapon. She did, but kept the gun down at her side. "We love Gunner. He left without warning and I think he's doing something bad. Billie said you were asking about me . . . and then an hour later, someone nearly killed her."

Mike shook his head and Andy cursed softly, then said, "It wasn't us. James was our family."

Mike looked at Andy and smiled and Avery knew two things then—these men loved each other, and they'd welcomed Gunner into their home, despite everything. Despite everything, they still wanted to protect him.

Mike cleared his throat and looked at her. "Josie was my daughter. Her mom, Amie, was my best friend. I grew up here."

"And I grew up in Texas," Andy said, his drawl thick and definitely not from Louisiana. His head was still pressed to the table by Jem, who was intent on listening.

"Amie wanted a baby, but she'd been pretty burned in the past by love. She decided she could raise a baby herself, asked me if I was okay with that. I knew I'd be away a lot with the Navy, and I knew she'd be a damned good mom. So I was always a part of Josie's life—she grew up knowing I was her dad and that I was gay and everything was fine. But then Amie got cancer—damn, it was so quick. And rather than relocate Josie, who was twelve at the time, or make her travel with me and Andy, which would've been damned near impossible with our jobs as SEALs, we moved here. I was willing to come alone, but Andy wouldn't let me."

"Best decision I ever made," Andy said. "We don't typically trade information on family, but you seem to want to help him, not use him. And you seem like you're in as much danger as Billie."

"Why'd you go to see her?" Avery asked.

"I wanted to talk to you," Mike said. "I knew James—Gunner—left New Orleans last month. What I don't know is why. Or at least I didn't. Now I think I know."

"He's in a bad place, isn't he?" she whispered.

"If he's back doing what I think he's doing, yes." Mike sighed, stared at the ceiling. "He's been in close proximity for years, but he never got in touch. For our safety, more so than his. He's got to be ruthless about cutting ties to his past."

Avery rubbed her wrists where the rope bit into them.

"Sorry about that. We're suspicious types."

"Jem, you could probably let Andy up now," Avery said.

Jem grumbled but did so. Andy got up slowly, moved away from Gunner. Avery put the gun back into its case then and Mike motioned for all of them to follow him farther into the deceptively worn house.

It was obvious these two men had a more than fleeting concern for security and privacy, especially once they were led through the living room, with the TV and the old couch into a room behind a locked door.

Andy sat in front of the large computer and began typing.

"Please, sit," Mike told them. There were several comfortable chairs and Jem collapsed into one while Avery stayed on the edge of her own leather recliner. Accepted a soda and turned it in her hands until they went numb from the cold and then the drink got warm, all in the space of the five minutes it took Andy and Mike to confer, wordlessly, about something on the iPad.

The men started slow, waiting to see if they could trust Avery and Jem. She appreciated that, even though she was frustrated with the pace.

They'd handed her and Jem a file folder marked CIA and confidential and branded with a red stamp that stated DESTROY.

"Someone didn't do their job," Jem muttered. He opened the file, since he was the best one to interpret the legalese and covertness of the CIA's writings.

He explained that, according to the agents who were working this case—one of whom had been Richard Powell himself—James Connor had fallen off the map completely at the age of nineteen. From the ages of sixteen until nineteen, he had a long list of crimes that he was implicated in but never captured for.

He appeared to have been working for a mysterious smuggler known only by the initials DL. The CIA had been watching him for ten years and only had a trail of bodies, explosions and money.

"James Connor is Gunner," Jem said. Because Dare told them that Powell used the name James when he'd greeted Gunner.

"Powell thought Gunner was dead."

"That must've been when he went into the Navy."

Avery nodded, but something was bothering her. "Where was James from birth to sixteen?"

"He was with his mom until she was killed. He was twelve. And we know he was with Powell for some of that time afterward—had to be."

"But he wasn't there when Grace got there. Gunner would've been fifteen or sixteen at the time," Andy added.

"So that's when he fell in with this mysterious DL character," Jem mused.

"And his own father was investigating him, not mentioning that this was his son?" Avery asked.

"Fucking bastard," Jem muttered. "Glad he's dead."

"And DL is Drew Landon, infamous smuggler," Mike added. "He's one of the biggest moneymakers—he smuggles criminals and their families out of the country. Any country. He gets them away from marshals, feds, whoever. It's a huge business, requires utmost secrecy. He only uses top operatives for certain parts of his business."

Smuggling was the reason Gunner had made so many connections. He'd made friends with criminals and innocents alike, offered favors even as he was an avenging angel to the human traffickers.

"There was a string of unexplained human trafficker deaths about ten years ago, when I was first with the CIA," Jem said. "You're saying that was Gunner?"

"As near as we could figure out," Mike said. "Whatever else Landon had him doing, Gunner was kicking ass."

"So Gunner is the man who actually escorts the criminals into their new country?" Avery asked. "Wouldn't that give him a way out of working with Landon?"

"Not if he wants to live," Jem said.

"But he had Gunner kill human traffickers. Because they were competition? I can't see Gunner working for someone like that, no matter what they had hanging over his head," Avery mused.

"DL is most likely hanging you over Gunner's

head," Mike said gently, then added, "Maybe Gunner doesn't know. Maybe it's what he needs to believe."

Avery rested her forehead in her palms, blinked back tears. "I can't believe . . . we did this to him. I did."

She and Dare had pulled Gunner into their problems, into helping them find their father. Ultimately, finding Darius meant that Gunner had to face his own father. Because of that, Landon had rediscovered Gunner. Knowing she couldn't have predicted the consequences did nothing to assuage her guilt.

Gunner stared out at the water, a bottle of whiskey and a shot glass next to him. Landon had had someone bring them by hours earlier, and Gunner hadn't refused them.

The guy had stared at his head, whistled and then offered to come in and share the bottle with him, after staring up and down Gunner's naked body.

Gunner just shook his head no and the guy offered his sister. Gunner just closed the door quietly. He'd gone numb the second he'd stepped onto this island, and no amount of pleasure was going to help.

He didn't want to close his eyes because every time he did, he saw Avery. He realized he didn't have any pictures of her, an old habit of never leaving a trail of people you loved for criminals to latch onto.

He'd never kept any of Josie either. But he had Josie's tattoo on his arm, the same one he pressed herbs against now. An offering, a prayer, a call for protection he knew he didn't deserve.

All the people you've helped in the meantime . . .

Didn't matter, he told himself ruthlessly. He'd wiped karma out with a single bomb on a job the night Josie was killed and he'd pay for it forever. Just the way it was meant to be.

He'd tried to be a part of the tight family circle that Gunner couldn't believe he was lucky enough to be a part of.

And you lied to them, time after time. As much as he told himself it was for their own protection, he knew that he'd been afraid they'd tell him to go to hell.

"What happened to you, son?" Mike asked, maybe two weeks later when Gunner was starting to get back on his feet.

Gunner looked him in the eye and started to make something up. Mike would believe it—and Gunner wished he could believe it too. Instead, he told the man, "I got out of something bad the only way I knew how."

Mike nodded.

"I've got to get out of here. I won't bring anything but trouble to you and your family."

"I don't believe that for a second," Mike said.

Josie continued. "Besides, that's what the ceremony was for. It cleared away the evil that surrounded you. Purified you."

Josie said this as though everyone knew that.

"So what, I'm like new now?"

"In a way, yes."

He'd gotten out of bed and nearly collapsed on her. She caught him, chided, "Come on, James."

"How'd you know that?" Because if memory served, he'd been wearing cargo pants and nothing else, had no ID or money. Nothing else when Landon's men dumped him from the car after beating him. Almost like a reverse gang ritual. He had no doubt they'd meant to kill him in one of the most painful ways possible.

"You told me," Josie said simply.

She sat next to him on the bed and Mike asked, "Are they going to come looking for you?"

"Considering they dumped him in the middle of the swamp, I guess they figured local wildlife would take care of the body."

"How long have I been here?"

"Two weeks."

"And nobody's come asking about me?"

"We're pretty well insulated from strangers around here. Between the geography and the Cajuns, any outsider steps foot in this parish and it's known before your shoe hits the dirt," Mike said. "Which is how we found you."

Chapter Eight

When Mike and Andy told her and Jem the story of finding Gunner barely alive in the bayou, Avery gritted her teeth together so hard her head ached.

"I don't know how he was still alive," Mike was saying. "He was . . . Jesus, I thought he was dead when the dog found him. Petey tried to drag him up the porch and then howled when he couldn't."

"Petey was a good judge of character," Andy added. "He'd bitten over half the damned parish, but with Gunner, he wouldn't leave his side, no matter how hard we tried to get him to leave the poor guy alone."

Avery pulled the blanket farther around her shoulders and sipped at the strong coffee Mike had made. "Did he remember anything?"

"I think he remembered everything, but he didn't tell us. Not then. Not until he'd realized he'd fallen in love with Josie. He came clean to us about his father and Landon then," Mike said. "He'd been through hell. But he had a drive . . . after everything happened, we tried to convince him to go right into the military. I wish we'd convinced him."

"He didn't want to?" Avery asked.

"Partly. And Josie didn't help. She wanted him here, with her. They were like two kids. I think it was the first time Gunner actually had a childhood." Mike smiled as he remembered.

"They were good together," Andy agreed, and then looked at Avery. "Sorry, hon—does this bother you?"

"No, it doesn't. Anything that made Gunner happy . . ." She trailed off and Jem put a hand on her shoulder.

"We'll get him back if I have to drag him by the hair," he assured her.

She laughed a little, then pointed to Mike's arm. "Did Gunner do any of those tattoos?"

He pointed to one. "This was one of his first. He learned from Josie."

"I think I really would've liked Josie," she said.

"You two are very different," Andy told her. "But I think you would've been tight."

That meant a lot to her. She felt as though she needed the dead woman's blessing to move forward with Gunner.

"Gunner was a natural with the tattooing. He's a great artist." Mike pointed to the wall behind her. She turned to see a charcoal drawing of a young woman, hugging a dog and smiling.

Josie. So pretty. So young.

I knew he loved you because he drew you, Billie told her in so many words. And Avery would hold on to that with everything she had.

Josie was the first person Gunner had sketched since he'd moved to Powell's island. He couldn't have stopped himself if he'd tried, found himself scratching the pencil on paper, watching Josie playing with Petey. She hadn't interrupted him, not until he put the paper down and stretched his cramped hands.

He'd drawn several versions of her, because he'd been rusty—and determined to get it right.

"It's beautiful."

"You're beautiful. My art needs work. Been a while."

"Why's that?"

He didn't tell her that killing people and art didn't exactly go together. "I haven't wanted to. Not until now."

"I can't really draw," she admitted. "I can freehand things when I tattoo, but it's basic stuff. Charms and things like that. But you've got talent."

She'd known some traditional tattooing methods, using sticks and ink and man, were painful but beautiful, and she was also handy with the tattoo gun. Her mother had dated a tattoo artist when Josie was small and she'd taken to it easily.

The first several weeks when Gunner was hiding and healing, she'd noticed him doodling and drawing on any scrap of paper he was near. He hadn't noticed—it was something he hadn't done since his mother had died. Before that, his mother used to tease him that any available space would be filled with his drawings.

When she'd died, he'd opened one of her suitcases and found a large stack of his drawings, from some of his earliest doodles to some of the most recent. He'd lost that suitcase after moving to Powell's. He had little doubt that Powell took one look at it, dismissed it as sentimental rubbish and burned it.

Thankfully, you couldn't burn memories as easily.

Josie had let him give her a tattoo, the first one he'd ever done. He'd been nervous, hadn't wanted to mar her beautiful skin. Hadn't wanted to make a mistake. But the bold, funny, raunchy woman told him that mistakes were what made life interesting.

"We can fix anything, James," she'd added.

He'd used the gun, not the sticks. It took him months before he was comfortable with that method, and it still wasn't exactly his bag. He'd let the buzz of the needle mesmerize him. She'd insisted that he use it freehand, tattoo the first thing that came to his mind.

He'd drawn a butterfly.

"I love it, James," she'd told him.

"I don't think you want to get involved with me."

"Then stop thinking," she'd said, right before she'd kissed him.

They'd made love for the first time that night. Lying on her mattress stuffed with cypress leaves and smelling like lavender and other scents that would forever remind him of Josie, he'd told her that he loved her.

Didn't know how he was capable of that still, but he hadn't wanted to question it.

Those were some of the good memories. The escape he'd made from the life with Landon into Josie's arms was one he'd never chosen, but he'd been happy with it. Would he have stayed that way?

He'd never gotten the chance to know.

"Maybe your past will just let you go," she'd said. And, for a year, it had. And then it had sunk its claws back into his life with a vicious vengeance that rocked his life to this day.

Don't go there, he warned himself, but too much whiskey brought up too many memories, and he was in the right mood to torture himself.

Josie had been raised by two men who were both SEALs. She knew how to fight, how to use weapons. She hadn't fought, hadn't seen it coming. She'd never been given a chance.

He wanted to run out the door, follow a trail to her killer before it got cold. But all he could do was kneel in slow motion beside her body and gather Josie in his arms. He didn't know how long he'd sat there holding her when he realized Andy was shaking him. Moving him aside so Mike could check the body.

"Look at me. You have to leave. James, do you understand? You have to get the hell out of here now," *Andy was saying to him. Somehow, even in his state of mourning, he heard that. Pushed himself shakily to his feet.*

"I'll go."

Andy propelled him onto the back porch. Started stripping him, and it was then Gunner realized his clothes were stained with Josie's blood. His body shook and he got sick over the side of the porch. Andy held him so he didn't fall over.

He wanted to ask why Andy was helping him. Wanted the man to punch him out. To stab him, shoot him, accuse him outright. But the being nice was the biggest and most effective dagger that sank directly into his heart.

He was paralyzed with shame and fear. And he couldn't admit to Andy where he'd been, although the man was far from stupid. He and Mike had to suspect something.

He let Andy strip him, take his clothes and burn them out in the swamp, where the remains would be quickly swallowed by the bayou. Mike brought out a packed bag, new clothes, while Gunner washed with the pump in the back so he didn't drag any more blood through the house.

"I'm going to call the police in a couple of hours. We're going to say this was a home invasion and that you're away, visiting a friend. I have a Navy buddy who'll provide the cover story for you," Mike said. "You have to leave. James, do you understand?"

"I'll go."

"James." He was forced to look into Mike's eyes. "We're not kicking you out. We're protecting you."

"Why?"

"Josie would never forgive us if we didn't."

He hadn't seen Mike or Andy since he'd left that night. They hadn't lied about helping him. They'd set him up to have shelter, to get new identification and paperwork, to create an entirely new life that led him into the Navy and then the SEALs and finally into a shop back in New Orleans where he tattooed people and helped mercenaries like himself in an attempt to pay back the penance he owed.

He'd learned lessons. Done what he could to erase a past he'd stepped back into.

But Avery was safe, and he'd never regret that.

It was almost midnight by the time they'd sat down to eat. Andy had cooked while Avery, Mike and Jem utilized different computers, Jem and Mike searching for any trace of Gunner, while Avery answered e-mails from Dare and Grace so they wouldn't worry.

She was starving and the food was delicious. Reminded her of how Gunner would cook for her.

"You should both stay here for now. Safer for all of us," Mike told them as he gave her and Jem seconds.

He was right and Jem, who knew it too, said, "I've got to move my truck."

Andy pushed his hand into his pocket and pulled out keys, tossed them at Jem. "I already put it into our garage and brought your bags in."

Jem grunted. "Could still take you out, squid."

Andy snorted and Mike looked over at her.

"Thank you," she said. She'd been quiet after they'd talked some more about what Gunner was dealing with. She was trying to absorb everything, and it proved overwhelming. "I should call the hospital about Billie Jean—let her know we're okay if she comes through. When she comes through," she corrected.

"I'll make sure she knows you're okay," Mike said. "I already checked with my contact from the hospital. She made it through surgery. Still critical, but they're hopeful. She's opened her eyes and she's spoken to the police briefly."

"What about his other ex-wives?" she asked, assuming that Mike and Andy knew about that too.

"I've got guys on both of them. One's in Europe—hard to find. The other's in Colorado. She's staying with friends, being careful."

"Good." She finished the rice and beans and sausage, ate more fresh bread and finished her beer. Now that her stomach was full and she knew that Billie was okay, it was time to turn her mind back to Gunner and the rescue effort. "How do we bring a man back who doesn't want to come back?"

"I've always found waterboarding to be pretty effective," Jem said, then stopped when they all just stared at him. "Not what we were going for?"

Mike and Andy looked at each other and shrugged. "We were about to try it on you," Andy told Jem.

"Not the worst idea I've heard," Mike agreed, and Jem nodded sagely, as though he agreed with the fact that they'd been planning on torturing him.

She took a long drink of beer, then asked, "You think that's really going to work on him?"

"I think it's the only thing he'll understand at this point," Jem said.

"He's only been with Landon for a couple of weeks, at the most," she pointed out.

"That's more than enough," Jem told her.

She asked the question she'd been dreading, the one she knew the answer to. "Do you think he agreed to go back because they threatened him?"

"I think he went back because they threatened you, Avery," Mike said.

"That's what I was afraid of. Excuse me." She pushed away from the table, went into the next room for some space. She blinked back tears, held herself together as she looked around at the pictures scattered on the table.

They were mainly of the men and Josie. A woman who was most likely Josie's mom. And, if she looked closely, there were a few of a younger Gunner. The fact that these men kept his pictures here after what had happened . . .

She turned away. This was like sneaking into someone's past, uninvited.

Can't change the past, Avery, Mom would tell her. *What's done is done.* But that didn't mean she couldn't change the future.

"What's going on, Avery?" Jem asked.

"Nothing."

He stared at her and she got the distinct impression she'd be next in line for light waterboarding if she didn't talk. "I saw him, Jem. Recently."

"When?" Jem demanded.

"A week ago. He came to my hotel room and . . ." She trailed off. "I didn't ask him where he'd been and he didn't offer. I didn't want to freak him out by asking him to stay, so . . . dammit. He made love to me and he left."

"That doesn't mean you suck in bed or anything," Jem said.

She crossed her arms and stared him down. "Thanks."

"Aw, come on, you know what the deal is with him now. The fact that he came back, even for a little while, is good news. But you have to stop holding shit back from me. I'm the king of shitty choices, Avery. I won't judge you." Jem put a hand on her shoulder. "You're still the key to getting Gunner back with us."

"Thanks for saying that." She paused, considering. "Maybe Gunner doesn't know Landon's trying to kill us."

"Or maybe Gunner sent them," Jem said.

"I can't believe he'd do that."

"I don't want to either."

She glanced at the picture of Josie and Gunner. "They both look so young. Innocent."

"Yeah, they do."

The fact that Gunner might've done this, given up his life, his love of tattooing, and gone to work with the worst kind of criminals because of her made her ache. She wrapped her arms around herself and stared at the picture of Josie.

"I won't let him down, Josie," she whispered as she ran a hand along the picture like a promise. "I swear I won't let him down again."

"You didn't let him down," Jem told her, but she knew better. She hadn't begged Gunner to stay with her out of some misguided notion that it had to be his idea to stay.

Gunner had been waiting for her to ask When she hadn't . . .

"Let's go find him," she told Jem.

"Atta girl."

Chapter Nine

No *contact, except for emergencies.* That had been Avery's rule, and Dare agreed with it, beyond his better judgment. He knew she wanted him and Grace to have time alone together. And it was much-needed time, he agreed. Their meeting had been a goddamned hurricane with a tornado thrown in for good measure.

Downtime would tell the tale . . . and so far, the tale was still damned fine.

"You're thinking about the team again," Grace said with a smile.

"So were you."

She shrugged, not minding being caught. The bikini she wore should be outlawed, because it was really just string and crocheted material and he would've been covering her with a towel if they were anywhere but in the privacy of their own beach. The resort he'd picked was known for its share of guests who didn't want to be bothered by anyone. Their food was cooked, left for them discreetly. They barely saw the people who cleaned their rooms while they were lounging on the beach.

"We're supposed to think about Section 8," she reminded him. "That's the point of Avery's forced vacation."

"She's really bossy, isn't she?" he grumbled, but couldn't hold back a smile.

"A family trait," she told him.

"Aw, come on, baby. That's not fair."

"I've never fought fair."

He stared up at the blue sky, sunglasses firmly in place. They'd all been to hell and back and none of them fought fairly when it was necessary for their survival. Typically, though, that happened when they were worried about one another's survival more than their own.

Which was exactly why this new S8 would gel so perfectly.

"You think they're all fine?" she asked.

He noted the concern in her voice. "You're worried?"

"It's just . . . a feeling," she said. And, yes, he knew her feelings.

"Grace?"

She pressed her lips together. "I'm probably just nervous."

He shook his head.

"Okay, look, it's not a nervous, *something horrible is happening right now* feeling. But . . . maybe we should put in a call. Tomorrow. Give me another night to let this settle."

Grace had premonitions for as far back as she could remember, until Rip, as she called her stepfather, had decided to see if she was as strong as she seemed to be.

Turned out, she had been, even though Rip had tortured her for a year, kept her locked up, let his men hurt her, but her gift of premonition had suffered, retreated so deeply inside her and refused to come out. Slowly, the premonitions were returning, but although they were unreliable as to when they would come, the feelings were spot-on.

At least she hadn't had any that were like the ones Dare first saw. Those were painful, made her space out and lose consciousness.

Now that Rip was out of her life for good, Grace felt she was able to come to terms with it all.

Except for what Gunner had been through. She knew Gunner felt guilty about her. And she worried that that could actually be all their undoing.

It wasn't an easy process. Avery knew that, with every week that passed, they were losing Gunner more and more.

Mike and Andy were amazing with comms. They'd made a lot of headway in tracking Landon, or rather, keeping track of him.

"Gunner must've been doing the same thing," Jem surmised. "Ever get a look at his computers?"

"Sure, but there was so much going on I wouldn't have known what to look for. Landon's info might've been right in front of my face and I wouldn't have known. My focus at that point was on Dare and Powell."

Tracking Landon wasn't the same as tracking Gunner at all. The men were never in the same place at the same time, and for good reason. And the reports that piled up about the jobs Gunner was doing mainly showcased him taking down notorious human traffickers and freeing the women and children who'd been captured.

"Why does Landon waste time doing this?" she asked.

"Why does a criminal do anything? Sometimes it's less of why and more of why not," Jem said. "But hell, this guy has to have a motive. This isn't ordinary stuff."

"Maybe they're trying to horn in on his business. Smuggling's smuggling. And the people who want to leave the country would pay good money."

"But it's two different skill sets. Trafficking to sell humans is different than sneaking a few away from the law and creating a new life for them. The women and children who get sold sure as hell don't need birth certificates and credit cards."

Landon seemed to be a master at reintroducing fugitives into the world with a clean slate. Of course, half the time the CIA caught up with them, although it took years and was usually because of transgressions performed under the new names. Because criminals didn't change. They couldn't, Jem had told her. *What's in your blood is what's in your blood. You're a prime example of that.*

What about Gunner? Powell was in his blood. But she didn't say it out loud, didn't want to make Jem answer. She'd bet he'd thought about it, though.

The only good that came out of waiting was that Jem was able to buy the properties back. He used a dummy corporation name and added extra security measures to the empty place and they stayed there in between searches. Avery was almost hoping they'd lure someone back who wanted to hurt them on Gunner's behalf, but no one came.

Finally, almost four months from when she'd last seen Gunner, they had their first solid lead. Along the way, she'd met more men and women of dubious character, made contacts, hung out with mercenaries and thieves, sometimes those who were one and the same, and generally tried to keep herself calm.

With Jem, that was easy. Somehow his bent to crazy calmed her. When he would get drunk, dance on tables, ride the bull, drink the worm, she would be the one dragging his ass out of the bar and into bed.

"Sometimes I think you're doing all this shit to keep my mind off the fact that we haven't found Gunner yet," she'd muttered to him one night.

He'd laughed drunkenly, touched his nose and then pointed to her. *Yeah, bingo*, she thought dryly.

In the morning, they'd take a small plane two islands over. Gunner was rumored to be doing a job for Landon, and that information was leaked from one of Landon's own men in return for the sole purpose of chartering a boat for said job.

Tomorrow, she'd be closer to Gunner than she'd been in months. She said a small prayer that they were doing the right thing and braced herself for everything to go wrong that possibly could.

Chapter Ten

The guards positioned on the beach were taken care of. The house loomed in front of him. He wiped the blood from his knife along the grass and shoved it back into its sheath. He secured it around his arm and continued along the dark beach.

It had finally happened. He'd stopped feeling. Again. He'd known it would happen, wasn't sure if he should welcome it or hate it.

This time, it had only taken five months. Five months of hell, in order to prove himself to a taskmaster he'd never wanted to impress in the first place. Five months to get back into the man's good graces.

He pushed forward like a machine. Couldn't remember the last time he ate or slept and he really didn't give a shit. All he needed to do was the job—this one and the one after it, get the people moved where they needed to be moved to and take out anyone Landon deemed unworthy.

Landon had made him the star of his show,

Let's Play God, Judge and Jury, all in his quest to take down human traffickers. The satisfaction he gained by helping the women and children go free after killing men who'd imprisoned them would wane quickly with every criminal he'd helped to sneak out of countries, across borders and away from justice.

It wasn't like the first time. Would never be like that again.

He glanced up at the light in the window ahead of him. It blinked twice and as he moved forward, it went dark.

When he blinked again, he was no longer standing on a beach looking up at a house where he'd seen the signal.

He was in a room that looked like a police station. Bare cement walls, what he assumed to be a two-way mirror and him chained to a metal chair in the middle of the room. The chair was semi-chained in place too. It had a little give, but there was no way he could get up and tackle anyone without slamming himself down to the floor in the process.

Mother*fucker*.

He tested his hands to see if there was any give. Legs too.

"Wouldn't bother, you asshole. I know how to keep someone from getting away."

Jem's voice. He stilled as he heard the man approach him from behind.

"I wouldn't count on it," he said, and for a moment, there was silence. Until he found himself with his cheek on the bare floor, his head aching from the blow, his body following suit on the unforgiving tile. "I will fucking kill you," Gunner promised.

Jem righted the chair unforgivingly, stood in front of him and taunted, "I'm right here, big boy. Come on."

He couldn't believe he'd let the former spook get the better of him. He'd gotten too comfortable, had immersed himself back into the life. He'd assumed S8 had let him go.

Instead, Jem had used a dart filled with sedative and now he used chains with prongs inside the wrist and ankle bands, which Gunner grudgingly admitted was a nice touch. He shifted his weight slightly. Being slammed to the floor had cut the shit out of his skin. Blood trickled down his fingertips, dripped to the cement floor. He'd been drugged, so he hadn't been able to count the miles or know how long he'd traveled to get here. Wherever *here* was.

He had no doubt they'd ditched his phone and his bag.

That was both good and bad. Meant Landon couldn't find him. Which meant he couldn't find Avery or Jem.

At least not yet.

He heard Landon's words, whispered in his

ear. *"If you go missing, I'll hunt you down. And you'd better pray I find you captured and not running. . . ."*

He had to get the hell out of here. Even if he had to kill Jem to do it. Which needed to happen as soon as he regained full consciousness.

He didn't know how soon after that thought it happened—Jem pouring water over his head. He sputtered. Spat. Cursed.

And then Jem did it again and again. What the fuck? Was the asshole trying to re-create hell week?

"I will kill you," he told Jem when he was allowed to breathe air instead of water for a full minute.

"You try, Gunner." Jem poured the water again. "Who're you working for?"

Gunner. Fuck. He'd managed to keep that name out of his mind for months, didn't slip when asked his name any longer. And in one breath, Jem brought Gunner back to life.

He choked out, "It's James. You're a failed agent, Jeremiah. Are you trying to get reinstated?"

"Fuck. You." More water. Never-ending fucking water as his chair was tipped back and the spikes bit into him and he welcomed the pain and the light-headedness.

As if Jem knew that, he stopped, dead. Demanded, "Answer me one question—did you set her up?"

"No clue what you're talking about."

"The flowers with the bomb—you sent them?"

There were two ways to answer that. Gunner chose the one that would make Jem hate him. "I did. Did it work?"

The backhand Jem cracked across his cheek didn't hurt as much as the pain involved in not knowing if Avery was hurt. And Gunner deserved it. He spat blood and smiled. "You didn't answer my question."

A glint in Jem's eye told him the test he was about to endure.

But that's what Gunner goddamn did. He endured.

He endured for hours. Days. However long Jem kept at him. The man didn't give Gunner any real way out—there were no right answers he could give. It was only torture. Meant to break him. Bring him back.

He refused to let it. Refused to ask about Avery, even though with every fucking beat of his heart he wondered if she'd been killed.

That didn't stop until Avery walked in, unharmed. Angry. Beautiful.

His chest tightened. He couldn't keep this up, not if she was here. But for her sake, he had to.

"You seem surprised to see me," she said, and fuck, he needed to learn to school his expectations around her. To date, she seemed to be the only woman he hadn't been able to lie to.

Scratch that—he had lied to her and somehow

she called him on his bullshit every single time. He thought about the orchids he'd sent in a moment of weakness, hoping they'd gotten to her before S8 moved out. He'd called from the truck as it barreled out of the city. And two hours later, he'd called to cancel the order, spoken to the wife of the owner who'd promised not to deliver them.

"You're working for Drew Landon. Again," Jem said.

Gunner shrugged. "He keeps me busy. Pays me well. What more do I need?"

Jem stared at him, the crazy man completely lucid, leaving Gunner to feel like he was the one who needed the mental institution. The higher the walls, the better.

"It's a job, Jeremiah. I'm good at it. What do you give a fuck what I do for the rest of my life?"

"Because you're not the same guy I knew."

"That guy never existed."

"Bull. Shit. And your running didn't help us. Landon's trying to kill us anyway," Jem spat. "Or maybe you knew that. Maybe you want us out of the way, since we know your secrets."

Gunner smirked again and Jem smacked him hard across his face, splitting his lip.

"Jem, I need to talk to him alone," Avery said.

Jem gave the chair one final kick for good measure and Gunner cursed a blue streak at him. His lip was split again, the metallic taste of blood filling his mouth. His body ached and he wanted to kill the crazy asshole who'd been torturing him for the past forty-eight-plus hours.

What was the fucking point? He was done with S8. Jem was telling him that Landon had tried to kill Avery and Billie Jean as a trick. Gunner knew tricks when he saw them, because he'd used them before.

But Jem was leaving and Avery was staying. He steeled himself against her, because nothing could've prepared him for the jolt he'd felt.

You thought you were dead inside. And just like that, Avery's presence gave him the jump start to his heart.

He hated her for that, and that hate was what he focused on. "Why don't you follow your friend and get the fuck out of here?"

Her mouth fell open, but only for a second. It was like steel grew in place of her spine, and when she straightened, her eyes snapped angry fire. "What have they done to you?"

He stared at her as obscenely as possible, refusing to break the gaze first as he spat blood in a straight line through his teeth. "They didn't do anything. This is me, Avery. I told you—go to Key and stay the hell away."

"I'm not with Key."

"You're fucking someone else, then? Good for you. I told you to *leave me alone.* What don't you get about that?"

Avery's chin raised defiantly. Instead of making her angry enough to walk out, he seemed to be succeeding only in making her will stronger. "There's a lot I'm not getting about you. Where've you been?"

"Around."

"Doing what?"

"Stuff. Christ, who the fuck are you, my mother?"

She ignored that, countered with a stack of files she held so he could see them marked CONFIDENTIAL. "I know exactly what kind of stuff you've been doing."

"So why ask?"

"Because I want to see if you have the balls to admit it."

He gave a short, dirty laugh, rocked his pelvis into the air. "You want to see those balls, go right ahead. Doesn't mean I have to make you wife number—"

"Five?" she finished, moved close enough to touch him and leaned in. "Wouldn't I be wife number five, Gunner?"

"James," he bit out. "And fuck you."

She reached out then. He thought she would slap him, but what she did was worse. She ran her hand through his hair, a gentle touch that honest to God nearly broke him.

He wanted to lean into her hand, rest his head on her, let her take care of him. Confess things she already knew and some she didn't.

"Talk to me, Gunner. Come back to me."

He closed his eyes, took a breath. He opened them, the fantasy ruthlessly pushed aside. "I was never yours to begin with."

"I'm not letting you go," she said, but she had to know that some part of him was already long gone. She held up the sale papers he'd left for her months earlier. "We bought it all back—the tattoo shop, the garage, the bar. All of it. And we're fixing it back up."

"Then you're stupider than I thought."

She picked up the files then and flipped through them. "The *El Coyote* was the first job you did after you left me," she said. It seemed like years ago that he'd done that. "And then we traced a line of crimes along the Ivory Coast and through the Sudan."

Brutal jobs. His bank account was fat with blood money. But Avery and Jem had been standing here safe in front of him, and he had to assume the same of Key, Dare and Grace. It was all he'd asked, and in turn he'd separated himself from them.

Fuck, being back here in Avery's presence was wiping away his carefully built resolve. He didn't want her to know all this shit. Didn't want her seeing into his past, his present, especially when she couldn't be a part of his future.

She tipped his chin up so he was forced to meet her eyes. His chin brushed the file she still

held, until she climbed into his lap, holding the
file behind the back of his chair. His dick was
hard and she ground against it while he ground
out, "Simple biology, baby. You want to fuck me,
go for it. Don't expect it to change anything."

"It already has, Gunner." She leaned in, licked
his earlobe. He fought a shiver, tried to stay cold
as fuck, but she was so goddamned warm. He
wanted to thrust against her, let her come against
him, calling his name. "I'm going to fight dirty.
And I'm not stopping until you give in."

"Why?" He heard a trace of despair in his own
voice.

"Because you wouldn't stop for me. Because I
don't think you want me to stop."

He looked up at the ceiling. She took the opportunity to kiss his neck. Run her hands over
his chest. "Come back to me, Gunner. Please,
come home."

"I don't have a home, Avery. Especially not
one with you."

She blinked at him.

"You told us we have to make our own decisions. I've made mine. You need to accept it."

"I won't."

Infuriatingly stubborn. He stared into her
beautiful eyes—she had an old soul and he'd noticed that from the moment he'd met her. She
could always see right through him. "Let me
go."

"I can't."

"You have no idea the kind of wrath you're going to bring down on your newly formed family."

"You're part of the family, Gunner."

"James. My name is James."

"Never to me. I don't know him."

"You're meeting him. This *is* me, Avery. Gunner was a facade."

Avery blanched and he knew he needed to hurt her, needed to twist the knife, sink it so deep she'd ache if she even started to think about him.

Gunner cocked his head, smirked when he told her, "Your family couldn't beat mine—in the end, it wasn't you or Dare who took out Powell. You needed me. Your own father couldn't do it."

Chapter Eleven

Avery blinked at him in disbelief for only a second at his callousness at Darius's death. Before she could think, she'd slapped him, twice, hard across his cheek. It didn't wipe the smug, satisfied look off his face, the one that said he knew he'd driven the knife deep.

The one that said he didn't care. But if he had to try this hard, he must care. Must be feeling threatened.

God, she hoped she wasn't wrong, but exhaustion and fear overwhelmed her.

Kidnapping him had been a mistake. She saw that now. Never before had the saying *if you love someone, set them free* seemed more clear. She grabbed the files, turned away from him and walked out, but not before hearing his soft chuckle behind her.

He thinks he's won. And he's right.

"Told you it wouldn't be easy, sweetheart,"

Jem said as he ate his lo mein with chopsticks. "You didn't cry in front of him, did you?"

She wiped the tears from her cheeks with her fingertips angrily and shook her head.

He tipped the carton toward her. "Want some?"

"Jesus, Jem, how can you eat now, after what he said?"

"Have to keep up my strength to beat some sense into him," he told her. "He didn't mean that."

"How can you tell?"

"Because I'm not Darius's kid. He's playing dirty. Mike told you this would happen."

She turned to stare through the two-way glass, the way she'd been for the past couple of days, refusing to cover her eyes or shut the sound off when things got bad. But everything Jem did to him seemed to make Gunner's resolve not to come back to their side strengthen.

"Let him go," she told Jem, her voice hoarse.

In turn, Jem dropped the container and his legs from the table and stood. "Are you kidding me? First of all, that's like signing our death warrants."

"Won't be the last time, I'm sure. If we're moving ahead with S8, we'll have to expect this. Although not from someone we thought was one of us."

Jem shoved a hand through his hair. "Sweetheart, love's made you blind and stupid. The goddamned way he looked at you when you walked into the room—how could you have missed that?"

He turned and rewound the tape, showed her the moment she hadn't seen, because she'd been too busy worrying about Gunner and how badly he was being hurt.

"He's in love with me," she whispered.

"Right. Now get back out there and make him fucking admit it. Because I can't do that lovey-dovey shit with him. Well, I could, but it might make you jealous."

She sputtered a laugh and it felt good. Maybe she did have Gunner where she needed him to be, in pain and lashing out because he was losing resolve. If he didn't care, he'd be sitting there, stoic, not allowing his emotions to poke through.

Jem caught her by the shoulders then, continuing the pep talk. "You've come this far. Don't back down now. We can't lose him to that man. You wouldn't have let Grace go back to Rip."

"Dare would never have let that happen."

Jem nodded. "I'll do the hard part."

"No. I'll have to do the hard part. He can handle the kind of pain you'll give him."

"But no man can deal with the kind of pain a woman can inflict," Jem finished.

"You're an asshole."

"An asshole who's right." He stared at Gunner through the two-way glass. "He's not going to know what hit him."

She waited another hour, turned the heat up in the room and watched him fall asleep. Then she turned the temperature back down, walked in quietly and poured freezing-cold water over his head to rouse him.

He woke immediately, blinking away the water, baring his teeth. Growling. He looked beautiful. Dangerously so.

"You are really pushing your luck."

"What are you going to do about it, Gunner?"

"I told you, my name is James."

"I'll never call you that."

"You will. And you'd better pray I'm not in front of you, making you say it, Avery."

"It was okay when I yelled your name in my bed, right?" she challenged.

"I don't remember. Guess it didn't mean that much to me."

"Oh bullshit, Gunner." She straddled his lap, pressing herself to his wet, bare chest. He might've been able to control a lot of his behavior, but he couldn't stop biology. His arousal pressed between her legs almost immediately. It was heady to know she still had that effect on him, despite his protests otherwise.

"What don't you get, *chère*? I was born to do this. Literally, born into this world. It's in my genes. I didn't need much training. Took to it like a duck to water, and I loved it."

"Really? Then why'd you stop?" she challenged.

"Extenuating circumstances."

"Like what? Falling in love?"

He scowled. "Who the hell told you that? I don't fall in love, sweetheart. I like pretty women and lots of sex. If they want to marry me, why the hell not?"

"Then why have three of them left you?"

"Because I can't help it if they think they can change me. What you see is what you get. I thought you realized that, honey, when you let me leave you in the hotel. You let me go," he said hoarsely, and her heart ached.

She'd been right—letting him leave that night had been something she should never have done. The fact that he'd actually admit it gave her more hope than anything, but she didn't show it, simply asked, "What did you expect me to do? Chain you to the bed?"

His gaze told her that he'd hoped she would've tried, but he refused to say anything.

"Forcing you to stay wasn't the answer."

He cocked his head. "What makes this the answer now?"

"Because you keep trying to kill us. Or else you're letting us think you are to try to make me hate you especially."

He started to say something but shut his mouth. She waited for him to deny it. Own it. Something.

Instead, he stared past her shoulder, straight ahead at the wall. She thought about how narrow her escape from the bomb had been. That if the flowers had hit the floor or the ceiling before she'd gotten herself into the steel panic room, she wouldn't be here.

She'd barely gotten the door shut behind her. She hadn't heard as much as she'd felt the vibrations of the bomb. And after finding Billie Jean, she'd been in shock, shivered for hours, unable to come down from the high that kept her alive.

"You want to think you know me. You all do. But that's not who I'm meant to be."

"What are you?"

He brought his gaze back to hers. "I'm a man who kills for a living. I take out bad men for another bad man. It's a dirty business, but it pays well. And I don't have to pretend to be something I'm not."

"We're so alike. You have to know that. We both ran from everything we knew and started over," she told him. "You started again with me. You still can."

"It's too hard," he ground out. "Don't you get it? I've done this before—started over."

"And you got a lot of good things from it."

"That's the problem. It was good. And every time I have to give it up, it's like ripping my goddamned heart out. I won't do it again."

"So you'll just rip mine out instead," she said softly.

"Avery, come on. Just fucking let me go." He jangled the chains.

"And you'll disappear."

"That's the general idea."

She played with the key she wore around her neck. Gunner watched it and she wondered if he'd try to overpower her. If he'd hurt her. *Hasn't he already?* "I don't want to let you go. I won't let you go again. Letting you leave my hotel room was a mistake, one I won't make again."

Gunner's eyes flashed. There was anger there, but maybe, just maybe, she spotted a slight bit of relief before he turned away. "You going to keep me tied up forever?"

"If that's what it takes."

"You have no idea what you're doing."

"Then tell me," she implored. "You know, S8 can help."

"Is that what this is about—S8?" His tone was angry. "S8 nearly got me killed. You and your team fucked me over good. I was in it before I knew what happened. So don't talk to me about taking one for the team."

"We're more than that and you know it."

"I know that I like to work alone. I'm built that way."

She grabbed the folder. "All these jobs you've done are just for you?"

"Yes."

"What about Drew Landon?" she asked. "He had nothing to do with this?"

He grimaced.

"He's pulling your strings and you're letting him. And I don't know why." She would push him now, because she did know. "You're not man enough to stand up to him, to tell him no. Does he scare you that much, Gunner? Are you that weak?"

After those words, everything became one big blur.

Gunner wasn't sure what made him angrier—the fact that he was scared of Landon hurting her, or the fact that he'd taken the least weak way out he knew. Avery's face blanched when she realized what was happening, as if she knew she'd gone too far, miscalculated.

It was probably his one and only chance to escape, once he knocked her out and beat the shit out of Jem.

He'd been working on the cuffs for two days. Getting Avery close enough to get a paper clip off the file to fall to the floor had been easier than he'd thought. A gift she hadn't known she'd given him.

And even though he could've gotten out of the cuffs half an hour ago instead of admitting shit better off kept to himself, he hadn't. Now he moved fast, his limbs protesting after being held in one position for too long. Didn't matter, because he wasn't losing the upper hand.

She tried to run from him, but he had her around the waist, then pinned to the steel table close to the double-paned window, aware that the cameras— and Jem—would see all of this. He didn't have much time before the man came in.

His body covered hers, one of her legs curling around his waist. He had to give her credit for trying to control a situation she'd very much lost control of. His hand splayed over her throat even as he pinned her tightly to him.

"You need to forget this. Forget me," he growled, hating the desperation in his voice.

"I'll chase you to the ends of the earth," she told him. Pushed up so her face was so close to his and he leaned in.

Would be so easy to kiss her. Sink into her. Let her promise she could fix everything when he knew damned well no one could.

Not even him.

"Don't do this," he told her as she rubbed against him.

"Why not? You used me as your scratching post once. Why can't I do the same?"

Because you're not like me, he wanted to tell her, but he couldn't. Dammit, she was dangerously close to breaking down the hard-won walls he'd built, brick by brick, over the past months.

He didn't move away though. "Goddammit, Avery—you can't—"

Jem burst in then at the same time Gunner

spun with Avery, holding her back to his chest and her throat with his palm still.

"You won't hurt her," Jem said.

"You're going to count on that?"

"Yeah, I am." Jem walked out, slamming and locking the door behind him, leaving him with a hostage who was the worst hostage ever, because she kept rubbing against him.

Frustrated, he let go of her, pushed away carefully, extricating himself from any and all contact with her body. "What do you want from me? An explanation? A promise to stay with S8 forever?"

"Sure, that's a start." He noted that her hands shook, despite how confident she sounded. He hated himself for being the one to do that to her.

Gunner didn't know what to do at all. Maybe if he was honest with her, really, truly honest, she'd forget him. Let him go. Realize that he was never right for S8, or for her, anyway.

He sat in the chair he'd been tied to. Avery watched him warily, hoisted herself up on the table so she faced him.

"Everything in that folder? It's true. And there are maybe a hundred more jobs out there that I've done too. I did them for the man I was given to by Powell. It was a way to get the guy you know as DL—Drew Landon—off his back, because he'd screwed the man in a business dealing. Giving him me seemed the best way to appease him."

"Your father . . . traded you? That's sick."

He shrugged. "In those circles, shit like that's more common than you think. Everyone just wants to stay alive, stay in the game. Most don't care what that takes."

"Powell thought you were dead. So did Landon, until . . ."

"Until cameras caught me on Powell's island," he explained. "Powell and Landon never really believed I was dead. For added security, they had their tapes sent to each other if the facial-recognition software alerted them to my presence. No amount of hair dye's going to avoid that kind of detection."

"You knew going back to that island would trigger this." She hopped off the table and moved closer. Knelt, her hands on his knees.

"I didn't have a choice. Not after what Grace had gone through. I couldn't let her lose Dare. I know what that's like."

He trailed off, and Avery was up, in his lap. Straddling him. Kissing him. This time, it was the best kind of torture and he knew he was true and well done for.

"I know you're trying to scare me away. It's not going to work. It's never going to work," she told him in between kisses.

He tried to hold out, to not touch her. To push her away. But in the end, he did none of those things.

He wrapped his arms around her and held her close.

Jem cleared his throat from the doorway and pointed at the two-way glass. "Dude, there's no way for me not to see what's about to happen."

"You could close your eyes," Gunner growled over her shoulder. Avery laughed softly, pulled back a little.

Gunner stared between Avery and Jem and wondered what the hell he'd done. He had to tell them the truth. Keep them safe.

"Damn you both—I was taking care of shit."

"Yeah, that was going really well," Jem told him. "We don't need you babysitting us."

"There are women involved," Gunner told him.

"I can certainly take care of myself," Avery echoed, then softened. "I appreciate the sentiment, Gunner, but Landon didn't keep his promise to you. Not this time, and not with Josie."

Instead of answering, Gunner got up and threw the chair across the room. It slammed into the wall and Jem said, "Dude, this place is rented. I want my security deposit back."

"Rented? From what—Interrogations R Us?" Gunner asked.

"Something like that. You know, that's not a bad side business." Jem rubbed his chin and Avery shook her head.

"We'll get right on that, Jem."

"Sarcasm. There's a new one," Jem muttered. "We don't have to pay for another full day if we vacate in the next couple of hours. Think you can pull it together before that, Gunner?"

"I'm still going to kill you."

"You had your chance. Do you know I broke you in less than two days? Christ, I would've lasted weeks," Jem said.

"Because your pain sensors are all fucked up," Gunner pointed out.

"Just jealous. But I do I have a question, G," Jem said.

"You did not just call me G."

"Did. Anyway . . ." Jem leaned forward on his elbows on the table. "Why not just kill the motherfucker and be done with it?"

"Landon's got a lot of enemies, but a hell of a lot more associates who make a hell of a lot of money with him. Taking him down would put an entirely new bounty on my head."

"How about giving him over to the CIA?"

"Guy's bulletproof. Other people, like me, do the dirty work. If I kill him, I might as well kill myself."

Avery grabbed his shoulder. "Bullshit. Don't say that."

"He's going to start looking for me. I have to keep working for him."

"Until we find a way to kill you," Jem finished.

"That won't work a second time."

"It has to. So either you die or Landon does. Personally, I'd take Landon out, but hey, what do I know?"

Gunner fisted his hands on the table. "He'll turn me in to the CIA if I try anything. He's got more on me than anything you've got in that folder."

Jem stood. "We've got shit to figure out."

Gunner nodded. "Let me make contact with Landon first."

Jem pulled Gunner's phone from his pocket. "You already have. I bought you a week and then he expects you in Bali."

"I've got a place," Gunner told them. "Can't risk flying, though, unless you've got a private plane I don't know about."

"I've still got several favors to call in, but I'd rather use them when we're closer to desperate," Jem said. "You two drive. I'll fly. Let me see if anyone's got my trail."

"I don't want you going alone."

"With my luck, I won't be."

Chapter Twelve

Avery held him the entire way up the narrow stairs to the small apartment above the interrogation room like she was afraid he would disappear.

He wanted to tell her that she'd brought this shit and everything that came along with it on herself, lock, stock and barrel, and they would need all the luck they could get. Instead, he let her help him, because he was beyond thinking. He needed to clean up and get her out of here.

He pushed into the shower she ran for him, let the hot water soak his sore muscles while she packed her things and brought him clothes. His clothes, from his house, he noted, then turned his face back under the spray for a while. Washed James away, as if it could be that easy to wash so much bad down the drain.

Avery was watching him and he was grateful she didn't join him. Not yet. It was too soon, everything too raw. When he finally emerged from the shower, he dried himself briskly and dressed. Ate some takeout she'd brought in for him too. Let her dress his split lip and a cut across his eyebrow. She dealt with the cuts around his wrists and ankles too, cleaning and dressing them gently like she was trying to make up for hurting him.

He didn't bother to tell her he'd deserved every second of it, and she didn't even know the worst of it.

"You still want me? On your team, in your life, after how many times I've fucked up?"

"Yes."

Yes. So simple. No reservations.

She brushed some hair out of his eyes. "You have to stop punishing yourself. You've made up for what you've done so many times over. You can't control things that weren't your fault."

"I made choices."

"You made the best choices you could at the time. I hate that Landon used us to force your hand."

"He knew what would work." He paused. "You haven't told the others."

"No."

"I don't want Grace to know . . . to feel like she's responsible. Because she's not."

"Gunner, we all feel responsible."

"I didn't have to go to the island," he told her. "I chose that. I knew. Didn't care, because saving her, Dare, Darius . . . it was important to you. And you'd already lost so much."

"Then don't make me lose you. Not when we just started."

He didn't trust his voice, so he nodded. And her arms wound around him. Hugging him. Healing him. Welcoming him home.

Within the hour, they were in a truck with bulletproofing and tinted windows. Avery pushed him into the passenger's side and he didn't argue. He was bruised and sore and he gulped down some ibuprofen.

"Jem was doing it out of love. You know that, right?" she asked as she tried to leave on a song that sounded like a cat wailing. "Hey, I love that song. It's Fiona Apple."

"It's depressing." He found some classic rock, AC/DC, then rubbed his ribs. "Asshole you claim loves me tried to waterboard me," he sniffed.

"I'm sure he'll make it up to you."

He leaned his head back and let the easy rhythm of the truck moving fast on the highway lull him into thinking everything was going to be all right.

"What are you thinking about?" she asked quietly after they were a couple of hours into the trip. She'd gotten them fast food at a rest stop, but that was the only break they'd taken. Couldn't afford to be out in the open, not at all.

"Everything." Because it was easy to let it all overwhelm him. He realized he'd lost count of how many jobs he'd done. There'd been no point in counting them. After he'd left Avery in the hotel, he'd completely immersed himself into James's old life and hadn't looked back. He had zero contact with anyone or anything from his old life. He hadn't kept an e-mail address or a phone number. Nothing to tempt him or make him think or wish he could've held on to something.

After a couple of months of carrying out orders, he'd stopped thinking or dreaming about Avery. In fact, he'd stopped dreaming at all. Dead inside was the only thing that would work.

None of the new jobs were as bad as the one that had nearly broken him all those years ago. But that didn't mean one wouldn't be. If Landon asked, he'd do it, because even though he was dead inside, he remembered the stakes.

He knew Landon was waiting for him to be dead enough inside so he wouldn't remember those stakes. And he knew what Landon would ask him to do, eventually.

Could he?

He guessed that remained to be seen.

"I meant what I said, about us both running from things. About starting over. I know it's hard—" she said tentatively.

"Do you know what it's like to live a lie?" he

interrupted. "When you ran, it was toward family. You started over, but you were still you. I've been living a lie since I was twelve, in one way or another. Gunner was who Josie wanted me to be."

He paused then, and she said, "I know about Josie, Gunner. Billie told me some . . . and then . . . Jem and I met with Mike and Andy."

"Fuck me," he muttered. That's how she and Jem had tracked him. It made sense now.

"I hear what you're saying. So show me who you are."

"It's that simple?"

"For me, yes." She paused. "Do you think I don't know you're capable of violence? You always were. Dare, Jem, Key . . . they're far from saints. So am I."

"What you did was avenge your mom's death. I was never able to do that for Josie."

"Until now," she reminded him.

"You really have no idea who you're up against."

"I do have some idea. He can't be worse than Powell."

He was, in a different way, though. "Landon was a tough taskmaster, but it was better than living with Powell any day of the week."

"What about your mom, Gunner? Mike and Andy didn't know much about her. They said you barely mentioned her."

"I still try to keep her life and death covert, the way she would've wanted it. She was killed when I was twelve. She was an SAS operative and she and Powell crossed paths a few times. I came out of a very brief affair. But she had no other family, didn't want me to have no one if she died. A lot of people never knew what Powell was like, even those who were supposed to be close with him."

There wasn't anything she could really say to make it better, but he gave her credit for trying when she said, "You made it out."

"I guess I did. Lot of backtracking along the way, though. I don't know what the hell she'd think of me. Of what I've done." He paused. "But anything good I've been able to make out of the bad situations Landon put me in ... well, that was because of her."

Planning the jobs was intense. Each one took anywhere from two to four months of meticulous research. Figuring out the trafficker's next move, predicting his next job. Buying intel without getting him suspicious. Sometimes even infiltrating the inner circle and working a job for them was the only way to get close enough. And sometimes, if it wasn't safe for the women and children Gunner would be looking to save, he would be forced to let an opportunity pass and wait for a prime one.

Because if he couldn't save them from the traffickers outright, he wouldn't risk killing them in an explosion meant for the real criminal. He was painstaking. Brutal. An avenging angel. It was the only way he could justify the greater good.

His mother would say that sometimes in order to do good you had to do bad.

His mother was always so conflicted. Couldn't have been more right. She'd been teaching him lessons, as if she was desperate for him to understand why she did the work she did.

He hadn't understood the full extent until Landon gave him her files. She'd been an SAS-sanctioned assassin, a top spy with a shooter's eye. One of the best there was, one of the best they'd ever had. Even without knowing what she did, he'd learned how to move quietly and stealthily, like a ghost. It was part technique and part genetics, that ability to move though a crowd and no matter how tall or attractive you were, not to be noticed.

She'd done it every day of their lives and somehow pulled him into that magic circle of space. Being with her was exciting. Comforting. How she'd balanced that kind of work and motherhood was summed up by what she told him every time she'd tucked him in and left for work.

"Going to make the world a safer place for you, James," she'd say to him before she went out on a job, even before he had any idea what she did for a living.

He'd done his best over the years to honor her sentiment. "I think she'd hate what I was doing."

"You're wrong. I think she'd completely understand. Everything you've done was to keep doing good. If you weren't under Landon's protection . . ."

He frowned. "Hear yourself? Suddenly you're a Landon fan."

"I'm a Gunner's mom fan," she said.

"Her name was Yolanda. She was awesome, Avery. She made me know we could do what we do and still have kids. She always protected me. She thought putting me with Powell, and giving me a trust fund he knew nothing about that I could access through a lawyer myself, would make me okay."

"Guess we were both raised by strong moms."

"Yeah. She traveled everywhere, but every single summer, we'd spend three months at the beach. All different places and she was there twenty-four-seven. I wasn't in one place long enough for traditional school, but she home-schooled me. And she taught me shit. And she loved me. And that's what I remember the most. She loved me."

"I'm glad you have those memories."

"Me too."

"What I'm not understanding is your loyalty to Landon."

"I didn't say I understood it."

"You believe that he didn't kill Josie?"

"Why wouldn't he admit it? He's got me by the balls. Wouldn't telling me he's taken away some- one I loved and trying to kill me keep me in line?"

"You'd think." She stared at him. "Gunner, if he didn't kill Josie, then who did? And if he didn't try to kill me or Billie . . ."

And with that, suddenly they had two prob- lems on their hands. And both were poised to bite them on the ass hard if they didn't run, either straight into danger, guns blazing, or far, far away.

Several hours later, Avery pulled the car up a long, hidden drive toward a pretty, sprawling house in Tennessee set on acres of land.

He obviously hired someone to look after it, because the landscaping and the inside of the house were spotless.

It was also hard-wired with security to rival Gunner's place in New Orleans.

"I'm cautious," was all he said when he caught her looking. Her heart tugged a little when he said that, and she put a hand on his shoulder as he punched in some codes and alarmed the place around them.

They were in their own little bubble now, a for- tress where they could presumably relax and try to regain some of the ground they might've lost.

"Jem's flight took off. No issues, according to him," she said after checking her phone.

He snorted. "Bullshit. With Jem, there are always complications. He's a walking issue."

"He seems to like it that way."

"It works for him, I guess. Come on, let's see what I can make us for dinner."

She followed him into the massive, state-of-the-art kitchen, her stomach suddenly growling for attention.

"I've got stuff to make us dinner here. Tomorrow, I'll bring in fresh supplies." He rifled through the freezer. "Got steaks. We'll do rice. Fuck the vegetables."

"Sounds like a plan."

Jem would arrive tomorrow. If anyone was following him, they'd be off his trail. She was worried about him and her life would always be one big worry from now on. She'd resigned herself to that fact the second she'd decided to go after Gunner and bring him home.

Home.

They were halfway there. "Let me help."

He snorted. "You don't cook, remember?"

"I can do . . . things."

"Yeah, baby, I know all about those things." His drawl deepened and he patted her on the ass. "You'd better go rest and let me get you fed."

Her stomach growled in answer.

"Go," he insisted. Tossed her an apple, which she crunched into as she walked through his house. She didn't have time for a complete tour, but she walked in and out of each room. She could see why Gunner came here to recover. It was the opposite of the shop in New Orleans. This was pure, masculine comfort. Down-home country, couches and beds that could lull you into the most peaceful easy feeling, and she found herself flipping through an old sketch pad that was next to the big bed.

There were some self-portraits. With the first ones, he hadn't drawn any tattoos on his neck. But as she got deeper into the sketchbook, they began to emerge. She could see the pattern of his re-creation happening before her eyes.

The final self-portrait in the book showed him from the waist up. He'd had a full sleeve by then. She recognized the specific pattern of twists and turns down his left arm, had spent nights memorizing them, mostly when he wasn't looking. But it was the one before that, of the woman with the secret smile that had a mouth that looked just like Gunner's, that held her interest.

She finally put the book down when she smelled the steaks cooking, the scent drifting through the open window. She stripped, went into the big master bath and showered, letting the tension of the past days and the road trip wash away with the hot water. Then she pulled on some comfortable clothes and padded into the kitchen in time to help him set the table.

The scent from the steaks on the grill drifted

through the open sliding glass door, and she breathed in deeply. It had been months since she'd had a home-cooked meal. And being cooked for by Gunner was something she feared might never happen again.

But here they were, playing house. Pushing aside everything and everyone else for just a tiny bit of normalcy that they both ultimately deserved. And when they finally sat down at the table, it was hot seasoned steaks and rice and cold beers. Perfection.

"Did your mom cook?" he asked.

"You mean, did she teach me how?" she teased, and he laughed. "She tried, but I had no interest in learning."

"Why am I not surprised?" he muttered.

"Hey, what's that supposed to mean?"

"So she ran a business, cooked and cleaned and all that good stuff? Like a real mom?"

That made her laugh again. "Yeah, like a real mom. God, I miss her."

"Sorry. Didn't mean to stir that up."

She reached out, touched his cheek for a second. "Don't be. It's a nice memory. I grew up watching Mom kick some serious butt, verbally and physically."

"And you learned that shit well."

"Knew it would come in handy one day." She paused. "She would've really liked you."

"Maybe. I have a feeling she would've kicked

my ass from here to the bayou, though." He ate some of his rice and then asked, "How'd she get into bounty-hunting to begin with?"

"She inherited the business from her parents, who inherited it from their parents. All on my mom's side."

"Makes sense why she'd be drawn to Darius."

"See, and I always thought the opposite. She should've known enough to stay away from the bad boy."

He gave a short laugh. "You haven't figured out by now that she liked bounty-hunting because it involved bad boys? Come on, now, Avery. Why do you think you took to all of this so easily?"

She wanted to say *survival*, but he was right. There was more to it than that.

Chapter Thirteen

Gunner took a drink from a longneck, letting the taste of the bitter beer mix with the home cooking. Two perfect flavors that went together. He watched her enjoying her food, tried to picture her working bounties, counseling criminals.

"Do you think you'd still be doing it, if none of this had happened?"

She stabbed a bite of steak, put it in her mouth and hummed around it. Held up a finger like he was interrupting a religious experience.

Yeah, he so totally fucking loved her. Had from day one. There was no backing out. He knew better. He could no more have walked away from Josie. It wasn't something to think about. It just was.

And he'd never thought it could happen again. But it had. And if he'd learned anything from Josie, and he had, it was that you didn't walk away from a gift. Especially one that chased your ass down.

She'd actually started in on his steak. "What? You're just sitting there all 'thinking.'" She waved the fork in a circular motion in front of his face. "And I need sustenance."

"Don't let me stand in your way."

"You won't," she assured him. "Mmmm, so good."

He knew what she meant. He'd been wandering and eating, of course, but not really enjoying food. It had been fuel. Now, in a calm place, back where he belonged, things had begun to have taste again.

But the worst wasn't over.

"You've got that *thinking of bad things* face," she told him.

"I don't have a face like that."

"You definitely do." She speared more of his steak on his fork. "Okay, to answer your question, if none of this had happened, I would've gone into the bounty business in the town I was born in. Exciting maybe five percent of the time and the rest was paperwork. Talking. Making connections."

She paused. "Of course, I would've taken that life for things not to have taken the turn they did. Horrible things shouldn't be the only things that force us into action."

He wanted to agree, but most people got and stayed comfortable, if not happy. And although he'd been through hell, being trapped and unhappy was something he didn't want.

"You know, sometimes I'm angry with Mom," she continued. "It's like she'd hidden a huge part of me from me."

"You don't think that part would've come out eventually?"

"It was always there, Gunner. Knowing that the way I felt was normal for whose kid I was. That made all the difference. Meeting Dare and learning about Darius made everything make sense."

He stared at her as her words sank in. "Right. You're born into something and you can't escape what you've become."

Her knife and fork clattered to her plate. "Gunner, Christ, that's not what I meant."

"It might not be what you meant, but it's what you said."

"You listen to me—you were born to two operatives. You have espionage in your blood. You're a warrior. Whether you use those traits to tip yourself toward the good side or the bad side is your own business. Your own choice."

Gunner pushed his plate away. "Not always."

"I can't say anything right today, can I?" she asked.

"You're just talking truth, Avery. No right or wrong in that."

"I know you did what you did for me," she said. "I would've done the same thing for you."

He saw the truth of that in her gaze. Her cheeks flushed and she looked so serious.

"I should never have let you leave that hotel room. I'm responsible for that. If I'd begged you to stay . . ."

"I want to say I would've, but that's easier to say than to do," he admitted.

"I wish we could forget our pasts, but that's what makes us who we are. You know that, Gunner. And even though you say you don't know who you are, I know. Mike and Andy know. Josie did too. Jem, Dare, Key and Grace. Are we all easily fooled? Are we all that wrong?"

"I don't want you to be," Gunner said.

Avery moved closer. Stood. Took Gunner's hand. "I'm done telling you. I'm going to show you."

She unbuttoned her shirt and let it drop off her shoulders as she waited in front of him. The tattoo he'd given her . . . from the moment he'd laid eyes on her, he'd pictured those flowers on her, a beauty that belied strength.

Now he ran his palms over his handiwork as she watched him.

"Why do you still believe in me?" he asked.

"Because if roles were reversed, you'd never stop believing in me."

He traced the tattoos he'd inked onto her skin, a perfect blossoming that trailed along her side, licking her rib cage, teasing her breast.

"If we'd been alone that night . . ."

She smiled at the memory. "For a while, we

were. And now it's like you're always with me.
No matter if you push me away, you're still here."

"Damn you," he whispered.

"You were the one who did it. And don't tell
me you didn't know what you were doing."

He'd known. From the second he'd hand-
drawn the flowers on her skin, he'd known. "I
was a fool to try to give you up."

"Yes, you were. Promise you'll never do it
again, no matter what."

"How about I show instead of tell?" He stood,
grabbed her around the waist and picked her up.
"Bedroom's too far."

"So impatient," she chided.

"For you, yes." He got her onto the soft leather
couch, crawled over her. "Need you naked."

She raised her arms so he could pull off the
T-shirt. He did, then immediately locked his mouth
onto a nipple, rolling it between his teeth and
tongue until she arched and called out his name.

His hand slid down her belly, into the wet heat
between her thighs.

"I'm not going to last," she warned.

"Good. Planning on making you come several
times," he assured her.

She was tugging at his jeans, helping him out
of them, telling him she needed him inside her.

"I've got to get—"

"Forget it. I'm on the pill. And I've only been
with you," she told him.

"You're the first in a long time, Avery. Before I left and after."

She spread her legs around him and took him inside her. He shuddered as he went deep and she raked her nails lightly down his arms. He locked his gaze with her as their movements got frantic, until she was coming hard with him inside her.

It took everything not to come—not yet. He waited until she was coming down from her orgasm, pulled out and away slightly. And then he rolled her to her belly, lifted her hips and entered her again. She was still hot and wet and her body gripped him. "Fuck, your pussy feels so good."

Her response was a long, low moan. Her body bowed as she moved against him. He lowered his face, licked between her shoulder blades, tasting her soap, the salt of her skin. He rutted against her and she gave back as good as she got. The night air from the open screen door settled around them, the stars glittered in the sky and he'd come home again.

Not many people got more than one shot. He wasn't letting this one slip through his fingers.

Avery traced the bruises along his cheek. She'd replaced the bandage on his split lip before she'd gotten comfortable against him again. She'd seen the contusions on his body and she realized she'd do it again—let Jem do it—if it meant ending up like this.

"That wasn't an act you were putting on at first, was it?" she asked quietly.

"No, not really. Did I scare you?"

"Yes," she admitted. "You were good at that."

"I guess that's some kind of compliment." He took her hand in his. "You were pretty badass yourself."

"I doubt my interrogation skills will be of much use in the future."

"Well, no, I'm not letting you use your best technique on anyone but me," he told her, tugging her back into his lap. "Because that was hot. For torture, of course."

"Of course," she murmured.

He leaned in and kissed the side of her neck, then nipped, then licked. She shivered. "I'm so easy for you."

"Nothing about this is easy, baby." He pulled back. "I never liked easy."

"Is that why you put yourself right back into Louisiana after you left the SEALs?"

There wasn't going to be any getting out of this. He'd known the interrogation wasn't really over when he'd left that room where she and Jem had him tied. It was just taking on a different—necessary—form. "I didn't come back to New Orleans right away. I stayed here for a while after Josie was killed."

"Why did you move back?"

"To test myself. To see if I'd really been burned.

I'd always have to look over my shoulder. I just wanted to know how much."

Avery nodded and he continued. "I wanted to be . . . close to her again. Closer to my family. And yeah, I realize how stupid that sounds."

"Doesn't sound that way at all," she said. "Mike and Andy are glad you came back. They don't blame you."

"How could they not?"

"Because it wasn't your fault."

"Yeah, it was. And no matter how good they were to me, how much I loved Josie, I should've left. Especially because of those reasons and no matter how hard they protested. I brought terrible danger to their doors. I knew it would happen, and trust me, I hated being right about that." He paused. "And then I brought it back to you."

"Jem and I were the ones who kidnapped you."

"I went to your hotel. I shouldn't have done that."

"If you hadn't, I still would've found you."

"Yeah, I bet you would've."

She traced a finger along his collarbone as he sank back into that world again. He was still close enough to taste it—dangerously so—and he expanded on what he'd told her earlier. Maybe it was an attempt to justify what he'd done, an attempt to justify Landon, to explain the man.

Drew Landon smuggled people—but people who wanted to be smuggled, mainly criminals and their families, drug lords and the like. He'd found his niche, and it worked well with his ability to counterfeit most major IDs and documents from all kinds of agencies around the world. He was well connected and built upon that in order to become the best at what he did.

He justified that the men and women he smuggled away from justice would eventually be caught—he was just taking their money, because someone had to. Plus, as Landon pointed out, sometimes he'd be helping out good people, those in witness protection who no longer trusted the government to keep them safe.

Gunner had once told him he wouldn't know any of the finer things if they bit him in the ass. He'd waited to get slapped. Put in his place.

He'd gotten fucking kindness. He'd vandalized Landon's place. Stolen from him. Gotten drunk. Acted like a wild kid. Acted like himself.

Landon let him, waited him out. Gave him things he'd needed in order to help with Landon's business. He gave him skills and an outlet—taking out bad guys.

"There are different grades of bad. And that's a seductive way to put it—I might be bad but I'm not hurting anyone." Gunner shook his head, rubbed the tattoos snaking up the side of his neck. "I believed what I wanted to believe.

Landon didn't make me that person. I made me that person. I didn't give a fuck about anyone or anything. And Landon liked me that way. I'd go anywhere, do anything. Blowing shit up was my favorite thing to do. If a human trafficker was involved, even better."

"You were young," Avery told him.

"I should've known better." He'd grown up in the world of shade, because no operative could ever be squarely on the side of the right. His mom tried. Once he was old enough to notice this dynamic, he'd watched her drag herself home, half distraught. By morning, the distress would be gone, the surface smoothed and calm. But Gunner knew now that under the surface, nothing ever truly settled.

"What made you get out?"

He laughed then. She was staring at him like he'd lost his mind. "I didn't leave. He kicked me out and I tried to get back in. I assumed he'd had me beaten as a warning. To teach me a lesson."

"Sounds about right."

"Except he says he never ordered that. And he claims he didn't touch Josie."

"Why call you back for that particular job?"

"To finish what I started when I fucked up the first time. A chance to make it right. To get back in. I don't know." He rubbed his face. "I was out of it for eleven months. I was in love with Josie. But I missed the action. So I figured, finish the job. Prove myself, and then I could get back in. Do it in moderation. But fuck, it doesn't work that way. And I never wanted anything to happen to Josie."

"I know, Gunner. No matter what, I know that."

"I thought I could have the best of both worlds."

"Sometimes you can, Gunner."

"I took a chance with her life. I never thought . . . If I was going to work for him, why would he . . ."

"How did he find you?"

"I took the SIM card from my cell phone before they destroyed it. He never canceled the phone number. It was on his account. I put it into a new phone after a couple of months and figured, if he wanted me back, he could find me. I guess he'd always planned on giving me a second chance. Guess I always wanted one. The only reason I went back this last time was because I made him promise to leave you alone."

He closed his eyes and pictured Josie, lying on the floor. "She'd died with the phone in her hand, trying to crawl to the door. Looking for me. I didn't get home in time. Not even close."

"Was it retaliation?"

"I don't know. To this day, I don't goddamn know. But whether it was retaliation or random, the fact still remains that I wasn't there. The worst thing I've ever done to get free from a man I hated and I did that for Josie. The night I was free, she was killed."

There was nothing she could say to make it better, so she didn't even try. Instead, she pulled him closer, ran her hands over his tattooed forearms as though the images would come alive under her touch. And maybe they did, because she and Gunner were kissing and although she didn't know how it started, she knew she didn't want it to end.

He couldn't do this. Not again and not to her. *She knows violence. Understands it.*

That didn't mean she should be married to it.

He heard the rawness in his voice, wanted to drown it out with alcohol until he couldn't see straight. "When I did that fucking last job . . . It was horrible." His face looked so pained, his neck muscles tensed, and she was sure he'd take off any second. "I can't even . . ."

She put her arms around him then. Shushed him. Told him not to say anything else. Somehow she had to make this all better for him. "You can tell me, Gunner. I think it's better if you tell someone."

"You can't ask me that. Take it back."

"No." Avery's voice broke. "I've done bad things too."

"You've done nothing close to my level." He pulled back and stared at her. "Does it matter? I did it. And it broke me. I lost everything. The only reason I didn't kill myself was because it hurt to stay alive. Good penance."

"Oh, Gunner."

"I was broken from the job," he said. He'd practically crawled home after it was done, and it had been like walking on hot coals. His entire body was aching with grief already, and seeing her on the floor, with Petey, was the final fucking straw.

"I wasn't there for her. I couldn't have been. I made a choice this time so you stayed safe. And that almost didn't happen. You're in danger just from knowing me."

"And I always will be," she reminded him. "That ship has sailed. So we have to deal with it, Gunner. Together. Because if there's going to be risk with or without you, I'd much rather be with you."

"Why?"

"How can you not know? The way you helped me. Let me mourn that night in the bayou. You know me. You always have."

He couldn't deny that. "You're so strong. Didn't need me to get that way."

"Maybe I need you to stay that way. Or maybe I just want you there." She paused. "Don't you worry about having to look over your shoulder every day for the rest of your life?"

"You're implying that I haven't been doing that already," Gunner said.

"That's kind of—"

"Realistic."

"You know that anyone who loved you would never want you to make yourself suffer, no matter what happened," she told him.

He didn't want to talk about this anymore. But Avery still had questions, legitimate ones, especially because she was now in this up to her neck.

"Why was Landon so intent on bringing down traffickers? They don't even tangentially interfere with any of his business. If anything, he had more in common with them than not."

Gunner shook his head. It was time to reveal secrets—his, Landon's. Everything had been rolled up into a big black ball of pain and it was unraveling. Finally.

It finally felt right.

"Landon had his reasons. He'd been in the smuggling business forever. Born into it. And his father screwed over a trafficker on one of his jobs, although not purposely. It wasn't even anything that led to a huge loss for the guy. And, yes, I researched it. Landon was transparent about it, but I wouldn't have just taken his word for it. But afterward the trafficker—George Mullin—took Landon's mother and older sister. Sold them both and Landon never saw them again. Never stopped searching. Every time I'd free people, I had their pictures, and I wore a necklace with a symbol they'd recognize."

"You never saw them."

"No. But Landon never wanted anyone's family to go through that. And then Powell traded me in exchange for the debt he owed."

"Landon took you in and really felt for you. Cared for you in the way he'd hoped someone had his own mother or sister."

"I told you it was complicated."

"And that's why it doesn't make sense that Landon would give you a second chance and then hurt Josie."

"Look, he takes what he considers betrayal very seriously. He didn't get to be where he is by not being ruthless. And he is. But there's a part of the picture I'm missing. And it's driving me crazy." He stared out the window. "I think I should contact him."

"And say what?"

"I haven't figured that out yet."

Gunner could see the wheels in Avery's head turning. He wasn't surprised, but he was glad he'd been able to give her some time away.

"Avery, we don't have to do this," he told her.

"What are the options? Do we kill me off?"

"Yes."

"It won't work unless he can kill me himself."

"So we'll disappear as best we can."

"No. If nothing else, I'm not letting you give up your life again."

"Maybe third time's the charm?"

"Maybe I won't take that chance. Even if it all ends there, we have to finish this job," Avery said. "I keep thinking, if we can just get rid of all our ghosts . . ."

"We'll be free and clear?" Gunner shook his head. "That's no way to live. Because you're always going to have a past. Someone who's going to want to hurt you for what you've done, especially if you've done it right."

"You're a very smart man, Gunner." She ran a hand through his hair. "Your mom's coloring?"

"It shouldn't go together, but it does. Makes disguises easy."

She trailed her hands over his inked arms. "But these aren't. You had to know they'd give you away."

On some level, he had. Maybe he knew that once he was found again, he'd have to make a decision.

"Will you tell me what your tattoos say about you?"

"All of them?

"All of them. First to last. I want to know the reasons behind each one. I want to know you better than anyone. I need that. Because you already know me."

He could do that for her.

"And the scars too. Everything."

He thought about the long scar on his lower

back. Easy to cover up, and he could probably get away with ignoring it, pretending he'd forgotten about it. But at some point, she'd notice it.

You're acting like she might not have already.

"Everything," she repeated, like she knew he was holding back.

"You're so much like Josie in some ways. And in others, not at all."

"Are those both good things?"

"Yes," he said softly.

"Gunner, why all the weddings?"

"I was trying."

"Trying what?"

"To feel. They seemed to love me. I don't know if they really did or not. And I figured, maybe I'd learn. Sounds so fucked up, doesn't it?"

She wound her hands through his hair. "Understandably so."

"I loved Josie. Was I in love with her? For what I knew about love? Maybe? I think we were a lot alike. I wanted to be as good as her. I wanted that goodness to rub off on me. When being in her proximity didn't change me or fix me . . ." He trailed off.

"You didn't need to be fixed, Gunner. Just shown a different way to keep doing what you like to do. You figured that out. I'm only sorry Landon used S8 to try to pull you back to somewhere you never should've been."

"I just need you safe."

"I will be. At first, I wondered how any of this could possibly work. I mean, look at Darius and my mom. She left when she realized what he did for a living. But her work was dangerous too." Avery rubbed her bare arms. "Grace wants to work with Dare."

"And you're okay with that."

"She needs training. And I think she'll be better in support roles so Dare doesn't lose his mind. But it seems inevitable that who you work with ends up being someone you have a lot in common with." She looked at him. "Could you have done this kind of work and gone home to Josie?"

"I wanted to try, but working for Landon was a lot different than working for S8."

"You've already worked with me."

"It's not that I don't trust you. I don't trust myself. You're not the problem—I am. The men in this group are the problem. I want to protect you, always have, always will above all else and not because you can't do the job. It's the way men are built."

"Some men."

"All the men in S8. The ones who'd be surrounding you," he reminded her.

"We'll all find a way to be comfortable," she said. "It's important to all of us."

"Yeah, it is." She stretched out on the sheets. "It's been at least a week since I've actually slept."

"And I feel like trying to sleep would be futile." She climbed onto him.

"When you put it like that, sure." He grinned. She loved seeing that. Over the next months, those smiles might be few and far between. But she'd take what she could get.

Chapter Fourteen

Jem had sent Key an *it's all good* message before he boarded the flight out of New Orleans. As usual, Key wouldn't believe him and would get pissed, and that was the way Jem knew that things were fine between him and his brother.

Key'd had a tough time coming back to the bayou. Seeing their parents' house had been more cathartic than either of them could've thought. Saying good-bye to their respective careers and delving into the shadowed world of black ops, and so far reporting to no one, was something both he and Key had been trained for. More than that, they wanted it.

Key was on a much-needed vacation and Jem was glad Avery had pushed the issue. Disturbing him was something Jem was unwilling to do.

He was several months–plus out of the last mental institution the CIA had sent him to in order to distance themselves from yet another situation Jem had created due to his overzealous, uncontrolled nature.

At least that's what he'd read when he'd broken into the shrink's files.

Jem had been labeled everything from manic to schizo, and the latter was only because he'd told one doc he'd heard the voice of God telling him to jump from roof to roof on two city buildings and then drop twenty feet.

"I caught the guy I was chasing and I didn't get hurt," had been his defense. Granted, he'd also been operating inside the U.S., where he wasn't allowed to—"not legally if you want to get technical," he'd continued, and yeah, they'd wanted to get technical.

The shrink had simply shaken her head and written shit on her legal pad. And so it went.

And when the plane finally touched down, ending his trip down psycho memory lane, he was fucking grateful. They'd landed on time and he grabbed his go bag from under the seat in front of him and headed to the front of the plane before other people got out of their seats.

The flight attendant who'd slipped him her number earlier didn't say a word, just smiled and wagged her finger at him. Once into the main terminal, he ambled along in order to make sure he was alone. He didn't have any weapons on him except the ceramic knife in his boot, a pen and his own hands, which were more than enough.

He hadn't noticed anyone tailing him in New Orleans and there was nothing suspicious on the plane. He pulled out his phone, slid by the *what the fuck is up with you?* message from Key and had just gone to check in with Gunner instead when the hairs on the back of his neck stood on end.

Someone was on his tail. He'd bet his life on it.

He pretended to make a call while slipping the SIM card out of his phone, just in case he was captured. He was going to find out who this asshole was, one way or the other.

He pushed out the door and walked through the crowds gathering with their luggage, waiting for taxis. He crossed the street, broke from the crowds and headed to the farthest long-term parking lot there was.

"I'll meet you by the car," he said into the phone, loud enough for his tail to pick up on.

He heard one set of footsteps behind him, then two. And there was a female coming toward him, checking her phone. Clueless.

Or maybe just playing at it, because something was off with this one. She was exuding confidence, but it wasn't working for Jem. He prided himself on reading people—less of a gut instinct and more of a spiritual thing. When he started talking about auras, most guys in the CIA rolled their eyes at him, but hell, he'd gotten most of their asses out of scrapes that way.

He'd lost partners because he tended to take

things too far, had little disregard for his own life, although he'd never let any of them take the risks he did.

Guess you understand Gunner a lot better than most.

To test his theory he grabbed the tall blonde in the short skirt around the waist as she went by him. Suspended in the air against his side, she yelped and hit him.

And then pulled a gun out and aimed it at his forehead.

When he laughed, it threw her. The fucking crazy always did. He grabbed her wrist and re-pointed the gun as she struggled to regain control, aimed and shot the two men coming up fast behind him. And kept shooting until he'd emptied the clip. Thankfully, she'd thought ahead and used a silencer, but even so, shit echoed in this underground part of the garage.

"How's that for a one-two punch, sweet-heart?" he asked before slamming her wrist against the nearest concrete barrier, breaking the bone and forcing her to drop the gun. No reason to give her any chance of reloading.

She elbowed him in the throat.

"Son of a bitch." He dropped her down, grabbed her in a headlock, because if she wanted to be equal opportunity, he would treat her like an equal. "Doll-face, you gonna tell me who sent you to kill me?"

"Fuck you."

"Is that a no? Because I can be really fucking persuasive." He dragged her toward a supply closet. "We're gonna have us a strip search, just in case."

"Don't you dare."

"Don't get modest. Besides, I like my women willing. This is all on the up-and-up."

In the closet, his hand slid up her shirt, into the front of her blouse, and bingo, he found her phone. "It's a good spot for it."

He checked the last several numbers. "Any of these Landon?"

"Please. I have a kid."

"This isn't a great job for parenting."

"He made me."

Jem noted the track-marked scars on her arms. She was painfully thin too, and this close up, she looked worn and pale, and older than she probably was. "Who's he?"

"He didn't tell me. Said you'd know."

"What's he got on you?"

She eyed him warily. "Enough."

"What the hell am I supposed to do with you?"

She pointed to her thigh, said hoarsely, "You're supposed to die."

He yanked her skirt up, saw the bomb taped securely to her thigh. She and the men were all part of a fucking distraction and he'd fallen for it. There were ten seconds left.

"Your kid—"

"Better off without me. Go." She shoved him away and he ran, slammed the door behind him, hit the dirt behind cars as the explosion blew the closet open.

He'd done a lot of things in his life and had pretty much zero regrets at the time, because how could you regret shit that at the time you ultimately wanted?

Had the woman been innocent? No. Was her kid better off without her? Probably. But Jem would be damned if he'd let himself get played like that.

He went for the first car with the door open and hot-wired it, because no one was going to notice a stolen vehicle in this fucking mess. But they would notice a man who looked like he'd been through the explosion.

He dialed as he drove, one hand on the wheel, away from the incoming sirens. "Gunner, fuck—"

"Landon has Avery."

"Fuck. He just tried to kill me. I'm on my way, but brother, I think your place was made a long time ago."

Gunner went to the store to grab some fresh food like he'd promised, leaving Avery home to relax in the steam shower. She got restless after ten minutes, although her muscles felt like butter. She wrapped herself in a big flannel shirt of Gunner's, not bothering with anything else.

It was beautiful here. For a little while, she was content to forget what was out there waiting for them. She just wanted to be. Since her mom had been killed, it had been a whirlwind. And she'd found a lot more good than bad since; she'd discovered her father, got to talk to him before he died. Got to be a part of saving him. And she found a brother. It hadn't taken long at all for her and Dare to grow close. She couldn't imagine her life without him now.

As she stared out at the expanse of lands, she thought about options. They'd already dodged two big bullets, had lost Darius, saved Grace. And now they'd gotten Gunner back.

She'd come so close to losing him, to losing herself. Lived a lifetime before hitting twenty-five. And she was thinking of committing a lifetime—a real one—toward more of the same. And asking the people she loved to come along for the ride.

It had seemed like such a simple and straightforward decision five months ago, when they'd been in the thick of it and come out the other side. But she'd just been in the thick of it again, come out a little worse for wear but with the man she knew she loved.

Tucked inside her suitcase were some of Adele's journals. There were too many to carry, and she'd left them in storage when she'd gone on the search for Gunner. The three volumes she

had with her had been read and reread what felt
like a hundred times over the past months. Grace
had been the one to give them to her, and they
gave a unique perspective on being a woman in
this kind of job, this kind of life.

*It can be done, but it's never going to be easy for the
men you work with, or the men who love you. Accept
that as something that will never, ever change and
you'll be fine.*

And if Avery couldn't accept that? Couldn't let
the men in her life constantly worry about her—
and Grace too?

She rubbed her arms as she pondered, the flannel soft under her palms. It smelled like Gunner.

What could they do? Work at the tattoo shop?
Open a restaurant? Never nine-to-five jobs for
any of them.

They were built for this, just as Landon had told
Gunner. What they did with that was up to them.

So much risk and potential loss. And that
could happen no matter what. She didn't want to
live her life in fear, couldn't let that rule her.

She couldn't figure out if her mother would be
disappointed in her or proud. Didn't want to
think about that for too long, so instead, she
pulled her phone out of the front pocket of the
shirt, where she'd slipped it earlier. She didn't
hesitate this time, like all those other times when
she'd ended up not letting the call go though and
ended up texting instead, the nightly check-in

they'd all agreed on. A code that they'd prear-
ranged to change weekly.

This time, she let the call go through.

Grace picked up on the second ring. "Avery!
What's wrong?"

Grace's tone was equal parts genuine happiness and genuine suspicion

"You're as suspicious as Dare. I just missed
you. Figured I should be able to break my own
rules about calling to say hi, or else what's the
fun of being able to make them in the first place?
And nothing's wrong."

"There's something, Avery."

"Is that a premonition?"

"I don't need premonitions with you. I know
that tone of voice. Talk to me."

Avery did. "I was reading Adele's journals."

"What volumes are you on?"

"S8's still viable."

"Right," Grace murmured. "Okay, so . . ."

"Do you think she's right, that this is going to
be harder on us? Make it harder on the men?"

"One hundred percent."

"Yeah, me too. It's making me rethink this for
the first time, and I don't think that would've
been Adele's intent in the first place."

Grace was silent for a moment and then said,
"Why do you want to be a part of S8? If you can
answer that, you can probably answer your own
question."

"At first, it was a way to honor Darius and Adele too. And then it became about more than that. It was like this was where I'm supposed to be, and this is what I'm supposed to be doing. A sense of destiny."

Grace would definitely understand that. Gunner did as well. But destiny could take you down the wrong path, get you in trouble, which is what she told Grace.

"I don't think making a decision with your heart is ever wrong," Grace said firmly. "There are always going to be things you didn't do. But that's what it is—a different path. Different, not right, and so it shouldn't be a regret."

"How'd you get so smart?"

"Born that way," Grace told her. "I think we're all meant to do good. Together, we can."

And just like that, Avery's decision clicked firmly back into place. "How're you enjoying your vacation?"

"Dare's already getting into trouble—he boarded a speedboat and almost got arrested," she said wryly. "Any more vacation and we're going to need a bail bondsman on the payroll."

"I've got contacts everywhere," she said. They hung up, and she was smiling. Lighter.

Gunner had told her earlier that the decision was hers. And she'd made it, again, and it was definitely the right one.

She'd read the next three journals as soon as

she could get her hands on them. Even though she knew how Adele's story ended, she still wanted to know the journey. That was the most important part.

Still grinning, she stared out at the lake. Heard the door open behind her and said, "That was quick."

"Glad you think so."

She barely had time to register that it wasn't Gunner's voice before she felt the pinprick of a needle in her neck. She faded fast, grabbed for the deck's railing as she started to fall to the floor.

She tried to fight, but her limbs weren't working right. She wasn't completely out of it, but she knew whatever she'd been given had immobilized her badly. She couldn't even scream.

She was aware of being carried, put into a car, and she tried to count to figure out how many miles she was being taken, but she went in and out of consciousness and her mind wasn't cooperating when she was awake.

Her eyes opened what seemed like hours later. She was staring at a ceiling, her head propped on a pillow on a bed, with a mirror above her. She was still in the flannel shirt, but it had risen and she was partially exposed. Her legs had been tied, and so were her arms, but she couldn't feel them.

"I wouldn't bother struggling. You've been immobilized." A man stood in the doorway. "Nice to meet you, Avery."

"Wish I could say the same." Her words slurred. Her head throbbed, a screaming pain, which seemed to be a side effect of the drug. She was virtually paralyzed and it was terrifying. She couldn't move, no matter how hard she tried. It was like being stuck in quicksand and her mind was still sharp enough to process everything. And panic.

"You're not what I thought you'd be," he told her as he moved closer, pushed open the flannel shirt. She lay naked in front of him, refusing to cry.

"You're Landon. Exactly . . . like I thought."

Drew Landon was maybe midforties. A good-looking man, although she could never give him that compliment, knowing what she did about his past.

"I hope you didn't think you were well hidden at James's house. Once he came back on the grid, finding properties associated with him wasn't difficult. Of course, the tracker planted on his phone made things easy enough as well."

"What do you want?"

"I want James, without the distraction of your group. You've gained quite the reputation after just one job. But really, you're the biggest problem. Women always are." His finger traced her lips, which she felt, then dipped lower. She glanced up at the mirror and saw his fingers were playing along her tattoo and she vowed not to look up again. Better not to know. "I think if I eliminate you—"

"He'll kill you," she tried.

"He might want to. But after Josie, you'd think he'd learn. But he didn't. He'll come back to me, the way he always does. I gave him a place to live, a purpose. You don't forget that for a piece of ass."

Something wasn't adding up here, but she had too many competing thoughts to figure it out. Add to that the crushing weight of fear and she had to force herself to keep her breathing even, not to panic.

He leaned over her and added, "By the way, I left an audio link behind so James can hear everything that's happening. So make sure you make some noise for him."

Tears ran down her cheeks. She hated that she couldn't wipe them away. The only thing she could do was spit directly into his face when he got close.

Her satisfaction at that was short-lived, when he pulled out a short but wicked-looking blade and tapped it against her breast.

She bit her bottom lip to keep from crying out. Stared into his eyes instead of watching the knife. "I will make you pay for this, Landon."

"Sweetheart, you're the one who's already paying."

She squeezed her eyes shut so she wouldn't look up by mistake. When she opened them because she'd heard him stop moving, he was staring down at her. And then he brought the knife back up into her line of vision.

It was bloody.

He was carving her up and she couldn't feel a thing.

The farmers' market was a fifteen-minute ride from his house. Gunner rolled the window down, turned the radio up and for the first time in months, he felt lighter.

There was still a lot of work to do, but there was a light at the end of the tunnel, and her name was Avery. And he couldn't wait to get back to her.

Leaving her wasn't his first choice, but she looked so damned comfortable, resting in the sauna. Besides, he knew he was Landon's real target, would always be until he took the proper steps.

For the moment, he shoved those thoughts down hard, parked and went into the open-air market with his cap pulled down low but no glasses. He'd still manage to blend into the crowd from the majority of the people there.

But there were people he couldn't hide from. And those same people would never be invisible to him either. It was a spook's instinct, an eerie feeling, like looking across a crowd where everyone else except the dangerous ones were frozen.

It took ten minutes for him to gather the food he needed. It was on that ninth minute when he spotted the guy in the Mariners hat—and that guy spotted him at the same time. They made eye contact as if they were the only ones there.

Could be nothing, another spook recognizing his own kind, another spy who discovered a newcomer to his territory. But if it wasn't . . .

He disappeared behind a large display, phone in front of him in case the guy came around the corner, and he dialed Avery. Got her voice mail.

Just because she doesn't answer doesn't mean anything's wrong. After they'd showered, she'd decided to stay in the steam room for a while. She was locked in a heavily alarmed house and she had a weapon.

He shoved the phone into his pocket and made a big deal about reading ingredients on a jar of honey. Bought it because glass always made a good weapon, if all else failed.

He turned and found Mariners Cap on his six. Still meant nothing. He'd follow a guy like him too.

He paid while keeping tabs on Mariners Cap. Still no return call from Avery. He hit REDIAL and got voice mail again as he headed to the parking lot.

He wasn't going to lead the guy to the rental car or back to his house, although he'd considered that he'd been followed from there. He was having trouble shoving his panic about Avery down, because every second that passed made him more convinced that something was wrong. He walked through the main lot, past the families with the kids, strode with the guy still on his six toward the back lot.

On a weekday, it wouldn't be full at all. And he kept walking through the mostly empty lot, filled with mostly employee vehicles.

In the farthest end of the lot, where a row of vehicles was blocking him from the road, Gunner turned. The guy had been following him, quietly, and now lunged the last several feet toward him.

Gunner reached out instinctively to grab him by the throat and put him down quickly, but stilled as he caught sight of the familiar face. The guy he had pinned had been involved in beating Gunner before dropping him in the bayou.

The car ride was oddly silent. Gunner had resisted getting into the car at all, but Landon wouldn't hear otherwise. He'd been in the States via Mexico after the fuckup—the major fuckup that could've been avoided had he not gotten cocky. That would haunt him, and the fact that Landon kicked him out and off the team was worse. He'd really had nowhere to go, and no one.

He'd been reeling. And when they'd switched cars, he'd gone along for the ride, hoping he could convince one of them to talk to Landon for him. But when it drove away, with him in the back, it took him a few miles to realize they were men he'd never seen before.

When he tried to get out, they Tasered him. Beat the

shit out of him when he couldn't move until he'd passed out. He lost track of everything, figured they were going to kill him. When he woke to a wet nose on his cheek and a low howl, he thought he was about to be eaten by some kind of wolf. And he didn't give a shit.

Now he pressed the man's head against the nearest car hood, an arm on the back of his neck. "Who the fuck sent you?"

"Same guy who sent me the first time."

"Guess you should've finished the job. Because this time, I'm going to." With the right pressure he knocked the guy out and cracked his neck as he fell to the ground. Gunner went through his pockets, took the phone and memorized the name on the ID, kicked the guy under the nearest truck and strolled back to his car.

A fucking forced stroll instead of the full-on run he'd wanted to do. As he walked, his phone rang and he grabbed for it without looking. "Avery?"

"Someone just tried to fucking kill me, Gunner."

Jem. "Me too. I'm going home to Avery—can't get in touch with her."

"I'll meet you there."

Chapter Fifteen

Jem pulled into the driveway twenty minutes after he'd hung up. Gunner met him on the porch as Jem demanded, "What the fuck's happening here?"

Jem was covered in dirt, and there were concrete pieces in his hair.

"Someone tried to kill you?"

"Suicide bomber," Jem said grimly as he followed Gunner inside. "What do we know?"

"There's a syringe on the back deck. Whoever took her left these two earpieces on the kitchen counter. They're not turned on yet."

"Fuck."

"I shouldn't have left her."

"Come on, Gunner—get real. And whoever took her couldn't have gotten far."

"I was gone an hour. An hour could get her far. On a plane, out of the country." Gunner swallowed his panic. "They left no tracks."

"Listen, they want to be in contact with us," Jem

turned over the earpieces in his fingers, then popped one into his ear. "I'll get in touch with Mike and Andy. And is there any doubt who took her?"

"None," Gunner said grimly. "I can call him."

"That might piss him off more. For Avery's sake . . ."

That was the only reason he hadn't called yet. He paced as Jem talked with Mike and Andy, forced himself to keep his phone in his god-damned pocket. Landon could be anywhere with her and his best course of action was to wait.

"What's he doing to her, Jem?" he asked at one point.

"He'd better not do shit to her," Jem muttered, and then he pointed to his earpiece. He turned on the tracking software and mouthed, *They're bouncing the signal. It's going to take a little time*.

Time Avery might not have. He held out his hand for the second earpiece and Jem shook his head. Paled.

"Gunner, we'll get her back," Jem was mouthing, pointing at the tracking software that was working furiously to pick up the location.

"Let me hear."

"No." Jem's voice was hoarse. He looked like he was about to be sick.

"You have to let me be with her. Now, of all times."

Jem cursed and handed him an earpiece. Gunner hesitated briefly, then slipped it on.

His ears flooded with Avery's whimpers of pain.

"No," he whispered, as if that could stop anything.

He heard sounds of grunting. Handcuffs. He tried to listen past it, to get any clues about where she'd been taken, but he couldn't get past hearing Avery cry.

He heard, "Bitch," muttered too low for him to tell if it was actually Landon or not.

"Fight, Avery," he muttered. The fact that she wasn't doing so could only mean one thing—she was drugged. Even tied, Avery would find a way to fight, scream, claw. Something.

Landon was determined to take everything away from him, to strip him down to nothing. To force him to be a machine.

He could never do that. Not after tonight.

He'd never forgive himself. Couldn't see how she ever would either.

Avery needed him to stop cutting her. The fact that she couldn't feel, couldn't know if she was dying or not was freaking her out more than anything.

"He talks about you, Drew. He understands you," Avery told Landon, trying to appeal to the man Gunner talked about, the one who'd saved Gunner from Powell. The one who'd been more of a father than Powell had been.

Of course, that wasn't saying much. But the Landon in front of her was a monster that maybe Gunner never saw, never wanted to acknowledge.

"That's where you're wrong, Avery. James doesn't know me, and you don't know him." His eyes were so dark and angry, the fury palpable even though his expression was outwardly calm. She tried to remain equally calm, but her fear bled through. And that was what he wanted.

She was a fighter and he'd taken that away from her physically. But inside, she was still strong.

Break them before they break you. She could hear Gunner's mom saying that to him.

"Yolanda, help me," she said out loud.

"I don't know who that is, but she can't help you."

I don't know who that is. How could he not know Gunner's mom's name?

"You're taking Gunner away from jobs he does best, Avery. He saves helpless women and children. Don't you think that's important?"

"He doesn't need you to help people."

Landon smiled, a cunning, chilling look. "You can't really believe that."

There was more blood every time Landon put the knife in her face. She whimpered because her body was cold now, numb and cold, and she was running out of time.

"Did your perfect James tell you what he did for me? What a good worker bee he was?"

"He was trying to save his wife. He was trying to survive." God, her voice was clearer now, which meant the drugs were wearing off. Soon, she might feel everything.

She didn't know how much worse that could be.

Landon smiled, that wicked, horrible smile that told her he was getting so much enjoyment out of this. "He'll do anything to survive."

"So would most people. But Gunner would never sell out the people he loves."

"No, he'll just kill children to protect them."

She blinked, wanted to call him a liar, but she knew that it was true, and that's why Gunner couldn't talk about it. "I'm sure that whatever he did, it's because you tricked him into doing it."

"I never had to trick him into doing what he was built for."

"You can't know him nearly as well as you think you do."

"He spent time in my life. My bed. I knew him intimately."

"And now I do. And I'm the one he wants." She drove that dagger in deep, smiling as she did so.

"He'll always come back to me. He always has."

"Not this time. Never again."

"You think James is yours?" Landon sneered.

"I think Gunner is his own man. I'll be damned if I let you force him to do your dirty work."

"Force him?" Landon bit out a laugh. "No one forces James to do anything. This job's in his blood. He's a legacy."

"I know all about legacies," she spat. "You have no idea what my pedigree is." She forced herself to calm down. "I want you to know that the next time you see me in person, you won't breathe longer than ten minutes."

"Threats, Avery."

"It's a goddamned promise." She'd been in that place before. She'd sought vengeance for her mother, killed the men who'd killed her, and she'd discovered it hadn't made things better at all.

In fact, it made them somehow worse. But this time, it would be different. She couldn't save her mother, but she'd be damned if she couldn't save Gunner.

But first, she'd have to save herself and survive this. She closed her eyes for a long moment, willing the courage she'd always had to come thrumming back through her body. She noted she was shivering. And her body was aching.

Oh God, it was wearing off. And he wasn't done cutting her.

"Is this the only way you can get it up, by killing the women Gunner loves?" she spat out.

Instead of answering with words, Landon held up the knife and pressed it to her skin.

She tried not to scream and failed.

"Playtime's over, little girl. You have no idea who you're up against. But don't you worry, I've got plenty of time to show you."

"No matter how long you take, you'll never show me." She didn't care about making him angrier. She'd take her power any way she could, would hang on by her nails, leaving deep claw marks.

Her hands moved as she thought about that. They moved—only slightly, but the tingle meant that the drug was metabolizing.

It wouldn't be fast enough. Because he was still cutting her, and she would wear those scars forever.

"Remember this. Every time you're with James, he's going to see these and think of me. And so are you. If you'd stayed apart . . ."

"If you'd done a better job of trying to kill me," she taunted. She wanted to pass out, but she couldn't. Adrenaline coursed through her body, made the pain bearable. Made her somehow unable to look away.

The blood welled from the deep cuts. She knew where he was going . . . her beautiful flowers.

She wouldn't beg, not even when Drew said, "If you ask nicely, I'll leave this alone."

She didn't believe him and she forced herself to stay calm. "What kills you more, the fact that

Gunner would rather work with me than you, or the fact that Gunner marked me first?"

That was the end of the conversation and the numbness, but only the beginning of the excruciating pain.

Gunner buried his face in his hands, knew what she was doing and why, but Landon was going to hurt her. The man had lost control . . . if it was truly Drew Landon, Gunner knew he was capable of carrying out his threats. He'd seen Landon torture people firsthand. A lesson he'd never forget.

"Find her, Jem."

Jem nodded, his eyes never leaving the screen. Ten minutes later he had a lock on her location, but Gunner wouldn't stop listening. He'd been deadly silent, fisting his hands so tightly they'd gone numb. Holding himself ruthlessly in check rather than risk losing the audio link, the only link they had to Avery now, was all he could do as Avery screamed in pain and terror. And then she went quiet, only whimpering occasionally.

He'd barely noticed that Jem had maneuvered him into the car, driven them back to the airport where the police presence was still heavy. He was still listening as Jem yanked him onto the private plane he'd called in that favor for.

They didn't know how sophisticated this audio link was, didn't know if they'd lose contact in the air, but they had little choice. "Tell him to go, Jem," Gunner said, after one particularly brutal scream from Avery.

"Fuck," Jem breathed, and then yelled, "we have to go now," and the plane began hurtling toward the runway.

"Who's the pilot?"

"Guy I used to work with. He'll get us there."

"Suppose he moves her?"

"We'll fucking find her, Gun. That's what we do."

The audio never cut out. Gunner and Jem didn't stop listening, even when things went silent on the other end. Silent, but not over.

"No more," he heard Avery say softly. She sounded . . . so far away. As if she was fading away and fast.

"You and James both think you run the show. This should show both of you just where you are on the food chain." Landon's voice was clear as a bell, which meant Avery was seriously hurt.

"We're landing!" the pilot yelled back. The cockpit door had remained open and Gunner knew they were going at a speed that wasn't allowed on any airline or private plane. How he was managing to stay off the radar, Gunner had no clue, but he'd owe this man everything.

As the plane touched down, a hard landing, Gunner could barely hear. As things settled down and the flight came to a stop, Landon asked, "Do you think I should let her live, James?" and Gunner gripped the arms of his seat tightly.

"I'll kill you, Landon," he said, with no way of knowing if the man could hear him. He and Jem raced off the flight into a waiting car that Jem must've arranged with the pilot. Gunner took the wheel, pushing the car with the sport engine up to one hundred on the dusty road as Jem tracked the link.

"We're close," Jem said. "Another couple of miles, Gun. Hold steady."

Jem already had his weapon drawn. His eyes held a life-or-death look that Gunner had only seen once before and it hadn't ended well for the man who'd gone up against Jem.

Gunner pressed his lips together, not wanting to say anything that could make Landon do something stupid. But his suspicions were confirmed when Landon said, "I'm sure right about now, you're threatening my life. Unfortunately, this audio only streams out. The thing is, James, I keep my promises but you didn't keep yours. You didn't stay away from Avery and her friends. You left me after I gave you a second chance. Now your friends will have to pay."

"Signal's split," Jem said. "One's moving away fast. One's still."

"We've got to check the one that's not moving," he said quietly.

"Then turn right up here. Up the hill."

Gunner parked the car with a slam as close to the old porch as he could. It was a cabin, nestled in a quiet, lush parcel of land that belied any ugliness that had happened here. He used his foot to kick the door in, and Jem went ahead, weapon drawn, clearing room after empty room.

They got to the final bedroom. Gunner stood in the doorway and blinked. The only thing he saw was blood everywhere. And his flannel shirt shredded on the floor.

Avery didn't know how much time had passed when she heard muffled voices. She pulled herself off the tile floor where she'd curled up, finally able to move. The pain was excruciating, but moving too much would make her lose more blood she couldn't afford to lose.

She'd just prayed for Gunner to come get her. Now she couldn't be sure who it was on the other side of the bathroom door and she grabbed the bloody knife she'd found on the floor of the bedroom after Landon left her. The knife he'd used on her—she had no choice but to take it and defend herself with it.

That sick fucking bastard.

She'd wrapped towels around herself to try to keep warm, and the blood had already seeped through. The adrenaline rushing through her was no doubt stopping the pain, but the dull ache between her legs was slowing her down more every minute.

She waited, crouched, as the doorknob turned. It seemed to take forever and then light flooded the small room and Jem was pointing a gun at her.

Jem. She sank to the floor as he came forward to her. She heard Gunner's shouts, murmured, "Don't let him see me like this," to Jem, but it was too late. Gunner was there, his expression of horror quickly erased by one of calm concern.

He moved forward, picked her up and walked her out of the bathroom. "I'm so sorry, baby. I've got you. Don't look," he told her as they passed the bed and she buried her face into his chest as he walked them out into the cool air and slid them into a car. She remained curled in his lap as Jem covered them both with a heavy blanket and then she floated in and out of consciousness once the car started to move.

She was safe. She'd survived. She'd made it through.

She'd let the need for revenge carry her the rest of the way through, would let it burn through her body like a fire that would stop the pain.

"She needs a hospital," Gunner said quietly at one point. "I can stitch her, but I don't have all the supplies with me."

"No. Too many questions," she murmured.

"I'll figure this out," Jem told them. "Plane had to take back off—air traffic control reported him."

The car sped up measurably and Gunner's arms tightened around her. She didn't know how long they drove, but at one point they'd stopped and Gunner was putting an IV in, applying pressure bandages where he saw blood and she was fighting him, telling him no. "I don't want you to see this," she told him, hated the hurt on his face. He didn't understand. She couldn't hurt him more.

And then they were back in the car, driving more. "Keep talking to me, baby. Just keep talking and everything will be okay." He'd repeat that over and over until he believed it himself.

"Tell me . . ." she started.

"What, *chère*?" Gunner prompted. "Tell you what?"

She needed something to focus on, something beyond the terrible, horrible tragedy that was now filling the truck, making these men too close to anger and panic. She needed to bring them back.

If you find the strength, your men will pull it from you. Find it. In your darkest of times, it will get all of you through. She swore she could hear Adele's voice telling her that, even though she'd never met the woman.

"How did you two first meet?" she asked, her voice slightly slurred. "Or is that classified, supersecret spy information?"

"You're kidding, right? You want to know that now?" Jem asked over his shoulder.

"Road, Jem—watch the road," Gunner told him. Looked at her. "Really?"

"Would help me. Please."

Gunner's jaw tightened, as though he didn't think he should be telling stories at a time like this. But that's exactly why she needed him to do it.

"It was my first year with the teams," he started. "We were in Beirut on a recon mission when we got the call about a hostage situation in the British embassy."

"I still don't know why the hell they called you guys in," Jem interrupted, and Gunner stared at the back of Jem's head, the familiar *I will kill you* expression on his face.

She would've laughed, but it would hurt too much. The truck's steady rhythm and Gunner's voice soothed her in a way not much else would've at the moment.

Get them to treat you normally, no matter how abnormal the situation. Reassuring them reassures you.

"Our objective was recon during the day, and then we were supposed to go in, grab the hostage, take out the gunman, all while the hostage negotiator with the CIA was distracting him," Gunner continued. "It was a good plan."

"It was a shitty plan and you know that now," Jem corrected.

"It was meant to minimize bloodshed and unrest," Gunner shot back.

"It was already too late for that shit."

Gunner stared at the back of Jem's head, then muttered to her, "He's right. The gunman garnered all sorts of unwanted attention—purposely—from the media and the locals. By the time my team got there, it was a barely controlled mass hysteria in the streets. The local police were close to losing total control of the situation. They'd called in soldiers to help, but that seemed to make things worse. The gunman was already agitated and unstable, and he started to lose it when the soldiers rolled up the street."

"In a goddamned tank. Tell her that," Jem prompted.

"You just did," Gunner pointed out. "The gunman—his name was Kassim—"

"I thought it was Amir."

"Does it matter?"

"I'm the one who got shot, so yeah."

"Jem got shot?" she asked.

"Just a little bit, honey," he told her.

"Anyway, Kassim shot out the window, yelled to us that he was taking the first one out," Gunner said. "The hostage negotiators weren't there yet—"

"Probably having lunch discussing the psychology of the hostage or some shit like that. Hostage negotiators are never there when you need them."

"That's the first true thing he's said so far," Gunner said.

"Who's crazy now?" Jem added.

"You still are." Gunner looked at her. She was smiling a little. "So anyway, all of a sudden, I hear some guy yelling, 'Fuck this shit.' And this crazy-eyed person steps through the crowd. Cuts through it like butter, Avery. I've never seen anything like it. Or maybe they were just backing away from the crazy."

Jem snorted at that.

"So this one guy—another agent, I think—says, 'Sir, we're waiting for the negotiator. Please don't make the situation worse.' And so Jem turns to him and says, 'I'm the negotiator,' and he keeps walking. He's beyond the police lines at this point and everyone just goes quiet watching him walk into the building. Even the gunman's looking out the window, and he's kind of stunned at the death wish Jem had going on."

"Again, the second true thing Gunner's said all night," Jem added.

"And so he's inside and the gunman's all freaked out, starts firing at him immediately, but he's wired and so his shots are going all over the place. And Jem's just walking toward him, weapon drawn, not firing. Just walking straight at him. And finally, he gets right up on the guy. Right in his face. And he just takes the gun from him. Tells the people to get the hell out of the building."

"Wait a minute," she said. "How did you know what happened inside the building?"

Jem started laughing, that crazy laugh she'd

come to know so well. "Tell her, Gun. Tell her how you followed me inside the building."

"Even then, I knew someone had to watch your back."

"I had it under control."

"What happened to the gunman?" she asked.

"Jem waited until everyone got out safely. Then he shot the guy dead and told everyone he'd done them a favor by saving them the cost of an execution. I visited him in jail," Gunner said wryly.

"I was only detained, not arrested," Jem told her. "Ridiculous red tape."

"He tried to get into the hostage negotiating team right after that. Used that as proof he'd do a good job," Gunner said with a roll of his eyes. "I told you—twenty pounds of crazy stuffed in a five-pound bag."

"But he's our crazy," she said with a smile.

"Yeah, he is," Gunner confirmed. "Crazy and I will get you through this."

"Crazy just found the perfect motel."

Under the cover of night, Gunner carried her into one of the adjoining motel rooms and put her on one of the beds. She was holding the blanket tight, shivering uncontrollably. Her body was wet with blood, although the cuts had stopped bleeding considerably, thanks to the pressure bandages.

"Come on, *chère*. Gotta let me help," Gunner urged.

"She doesn't want you to see this, man," Jem told Gunner.

"I don't have a choice. I need to help her."

"Get her comfortable and give me half an hour."

"What are you going to do, find a doctor?"

Jem pointed and for the first time, Gunner noted they were across the street from a clinic with an ER. "Gotta be someone in there who'll help and keep their mouth shut."

"Jem—" Gunner started, but the man was already out of the room, shutting the door behind him.

Gunner focused on Avery, who was trying to make sure the blankets were covering her. Keeping her calm and from going into shock were two things he could do. Uncovering her now would make things worse, although he wished to hell he'd brought his medic bag. Being helpless never sat well with him, but this . . .

"I'm . . . okay," she managed to say.

"You're comforting me?" he asked. "You never cease to surprise me, Avery."

"I promise I'll be okay. You're what got me through."

I'm the one who got you into this, he wanted to tell her. Instead, he said, "I was with you, every step of the way. You're so fucking strong."

"For you," she murmured.

Chapter Sixteen

The twenty-four-hour clinic had seen better days. Jem eyed the staff, assessing them quickly, and focused in seconds on the female doctor who was talking to a young woman in the waiting room.

Her hair was in a messy bun, a pencil stuck through it. She was touching the woman, who looked like a prostitute, kneeling in front of her. Reassuring her.

She'd be perfect. Especially because it didn't take her long to get up and walk away from the main part of the clinic. He slid past the waiting area where there was too much chaos and not enough security for anyone to notice him and followed her into the back room.

He would recruit Dr. Drea Timmons as urgently and persuasively as possible.

When she whirled around to face him, she looked more angry than terrified that he'd followed her in here and blocked the only exit. The locker room was small and crowded, with a cot in the corner.

This had happened to her before, and he was suddenly oddly protective of someone he was attempting to kidnap.

She didn't say anything, didn't try to scream. Simply went to punch him in the jaw, landing a semisuccessful and damned good right cross, but he subdued her in seconds. At that point, she looked suitably impressed and fearful. And then irritated when he drew his weapon.

"I'm not going to hurt you," he started, and she snorted. "I have a friend in need of medical attention. You come with me and I'll make sure you're more than suitably compensated."

Her amber eyes searched his. Beautiful eyes, like a wary lioness. Her hair was long and blonde and wavy, although it was now tucked into a loose ponytail, sans pencil. She'd only managed to take her white coat off before he'd come in, and she wore a plain black T-shirt and blue scrub pants.

"I don't want money from you," she said evenly.

"Either way, sweetheart, you're coming with me." He pointed to the phone. "Excuse yourself from work."

"I'm off the clock now," she told him. "No one's going to miss me."

He wanted to tell her that was something she

should never, ever say to someone, but who was he to lecture people about doing stupid things? "Come on. I will pay you."

He released her, a show of good faith.

"I don't want your money. Donate to the clinic," she said as she grabbed her bag, stuffed it with supplies like IVs and the like.

"You'll need stitch kits. Several of them."

"Blood?"

"Maybe."

"Bullets?"

"No. Knife. And a rape kit," he said quietly. The anger dissipated for a brief moment.

"Are you criminals?" she asked.

"No. We're the good guys," he told her. Couldn't tell if she believed him or not, but he hoped she would walk out with him, not alert anyone that she was leaving under duress.

As if to reiterate that point, she turned to him, pointed at his chest and hissed, "This is my choice. Just remember that. Put that goddamned gun away."

He did.

"Please. My friend, she's really hurt." He locked the door and she went to her locker, but not before he showed her that he'd taken her phone and her beeper.

She took her bag out of her locker, along with a black medical bag like the one he'd seen Gunner haul around.

"Is this what you consider something good guys do?" she asked quietly.

He thought about that carefully. "Yeah, it is. Because sometimes being good requires you to do some of the most fucked-up things you've ever seen."

Drea stared at him, blinked. It was like some kind of debate settling itself behind her eyes. "At least you're honest."

"Some of the time. At least about that. Come on now." He led her toward the door. "Do the people who work here know you well?"

"What do you mean?"

"Do you talk about your personal life?"

"No. Never."

She was telling the truth. "Well, you're about to walk out holding hands with your boyfriend, so we can move past security."

He put his hand out and she took it. Glanced up at him for a long second before they passed the security guard, who opened the door for him.

"Night, Dr. Timmons."

"Good night, Ray," she called, caught Jem's eye and smiled. He held her hand as they crossed the street. He pointed at the diner and they swerved in that direction until he was sure the guard was distracted by other patients entering the clinic.

Then they moved behind the diner to the motel. She stiffened for a second outside the door, until he whispered, "Avery really needs your help badly. Please."

He held his breath because he really didn't want her to do this under the duress of a loaded gun.

"Let's go, then," she said, her voice sure.

He opened the door. Gunner stood, not letting go of Avery's hand.

"This is Dr. Timmons. She's agreed to help."

"Drea," she said. "You can call me Drea." She moved to the bathroom to wash her hands, kept the door open.

Gunner raised his brows.

"What? She came of her own accord," Jem said.

"I'll believe that . . . never."

"Whatever. Avery getting help's what counts, right, G?"

"You have to stop calling me that," Gunner muttered.

"I'm going to need some help," Drea said.

"Not him." Avery pointed to Gunner. "Please. Just . . . if you can do this yourself . . ."

Her voice was a plea. Jem watched Gunner nearly crumple. He took his friend in hand, forced him to sit watch by the window in the second room so he was far enough away. He bolted the door, boarded the window behind the curtain so it wasn't visible to anyone from the outside. He rigged it so it was alarmed and handed the small camera to Gunner. He also rigged a makeshift curtain between the bed and the rest of the room, where he could still see Drea and Avery, but there would be some semblance of privacy.

He caught Drea's eye as he did so. She nodded her approval and gloved up. "If I need you, I'll let you know," she said quietly. Calmly. Then she turned back to Avery, her competence shining through. "Avery, I'm going to help you and you're going to be fine."

Jem knew he wasn't the only one in the room who believed that.

Chapter Seventeen

While the doctor named Drea was washing up, Avery resumed her stare at the ceiling. She'd been doing that while Gunner was running her IV, grateful that the ceiling wasn't reflecting back at her. The stark whiteness was a relief, as was the fact that Gunner hadn't pushed her to look under the pressure bandages.

He'd seen enough, though. Seen the ugly gashes in her skin. Seen the cuts through her beautiful tattoo. All of those marks hurt her more than anything.

Gunner thought he'd heard everything, but he hadn't.

She closed her eyes and tried to remember the exact coordinates on the paper Landon had held up in front of her. Her mind had been swimming, a combination of the drugs and blood loss and fear making her unable to focus for any length of time, especially on tiny numbers that seemed to swim on the page every time she'd tried to focus.

And Landon had laughed. Since he had complete control of the audio, he'd lowered his voice, turned away from the speaker and mouthed, *All the information is here, Avery. Come on, don't you want to help these people, the way James had been doing?*

She'd cursed at him, viciously. Her hands had been able to make full fists by that point, but the assault had been too far under way.

He'd held the paper closer. Whispered, "These are exact coordinates of the boat that leaves late tonight. Your drugs will have worn off by then. If you survive this, you'd be in time to help them. Then again, if you'd left James alone to do his job, this wouldn't be your problem."

Landon's words echoed in her ear now. *Because of you, there are women and children who are suffering.*

And while she knew it was complete bullshit that it was her fault, the fact that she'd had tangible evidence of a cargo ship containing unwilling, kidnapped people that was too late to stop because she couldn't read the information chilled her.

It could've been a lie, but she'd seen the container invoice. The stamp with the approval number as it left Mexico. He'd pointed to the date—read it out loud to her. Taunted her with the arrival time. That cargo ship could've been docking anywhere in the world, and it would've been coming in right about now.

She'd considered telling Gunner this part of it. It was important, but since there was nothing any of them could do about it, because he and Jem felt guilty enough for something they had no control over already, she decided she was best served living with that guilt all by herself.

Stopping human trafficking was the one thing that made working for Landon bearable for Gunner. The fact that Landon would throw that in his face proved to her how depraved he was.

Drea was watching her. Avery tried to school her expression and figured she'd failed miserably when the young doctor put a hand over hers and said, "It's okay if you cry or yell or curse. Sometimes it's better."

She wanted to, but she glanced past the curtain, could see the open door, although not Gunner or Jem.

In response, Drea turned the clock radio on, low enough to be able to have a conversation, but loud enough that Gunner and Jem couldn't hear.

Avery realized her fists were balled tightly against her sides. She'd been holding her body so taut against the threat of pain that it ached to move even a little. "He didn't . . ." She paused, licked her lips. "He cut me. He didn't rape me."

She swallowed.

"You were still violated, Avery. You have every right to be angry at what he did to you."

Her body eased as Drea gave her that permission for the anger that had built to an unbearable level. It was as if the cork had been pulled from the bottle, simultaneously making the anger a living, breathing monster, but easing the intensity at the same time.

It was a livable, focused anger. She could do something with that. And the first thing she would do was get through the next several hours.

Drea gloved up and asked, "Can I take this?" pointing to the blanket wrapped around her.

Avery nodded, still not trusting her voice, and watched as Drea carefully replaced the bloody blanket with clean sheeting and disposable chucks. The sheet went over Avery lightly; the chucks were slid with care and precision under her so the bed wouldn't get soiled from the Betadine.

Gunner called this battlefield medicine. Drea appeared to have experience with it, judging by how efficient she was. Avery let that soothe her—she was in good hands.

It also made her wonder why Drea had this kind of experience. "Where . . . do you work?"

"The clinic, right across the street," Drea answered, her expression softened. "Your friend asked me to come help you."

Asked. Avery could just imagine how Jem had asked but let the subject drop for now. She'd only be prolonging the inevitable.

Drea laid her instruments on the night table

she'd covered and pulled the chair Jem had gotten for her right up to the bed. Avery shifted so she was closer and winced even as Drea put her hands out to stop her.

"Avery, you've got to let me help you. That's what I'm here for. You can cut the tough act, at least in front of me. You've got nothing left to prove."

Drea's voice was warm and understanding but also made Avery nod and agree that she wouldn't move again until Drea helped her. "Thanks, Drea. I'm so sorry about all of this. I don't know how Jem asked you to come here, but knowing him . . ."

She trailed off and Drea gave the ghost of a smile. "It's not the first time I've been recruited. But you need to tell me if the men in this room hurt you."

"No, they rescued me. Jem and Gunner, they're my friends. Don't want Gunner to see me like this. Both of them feel guilty enough already."

Drea leaned in. "Are you sure? I can call the police. I will get you out of here if you need that. I'll make sure you're safe."

There was something in Drea's voice that made Avery want to hold the doctor's hand. "I'm positive. They're good men." She heard the catch in her own voice and stared up at the ceiling, blinking. She would not give the fucker who did this to her any more of her tears.

"And whoever did this to you isn't," Drea said firmly. "Do you want me to do a rape kit?"

"That's not necessary. Besides, a court of law's not going to be the one who convicts the man who did this." Avery heard the vengeance in her own voice and after a brief pause, Drea nodded approvingly.

After a moment, Drea held up a needle and Avery almost fell out of bed trying to get away from it.

"It's okay, Avery. Please, breathe. I'm putting the needle down," Drea told her. "I don't want to hurt you any more than you've been."

"It's okay. I didn't feel anything when he did it. That was . . . horrible." She stared at Drea as if willing her to understand. "I need to know it really happened. If I don't deal with it now, it's going to come back and bite me. I need to feel the pain."

"Oh honey," Drea said sadly. "It's my job to stop the pain."

"Only if you can erase it forever. Really, I can take it."

"If I can't get you stitched up properly, I'm not going to have a choice," Drea warned her, but went ahead with what she needed to do.

It hurt. Burned. Avery stared at the ceiling and thought about all the ways she would make Landon pay, for everything. By the time Drea was done, at least an hour had passed and tears had streamed down Avery's face.

Except for murmuring, "You okay?" several times during the procedure, Drea was completely focused. She covered the stitches loosely with a dressing.

"There will be some seepage for the next forty-eight hours, which is normal," Drea explained. "I've started you on an antibiotic already. A strong one. I'd like to clean you up, get you dressed."

"I don't . . . have clothes," she murmured, not answering to what Drea was saying.

"I've got some scrubs in my bag I can give you," Drea continued. "They'll be comfortable."

"Thank you. I'm sure this wasn't how you expected to spend your evening."

"I've learned to take life as it comes." Drea took more things out of her bag. "I'm going to clean you up and make sure I'm not missing anything."

"Please. I want to wash him off me," Avery said, teeth gritted. Drea nodded, got up and went to the bathroom. She came back with a basin full of warm water, washcloths and gloves.

She cleaned Avery up gently, but even that hurt. Avery clenched her teeth and bore it. Drea looked up at Avery, nodding, realizing that Avery hadn't been lying about not being raped. But Avery was still grateful to have as much of the experience wiped off her as possible.

Drea looked over the other bandages after dressing her in the scrubs. "I went slowly with the stitching because I was trying to minimize the scarring. After it heals, I'm betting a plastic surgeon could work miracles."

"Thanks, Drea."

"I'm going to talk to your friends about getting you some food. Can I put a mild painkiller in your IV? You won't be numb. I won't snow you."

"Yeah, that would be good," Avery said. She needed sleep. Needed all her strength to get through this. "Food, maybe later."

"Definitely sooner than later," Drea advised. "You did great. I'll send Gunner in now. I'm surprised he's stayed out this long."

Through the curtain, Gunner watched Drea's fingers flying over Avery's skin. Jem set it up so he could easily see both their outlines, and although it wasn't close enough, it was better than nothing.

Avery was holding back her whimpers. She'd refused pain meds.

"Dude, you gotta unclench," Jem said quietly, passed him a cigarette.

Gunner lit it and inhaled the smoke deep into his lungs, blew it out toward the open window, because he couldn't do anything else. "I want to kill him. If he was here in front of me . . ."

"I know. But going off half-cocked isn't going to help the plan."

"What *is* the plan? I still can't believe Landon would pull this shit. It doesn't make sense. Hurting women's never been Landon's style." He had to think about it rationally, or else he'd start smashing everything in the room.

"But these women are standing between him and you," Jem reminded him. "Makes sense in a very fucked-up way."

"Landon's all about seduction, no matter the form it takes," Gunner told him. Jem had been an undercover operative for years, had been in situations where he'd had to do things for the job that weren't to his personal bent. "When he got angry last time, he took it out on me. But he's still denying that. Why?"

Jem raised his brows but didn't say a word as Gunner continued. "I never believed he killed Josie. Call me a fucking idiot but—"

"Fucking idiot. What? You said to," Jem pointed out. "What about the brother?"

Gunner stilled. "Donal?"

"Yeah. I found his name in the folder that Mike and Andy had. What's he like?"

"The only thing I remember is seeing him walk away toward the plane. Landon had him leave when I got there. Don't know why, never asked. At the time, I wished I was going with him. Maybe Landon was hiding something?"

"Everyone's got something to hide. Something they're ashamed of."

"Even you?"

Jem gave a short laugh. "Brother, my shit's on the table for everyone to see. I've got a crazy family tree, dressed with a dose of mean as shit, addiction sprinkled in for good measure. That's the great thing about being nuts. You scare people just by being you."

On the surface, Jem appeared to be a fun-loving good old boy without a care in the world, one who talked a good game about being crazy.

Guy was fucking nuts. Gunner had seen him take point on missions. He was a wild man, took chances no sane person would ever take—or want to. That was the true sense of crazy, that it would live right next to you and you'd never know it.

Crazy always had the element of surprise.

"You think Donal sees me as some kind of rival?"

"As good a theory as any," Jem said.

"Mike's been able to track him down?"

"Never. He only knew about him because he talked to someone who knew Landon's father. Then he pulled the birth certificate."

"I know as well as anyone what happens when a guy disappears."

"If anyone can find him, it's someone who knows how to bury himself. Between you and Mike . . ."

Gunner shook his head.

"Gotta face them at some point." Jem's voice softened. "They helped you. They don't fucking blame you."

"Wouldn't you?"

"Fuck, Gunner, I don't even blame my parents and they were the biggest jackasses on the planet. But yeah, I'm sure they thought about blaming you. I'm guessing they're over it, since they're the ones who helped us get you back. They've always known where you were." Jem shook his head as Drea poked her head out from behind the curtain.

"Is it okay?" she asked, motioning to where they sat.

"Please, yes." Gunner stood, waited for her to move closer. "How bad is it?"

"If it doesn't infect, she'll be okay in two weeks. Not great, but okay. She can't do anything for herself until the cuts start to close—give it three days at the least. They were deep enough to scar, but whoever did this knew exactly where and how to cut to create maximum scarring and blood loss without hitting any internal organs or arteries."

Gunner could only nod, his fists tightening with anger.

"She'll be all right, but she's in a lot of pain."

"I heard the whole thing when it happened. I couldn't get to her, but I had to be with her."

Drea blanched. "I'm sorry. But she's strong.

Even so, she'll need to talk to someone about the attack. And I mean someone besides you."

"I hear you, Doc."

"She needs to eat. I've got an IV running, but the sooner you can get food into her, the better," Drea told him. Jem handed him the bag he'd grabbed from the diner. Pure comfort foods, and Gunner took it and left the two of them alone to sort the rest of the shit out.

He got why it might be easier to let a total stranger help her. She was more worried about his welfare than hers, and that made him want to strangle Landon in the middle of the police station and make sure it was televised.

He'd already allowed the man to lie to him about fucking with the people he'd loved.

You believed a criminal and you're surprised that he lied to you.

"I'll get him, Avery. If it's the last thing I do," he told her sleeping form quietly as he sat on the chair next to the bed.

She looked so small lying under the covers, but she wasn't as pale as she'd been. Her bare shoulder poked out from under the sheet and he drew the covers up over it. She shifted, her eyes still closed, her hand reaching out to find his. When he took her palm in his, she tugged, wanted him next to her. He moved the covers so they'd stay between them but not pull on her bandages, and he crawled in next to her.

Chapter Eighteen

Drea had loosened her hair. It hung halfway down her back in tawny waves. Her eyes were lazy, amber, lioness eyes. She moved like one too, an easy predatory lurk that he liked to watch, and if it had been any other situation but this, Jem would've already hit on her.

Correction, he'd have already been sleeping with her.

"You're going to have to stay," he said when she started to grab her jacket. His chair was already halfway blocking the door, and his weapon was held loosely in his lap, not for her so much as anyone who tried coming in. But the effect wasn't lost on her.

She dropped the jacket back onto the chair and her bag to the floor.

"Don't be like that, Drea. I got you some food."

"Oh, food in exchange for being kidnapped. Awesome. And my friends call me Drea. You can call me Andrea," she told him.

"Guess you told me."

"What do you expect?"

He shrugged. "I'd expect you'd want to stay with your patient and make sure she's okay."

"I could be across the street working on other patients and come back here in two minutes if there's a problem."

"You could also call the police, and I can't chance that."

"I thought you said you were one of the good guys."

"We're often misunderstood. Sometimes it's hard to tell us apart from the bad guys." He shrugged. "Besides, you checked out for the night, remember?"

"Give the man points for being attentive." She sat and accepted the food and coffee he put in front of her. After a couple of bites of the turkey club, a few fries and some caffeine, she looked slightly more relaxed. "She's going to be okay."

"I know."

"What happened to her?"

"Beyond the obvious? A sick bastard wants to make that guy pay for being alive." He motioned to Gunner, who was sleeping next to Avery, a hand on her arm.

"That's why he kept her alive," she murmured.

"Pretty much. Look, Andrea, by this time to morrow, your life will be back to normal and you can forget all about us. I'll make sure the clinic gets a good donation for your time."

He wanted to ask her why she was working at a clinic rather than a hospital, but he didn't need to get involved any more than he already was.

"Avery's going to need counseling. You know that, right?"

"I heard you talking to her. You sound like you've had some experience in this, Doc," he drawled. He blew smoke out the open window. His weapon was held loosely on his thigh as he kept an eye out for any disturbances in the force.

"Would that matter to you?"

"Maybe." He leaned forward. "I hope I'm not dragging up bad memories for you."

"Really? Now you have a conscience?"

"Only a quarter of the time. Keeps my life much simpler."

She dipped a fry in ketchup, paused before eating it. "I don't buy that at all. I'm betting there are things that keep you up more nights than don't."

"In this game, there's always something bur-rowing in your brain, refusing to let go."

"Like?"

"Like . . . what if you play the game like you've got nothing to lose, but you end up losing something big? Is that worth it?"

"Let me know when you find the answer." She ate in silence for a few more minutes, then asked,

"What do you guys do that makes you the good guys?"

"You takin' a survey?"

"I'm trying to figure out if I should hate you or not," she countered. And yeah, he really liked her.

"We help innocent people. And sometimes we get caught in the cross fire. Speaking of." He pulled her cell phone out of his pocket. "Is there anyone you need to call? Anyone who'll worry?"

She stared at the phone, and her face flushed. At first, he thought it was anger that he'd gone through her bag and taken her phone without her noticing. He also had her wallet but figured now wasn't the time to tell her so.

"There's no one," she said quickly.

"You're sure?"

She pushed the unfinished food away. "Yeah, I'm sure."

"You're not close to your family?"

"Are you?"

"To my brother. I consider those two family. Couple of others. The group's small but worth it."

She drank more of her coffee. "Are you really going to let Avery go after the guy who did that to her?"

"With Avery, *let* isn't exactly the right word. I don't think there's any way to stop her. But she won't be alone." He shoved Drea's phone back into his pocket. He'd already gone through it, made a copy of the information he'd found, just in case. "Do you need any other supplies to get her through the night?"

"I'd love a monitor, but it's probably not necessary. She's breathing okay and she wouldn't let me give her much in the way of drugs."

"No, I'd expect she wouldn't have. White-knuckling it seems to be our specialty," he muttered.

Drea stared at him for a long moment before saying, "It's an endearing quality, even if I'm here against my will."

"And you're sure no one out there's looking for you?"

"Yeah," she said, but she was lying. He didn't push it, because it hadn't triggered any bells and Jem would go down living and dying by his gut. "Is there anyone out there looking for you?" she countered.

"More than you could hope to count, sweetheart."

"You like it that way, don't you?"

"Very much."

"I think you're crazy," she told him.

"Like I don't have papers from the nuthouse to prove that, sweetheart." He took a long drag from the cigarette, blew the smoke out the half-open window that gave him a clear view into the lot. Gun and Avery were sleeping peacefully, and he'd let them remain that way until night. Then they'd move the hell out of Tennessee.

He felt his phone buzz, knew it was Dare or Key demanding explanations as to why he was bringing them in. Not answering them would piss them off and get them here faster, both of which he was in favor of. The shit had officially hit the fan, and the blowback was already a killer.

He'd told Key to find them a secure location, scout it out and leave him a coded message. He'd already ditched the truck and found another while Drea was working and Gunner was watching to make sure she didn't run.

Now he typed Drea's name into his laptop and came up basically empty. Which meant one of two things on an initial search—either she completely shunned social media and had no friends or she wasn't who she said she was.

But she was a practicing doctor—that wasn't something a clinic would allow her to fake, not even a clinic here.

He was about to go further into his search when Drea put her coffee down on the table and he felt her eyes boring into him. He glanced up, raised his brows.

"She almost died and you're tapping away on the Internet. I don't get it."

"Didn't ask you to." And, yes, he was definitely running a search, because she was trying to distract him from it.

"You're just . . . Is everything so easy for you to shrug off?"

Even though he knew what she was doing, it still took him a long minute to push back and swallow back the big burst of anger that threatened, leaned into her and smiled.

"I just heard one of the best friends I'll ever have, one of the best women I've ever met, get tortured," he said with a bluntness he knew didn't match the smile. "I'll never be the same."

And then he moved away from her. "Answer your question, Doctor?"

She tightened her arms around herself and he threw a blanket her way. She pulled it across herself and glanced out the window as a couple of motorcycles rolled by. Loud and proud, their engines rumbled, motorcycle gang members just roaming the town.

She didn't tear her eyes off them until they'd moved past the clinic and were far enough down the street so they couldn't be seen. And yeah, there was most definitely a problem here. And fuck it all, Jem knew how to pick them.

"You know them?" he asked.

She turned back to him, like she was pissed he'd caught her. "They come into the clinic sometimes after they've been fighting. Usual drunken bar brawl stuff."

I'll just bet. "You like your job?"

"I'd better. I have a lifetime of loans to pay off." She gave a small smile. "It's all I could remember wanting to do."

"Good to have goals. Life dreams."

"Is your job yours?"

"Sweetheart, my life's goal was to get the hell out from under my parents' rule and do whatever I wanted. So yeah, for the most part, I got that, aside from a few blips where people try to pretend I'm going to obey them."

She smiled again. Fuck, he liked her smile. He could tell it was an underused expression of hers and it lit up her eyes.

Her hands were long, slim fingered and nimble. Even though she'd stitched Avery carefully, she'd worked fast. She knew what she was doing. Probably got enough practice with the clinic, judging by the clientele he'd seen in the waiting room.

He wondered if the MC gangs had pulled her into service like he had once too often. It would make sense as to why she wasn't all that surprised when he'd done it.

"What kind of work is this that gets a woman attacked that personally and viciously?" she asked suddenly. "If this was a government job, you'd already have a doctor on your payroll."

"It's not government, but it's definitely not against the good old U.S. of A. We've got standards." He paused. "We're specialists. Gunner's a medic. So far, that's gotten us through."

"And when it doesn't?"

He shrugged. "Try not to dwell on the negative shit."

"Take me with you," she said suddenly. And she was completely serious.

"I can't."

"Why? You have doctors you kidnap in every city?"

"I just told you, Gunner's a medic."

"He can do a lot, but not what I can."

"True. But you wouldn't even let me call you by your nickname half an hour ago. Why would you suddenly want to do that?"

"You seem like an impulsive kind of guy yourself," was her answer.

Chapter Nineteen

It was like waking from the deepest sleep Avery had ever had. It took her several moments to realize where she was . . . to recall what had happened. She was still half numb, but the pain had begun to seep through the edges.

Whatever Drea had given her had taken away dreams, and taken the threat of nightmares with it. She had a feeling they wouldn't stay away for long, but she was grateful to the doctor.

She knew Gunner was in bed with her. She hadn't fallen into a full sleep until he'd gotten in next to her. The warmth of his body gave her that final push to nod off.

"Gunner?"

"I'm here, baby," he told her, his drawl thick with sleep. "I've been here the whole time."

"I know."

"Do you need more pain meds? Drea left them for you."

"She's gone?"

"Yeah." Gunner paused. "Jem said she asked to come with us."

"You should let her," Avery said sleepily. "She needs us."

"You're psychic now?"

"I could tell."

Gunner pressed a hand to her forehead, checking for fever. "You need to eat and drink something."

Her stomach churned at the thought. "Can't."

"At least drink." The bed rustled and a can of Coke, complete with a straw, was in front of her face.

She did, because she was thirsty. The soda was cold and sugary and went smoothly down her throat, easing the ache she had from holding back her screams for so long.

She closed her eyes to shake away the memory and saw Landon's face flash in front of her eyes. Heard his laugh. Felt his hands.

Shit. This had to go away.

"You'll get through this, Avery. If it's the last thing I do, I'll make sure of it," Gunner told her.

"You already got me through. All I kept thinking about was you. Being with you. That you'd come get me. And then I'd kill Landon for you. For both of us."

The bed shifted and Gunner moved around so she couldn't not look him in the eye. He knelt down by her side of the bed, rather than trying to make her move. "I won't let you."

"I already have blood on my hands," she reminded him.

"Not like that." He took her hands in his, kissed them. "I'll never let you have that on your conscience."

"Landon deserves what's coming to him, Gunner. My conscience will be just fine."

He shook his head and she knew what he was thinking. "It was different with my mom."

"You thought it was going to be," he said quietly.

"Right now I hate that I told you things."

Drea didn't try to do anything for the rest of the night, especially not talk to him, Jem noted. But she did check on Avery, quietly, not waking either her or Gunner as she did so.

Avery was tough—Jem knew she'd get through it, but Gunner would have to avoid the whole alpha *I can fix this shit* and just be there for her. This wasn't the time for Gunner to retreat into medical jargon—it would be too easy for him to distance himself with what had happened, and Jem knew from experience that distance from emotions was bad.

Of course, that was also coming from someone who was way too much in touch with his own.

He shifted, stared out the window again. The

bikes were back again, the way they'd been all night. There was a strip of bars down the road, so this could've all been a normal, nightly thing, but . . .

But Drea practically went out of her way to remain too casual every time she heard the rumble of the engines. The subtle signs, the shift in her seat while pretending she was just getting comfortable, the avoidance of eye contact . . . the fact that she was more than willing to let a group of strangers who'd kidnapped her take her the hell out of town . . .

"You okay?" he asked for the millionth time, and she nodded. Sipped the Coke and stared at the TV.

He checked his watch. It would be time for her to go in the next hour. Time for him and Gunner and Avery to get the hell out of Dodge too, once Key got here.

God, Key was pissed. Jem was sure Dare and Grace were too, but he wasn't even looking at their messages, much less answering them. At this point, his phone was like a fucking vibrator in his pants and even Drea was starting to look at him funny.

When she was pretending not to look at him.

He glanced down at his phone, then hers, and realized that his wasn't the only phone blowing up. "Thought you said no one would worry about you."

She stared out the window, tightened her arms

across her chest for a second before loosening them. "No one I care enough about."

"Fuck, Andrea, that's not what I asked you before." There were more than twenty text messages from two different accounts, not including e-mails and missed calls. She might've had him beat on the *people are pissed at you* contest.

"None of them are going to bother you." She held her hand out and he gave her the phone. This time, he didn't stop her when she pulled her jacket on and she didn't ask to stay. She wouldn't a second time, had too much pride.

But a part of him wished she didn't. "Need me to walk you across the way?"

"I don't think so." She paused, hand on the doorknob. "Tell Avery I hope she gets what she needs."

"Andrea," he said more sharply than he meant to. "You don't have any training."

She pushed her lips together tightly, like she was trying to keep information inside, then simply said, "Right."

And then she was gone.

"Fuck me," he muttered, watched her cross the street back toward the clinic. Instead of going into the front door, she went around the back and a few minutes later, a motorcycle pulled to the edge of the lot. "And that is really fucking cool," Jem muttered to himself. Wanted to get on the bike behind her and beg for a ride.

Yeah, he'd have to find out more about Dr. Andrea Timmons. What would make her want to pick up and hang out with a merc group, especially one that kidnapped her?

She roared away, her ponytail trailing behind her out of the helmet, and at the last second he noted her bike's logo. He recognized it from the bikes he'd seen riding by the clinic earlier—the symbol of the Outlaw Angels, a one percenter biker gang with charters all over the States. Now that was interesting as fuck, and maybe one of the reasons she was so keen to stay on with them.

And that was trouble they couldn't afford at the moment.

He'd almost turned away when he heard the rumble of more bikes. They were trailing after her, had been lying in wait in the parking lot next to the motel.

Ah, fuck, couldn't be good. Not when another couple of them pulled into the motel lot.

"Gun, we got company," he called quietly.

"Trouble?" Gunner came out from behind the curtain, rubbing sleep from his eyes.

"Outlaw Angels."

"The hell?"

"I think our doc might be tied to them."

"That why she asked to come with?" Gunner asked as he glanced out the window. "Yeah, I spied on you. You've got game, brother."

"And I wasn't even trying," Jem pointed out. "Cavalry's here."

Cavalry in the form of Key, and he looked pissed as shit. He was on an old Harley Fat Boy and he slammed past the bikers and pulled in front of the room. They surrounded him and he looked toward Jem through the window. Jem nodded and then Key turned slowly back to the menacing group.

His anger was palpable, directed totally at Jem, but when Key turned it outward, it was a sight to see.

"Baby brother's got this," he told Gunner. "Go back and get Avery ready to go."

"At least we know for sure this isn't Landon," Gunner said. "But what the fuck, Jem?"

"I ask myself that every single day," Jem muttered, turned back to watch Key getting three beefy OAs under control. "That's good. Get your anger out on those good old boys."

He had Drea's address, dialed her phone number and got her voice mail. Didn't want to leave her one in case other OAs were checking her phone.

After ten minutes of Key's reasoning techniques, the OAs up and left, speeding off into the night. Key slammed into the room. He was tan. His hair was longer, pulled back, and he had several days' growth of beard.

"Dude, you trying for a spot in the MC?" Jem asked him.

Key ignored that. "Want to tell me what that's all about?"

"Yeah, right after you go with me to pick someone up. We'll send Gun and Avery ahead—can't leave them here."

Key narrowed his eyes. "Is this about a woman?"

"Isn't it always, brother?"

Chapter Twenty

Drea's rental house was small, well kept and in a decent enough neighborhood. No sign of the bike anywhere, but there was a light on in her house.

"I'll go in." Jem got off the back of Key's bike.

"Sure, leave me outside to handle more shit," Key muttered.

"Just don't sign any contracts in blood," Jem told him, then headed up the front walk. He didn't bother knocking, walked right into her living room and heard the shower running. "Andrea! It's Jem. And you'd better be alone in there."

He pushed the door open a little and the shower stopped. In seconds, the curtain pulled aside and she stepped out, wrapped in a towel. Which was disappointing.

Worse, she'd been crying.

He moved aside to let her pass since she wasn't exactly stopping to greet him. "Not surprised to see me, doll-face?"

He turned to watch her go into the bedroom right across the hall. Not bothering to shut the door, instead she dropped the towel and started to get dressed. Fuck, she was beautiful everywhere. Confident as fuck too.

She turned to face him as she pulled on a T-shirt, sans bra. "No, I'm not. I figured that was you who called. And I know the OA came to see you."

"What do they have on you?" he asked. "Never mind. That's why you want out."

"Even if I go with you, I can't escape. Can't change my name and keep my medical license. That's how they'd track me. They have charters everywhere." She paused. "You're in one piece. They didn't hurt Avery, did they? They promised they didn't."

"My brother fucked your guys up."

"They're not my guys. Trust me." She stood in a pair of tight jeans and a black T-shirt, face free of makeup and a sleeve of tattoos ghosting down her left arm.

"Grab your shit—I can't leave you here. Not after Key beat the shit out of them."

"You're not doing this out of pity, are you?"

"Safety, not pity. The OA probably thinks you're working with us, and they don't know who we are."

She didn't hesitate, swore under her breath as she scooped some things from her night table into a bag on the floor. She'd been planning on leaving either way, and because of what she'd done for Avery. "I'm not leaving my bike behind."

"We'll get the symbol taken off ASAP. But you don't have to leave it behind, no."

Her phone rang and she glanced at it.

"Go ahead—answer," he told her. She did, put it on speaker as a graveled voice said, "Drea, what the fuck?"

"It was a favor for a friend, Dallas. Don't get yourself twisted."

"You don't tell me what the fuck to do, right? Get your ass to the clubhouse in five or I'm comin' to get you."

"Okay," she said, hung up and grabbed her bag. Jem took it from her and put it on the back of Key's bike, since he'd be riding with Drea.

"Go up the highway—get off two exits down and we'll back-road it for a couple of miles. Gunner's waiting an hour up and we'll just pack the bikes into the van he'll rent and move from there," Key said. "And then maybe one of you can tell me what the fuck's going on."

"I'm driving my own bike," she told him, handed him a helmet.

"Don't worry, sweetheart. Wind in my ears can only improve shit in here." He refused the helmet but climbed on behind her.

"Jem, earlier, when I called you crazy . . ."

"I do have papers," he told her. "Not on me, of course. Now come on, sweetheart, give me the ride of my goddamned life."

Gunner loaded Avery into the front seat, lowered all the way down. She was so sleepy and he didn't want her bouncing around in the back. Key and Jem followed them until they got on the highway to make sure there was no tail on them, and then they branched off to go find Drea.

"Jem's going to get Drea back, isn't he?" Avery asked in a sleepy voice.

"You don't miss anything, do you?"

"You all talk very loudly," she sniffed. "Is she okay?"

"There's something involving the OA."

"The motorcycle gang?"

"They call themselves a club," he said, heard her mutter, "Bullshit" and then, "Are Dare and Grace okay?"

"Key said they're waiting for us. We're an hour out."

Now that the imminent danger of both the threat and her dying was over, she could feel the tension vibrating through Gunner. She was woozy from the drugs, and the adrenaline rush from earlier had most definitely passed.

The thought of seeing Key, Grace and Dare made her stomach clench. The fact that she couldn't recall anything from the files Landon showed her made her angry, and the guilt about not telling Gunner or Jem about it was crushing.

"I hate seeing you look like that," he said quietly. "I know you're thinking about him."

She couldn't deny it.

"I will kill him, Avery." He could barely get the words out. They were clipped, forced, coming through gritted teeth. It was the way he'd spoken to her when she and Jem were interrogating him, and she didn't want that.

"No. You'll go to jail."

"It'll be worth it."

She pulled in a deep breath, despite the fact that it hurt, and blurted out, "I'm going to be the one to take him down. I'll need all of S8 to do it, but I will be the one who disgraces him and pulls the trigger. It's not just for me, Gunner. It's for us. I won't let anyone get between us again, and that's exactly what he's done."

Her voice was firm and Gunner's jaw clenched, but he didn't say anything more. She closed her eyes and let the pain meds wash over her.

She wouldn't remain a broken woman. She would save herself, Gunner and Section 8. And she would take the consequences, no matter what they were.

"I don't want you taking on my burdens, Avery," he said finally.

"Our burdens," she told him, reached for his

hand. The hum of the road quieted them both for the rest of the trip as she drifted in and out of sleep. She didn't know how long it took to get to the next safe house, but she woke, blinked blearily as they pulled into a lit garage. Gunner watched the rearview mirror until the door closed firmly. She heard the beep of a house alarm and he said, "Dare and Grace are here. Jem and Key are close behind."

"They have Drea?"

"Yeah, she's safe."

"Good." She wished she could go into the house on her own steam, because that would go a long way in reassuring both Gunner and Dare that she was fine. Grace would know she was full of shit either way, but dealing with the men required a little more subterfuge.

Even if she could have walked on her own, Gunner wasn't having it. He carried her the short distance from the attached garage through the doorway into the kitchen and finally into the living room where her brother and Grace waited.

"I've got the bedroom over here all set up," she heard Grace say, then felt the woman's cool palm grip hers. She knew if she looked into Grace's eyes, she'd lose it, and so she didn't. Just squeezed Grace's hand and Grace squeezed back.

When Gunner put her down on the bed, Dare

was hugging her gingerly. "Avery, fuck, you have no idea . . ."

His voice broke and she did know. They were the only family each other had, barring S8. And they'd only found each other months before. "I'm okay, Dare. I will be. Please . . . it's not Gunner's fault."

He didn't say anything about that. But he knew enough to avoid touching her in any of the places she'd been cut. He eased away from her, helped her back onto the pillows and she saw they were alone in the room. "Avery . . . don't do that to me again."

She'd feel the same way if Dare had done something like this. "I had reasons."

"Not good enough. You're my family." He squeezed her hand. "You rest, okay? We'll deal with all of it when you're better. I don't want you to worry. About anything."

She nodded and then Grace was in the room and Dare was leaving. She grabbed Grace's wrist, told her, "Don't let them treat me like . . ."

"Like a woman?" Grace finished. "Good luck with that."

There was a knock on the door and after Grace called, "Come in," the door opened and Drea stuck her head in hesitantly.

"Sorry, I just wanted to see if you needed anything."

Avery waved the woman in. "Grace, this is Drea. She's the doctor who helped me."

"We owe you, Drea."

"And now I owe all of you." Drea hugged her arms around herself.

"Seems to be an epidemic around here," Grace murmured.

Chapter Twenty-one

Drea had stayed in the room with Avery and Grace until the meeting with the guys had broken up. Without Grace or Avery there—especially without Avery there—it hadn't felt right.

But at least they were all in agreement that she needed a part in this. That none of them would ever rest if they'd been in her shoes.

Now Drea came out of the bedroom behind Grace, after Gunner went inside and closed the door. Grace took Dare's hand and Jem motioned to the couch. "It pulls out. You can sleep there and I'll take the chair, okay?"

He'd given Key the last bedroom, mainly because he needed to figure some shit out about their newest houseguest. He pulled out the bed—Grace had already put sheets on it, and put pillows and a comforter on the chair. When he finished, she stripped out of her jeans and crawled under the covers.

He snagged a pillow and made himself comfortable in the recliner closest to the door, his weapon tucked in by his side. The security cams were in easy viewing range and so far it was all quiet.

"Was Avery okay?" he asked.

"I think so. She and Grace have both been through a lot, it sounds like. They're . . . nice. I didn't expect them to be so nice to me," she said honestly.

"They're good judges of character."

That got a small smile from her. "I feel like I've lived a thousand lifetimes in the past twenty-four hours."

When she'd left the house, he'd destroyed her SIM card and left her phone behind. No reason to let the past follow her. A clean break was what was required and necessary, for her safety and her sanity.

Now he just needed to know what, exactly she was running from.

She wiped a tear away. "Sorry. Just . . . hearing Grace talk about what she went through and Avery . . . I know what she's been through. Brought up a lot."

She didn't elaborate and he didn't push. Hopefully, she'd talk to Grace and Avery about it, if for no other reason than catharsis.

He knew that Landon hadn't raped Avery. But, as Drea had told Avery earlier, what he'd done to her was most definitely a violation. No mistake on that. "Did something similar happen to you, Drea?"

"In a way." Her voice had that quiet strength he'd come to expect from her over the past twenty-four hours. He wondered if she'd always been this strong, or if life had forced that strength into her.

He didn't push for a better answer. "Been a shitty couple of days for all of us."

"Tomorrow, I can find someplace to stay. I have a bank account set up for this eventuality, and I have other IDs. I can use that for a while . . ." She trailed off. "Or, I mean, I'll take care of Avery until she's healed and then—"

"Drea, we don't expect anything from you. We got you out of there because we compromised you. I didn't know your ex watched your every move. It's our fault and—"

"What? You're not going to force me to perform medical services," she asked wryly.

"Something like that." He paused. "You were in danger back where we found you, but you're in danger with us too."

"Because whoever did that to Avery is still out there?"

"Yes."

"So you're not kicking me out?"

"No."

She stared at him, her gaze a cross between grateful and suspicious. "I want to ask why, but really, I should just shut up and be grateful."

"Why suspicious?"

"Because the last time I let someone help me out of a bad situation, I ended up in something much worse." Her hands were fisted in front of her on the blanket. She was sitting up, refusing to get comfortable. She looked like she didn't know the meaning of the word anymore.

He hated that. Wanted to make it his mission in life to make her goddamn smile, just for the way she'd helped Avery alone. "This isn't anything like that, Drea. I can promise you that."

And he could, because he had connections. He could make sure, even if shit rained down on S8, she could escape without a scratch.

"Don't, please. Promises . . . I don't believe them anymore. Just tell me you'll try—I'll believe that much more."

"I'm a man of my word. I don't think you've met many of them—any of them—so you might find it hard to recognize them. Recognize."

She stilled and stared at him. Raised her chin like she wanted to defy him, but fuck it, he wouldn't let her—not for something like this. "I'll try."

"Talk to me, baby. Tell me what I need to know. Always helps to know what I'm up against and why."

"I figured," she said softly. So reluctant and he couldn't blame her.

He started, leading her. "What's your connection to the OA?"

Drea stared up at him, her amber eyes troubled. "Danny's my ex. Danny Laurel. He's the enforcer of the New York chapter of the OA. Wherever I move, he's got people . . . following me."

"Because he doesn't want to be your ex?"

She nodded, chewed her full bottom lip for a second. "You bought a world of trouble when you kidnapped me, Jem."

"Don't you worry about me."

Her face clouded when he said that, but she schooled her expression quickly. "Right. Because this is what you do. You save people."

"Right."

"So you guys could just put me somewhere to start over. Maybe you know someone who could just switch the names on my medical license? It's not like I didn't earn it."

"I know someone who could do that," he agreed. "But if you stayed with us, you really wouldn't need to. Course, you couldn't work in a hospital either, but I'm betting we could keep you busy."

She nodded, relaxed her hands a little.

"We're getting ahead of ourselves. Tell me more about Danny. I know you didn't just meet him one night and ended up not being able to shake him."

"No, that's not the way that happened. We went to school together in New York. I was raised in Hell's Kitchen by my grandmother. At least until my mom got her shit together—pretended to. Grams never would've given up custody, but she had a bad heart. She died when I was twelve and I went to live with my mom. God, it was horrible."

He'd been there. Wanted to get into bed with her and give her a hug, but couldn't afford to let her stop talking. And if he got closer to her, he'd be kissing her.

"Danny was . . . he saved me when we were in high school. He got me out of my house when I was just a freshman. And I couldn't have stayed there, not much longer. His father was a member of the OA, so Danny was a legacy, although he still had to prove himself. But his father didn't care that Danny moved a girl into his bedroom. And I was never so grateful for that kind of permissiveness. When my mom came around, demanding I come back, Danny and his father . . . they made sure she was too scared to ever try to get me again. Talk about out of the frying pan." She had her arms wrapped around her knees, and her hands were white because she clutched them together so hard. "At the time, I needed him. He was my whole goddamned world. And as long as he stayed that way, we were fine."

Her voice got thin in the dark. He reached over and turned the light on dim, and she nodded her approval, looked around as if she expected to see Danny in the room. And Jem would motherfucking kill the bastard when he saw him. And he would make certain their paths did cross again.

"I tried to separate from him. He knew I wasn't comfortable with the club stuff. Didn't want to become anyone's old lady in any way, shape or form. I had to pull myself up and out of that shit. Too much poverty. I had to break the cycle. And I did."

"You were in the Army."

She didn't seem surprised that he knew. "I was a reservist. Paid for my schooling."

"You lied about the loans."

"You were doing background checks on me. I'm surprised you didn't find that."

He grinned. Held up his phone with her Army record. "I did."

She shook her head. "Maybe I should've stayed in. Danny couldn't touch me there."

"So why didn't you?"

She shrugged. Didn't want to tell him, not yet, and he'd respect that as long as he could. But if it meant the OA would come knocking at his door sooner rather than later, Drea would have to spill.

"Danny's still in New York, right?"

"Yeah, but he finds me every time, because of my medical license. I chose Tennessee because the charter's pretty small. I figured they wouldn't bother me all that much—their violence seemed pretty low-key. More petty stuff like robbery. Small-time. But it didn't stay that way. They saw pretty quickly that taking care of me the way Danny wanted entitled them to a lot more of the club's respect. Danny made sure they got in on some of the drug business. Pretty soon, I was on call constantly for them."

"Dammit, Drea. You should've gotten out of there."

She glanced at him. "I don't like running. And I can take care of myself, you know. Those guys . . . they don't force me to do anything but fix them up after they've been fighting. A few bullet holes here and there."

"I'm sure dating's a real bitch."

"Honestly? I haven't even bothered trying."

"Worried about him?"

"More like burned by him. I dated him in high school and it's still haunting me, Jem. One mistake like that and . . ." She shook her head. "It's been thirteen years and I can't shake him. My past will not stay past. Do you know what that's like?"

He glanced up at the ceiling and gave a full-body sigh. "Little bit."

"Did your brother really beat up three OAs?"

"Without breaking a sweat." She gave a low whistle and he smiled. "Sometimes the good guys do win, you know."

Of course, they had to have enough bad in

them to do so, but he kept that part to himself. She'd discovered that already.

"You've got a lot of security here?" she asked now.

"You mean, besides me?"

Her next words were so soft he barely heard them, but they were enough to make him go cold. "If they find me, they'll break my hand, smash it with a hammer until they pulverize the bones. And they make good on their threats."

He was out of his chair and next to her in seconds, her hand in his as he stroked the nimble fingers. "I will kill them before they touch you."

"Can't keep me in your sight forever."

"Watch me." He got into bed with her. Pulled the covers off and yanked her close to him, her body so hot against his.

"Boundaries?" she inquired.

"Were made to be crossed," he finished. "Consider yourself crossed."

"Why don't I mind hearing that from you?" she asked, then pulled him in for a kiss before he could do so first.

Chapter Twenty-two

A week passed. A week of Avery sleeping for most of the time, thanks to pain pills and Drea's insistence that she listen to her body, because sleep equaled healing.

The antibiotics that were preventing infection were also not helping in the staying-awake department. She was aware that Gunner rarely left her side, only conceding when Drea and Grace came to check on her. They'd bathe her and change her bandages . . . didn't make her feel helpless, which she appreciated, even though she was helpless, and more than a little high from the meds.

"Gunner's mad I won't let him do this," she remembered saying.

"Honey, he understands," Grace reassured her.

"Things are healing well," Drea told her another time when Avery complained she was itchy.

Now she realized she was wide awake and

staring at the ceiling. This was good that she wasn't in a fog any longer, but she was still tired. And every time she closed her eyes, she saw Landon's face. Heard his voice. It made her body throb more.

She glanced over at the night table, where Drea had left her pain pills. She'd started reducing them, with Drea's help, and the two she'd taken earlier that afternoon had obviously worn off. Although she wanted to do it without their help, there was no way.

"No reason to suffer, baby. Take the goddamned pills." Gunner's voice, low and rough, still made her tingle, even now. She took that as a good sign.

"Here, let me." The bed dipped and he came around to her side, fixed the pillows so she was more upright, which actually made the pain lessen. Then he handed her water and pills and watched her take them. "You hungry yet?"

"Not really."

He produced some crackers that he must've brought in with him earlier. "Have a couple—can't take too much of that shit on an empty stomach."

"Thanks." She nibbled on one as he got back into bed next to her. The glow from the TV was enough light, the house was alarmed and no one was getting past Jem or Key or Dare—she knew they'd be taking shifts watching the house tonight.

And obviously, Gunner wasn't planning on sleeping. "I don't know if I can do this."

When the words slipped out, they surprised her. She hadn't been thinking about S8 or anything like that, just eating the cracker. The pills hadn't even started taking effect yet, so she couldn't blame them. And even though what she said could've been construed as anything, Gunner knew exactly what she was talking about—she saw it in his eyes.

"Forget it. I don't mean that," she said quickly, but Gunner's gaze held hers, his blue eyes locked on to hers.

"I'm not forgetting anything, Avery. You have every right to say that, to feel that way."

"I might feel differently tomorrow."

"No one said you're not allowed to change your mind." His voice was gentle, but his eyes held an anger she knew wasn't directed at her. And he didn't seem surprised by what she was saying. "We're all in this together, just like you said."

"Just because I said it."

"You know that's not true—not with this group."

The pain pills were working, the empty stomach aiding that along. But she continued eating the crackers, mainly because her stomach was growling. "Is everyone okay?"

"Worried about you, but they're all fine. No

signs of anyone or anything suspicious. We're in a good place. Everyone wants you to take your time and heal."

She wanted that too, thought she'd want revenge so badly that it would heat through her like a white-hot fury, forcing her out of bed and into planning mode. By now she should've been insisting that they find Landon, stop him from ever hurting anyone again, the way she had that first night.

Instead, she was thinking about giving up S8. The fact that she could think about letting Landon take something else from her pissed her off.

"I have to tell you something, Gunner," she started, and she looked wary.

"I'm listening."

"When Landon was attacking me . . . he showed me a folder. He whispered, so you wouldn't hear. The folder showed a list of times and coordinates that a cargo ship with underage women was leaving Mexico for . . . shit, I don't know where. Or when. He said it was soon and I couldn't concentrate, couldn't see . . ."

He pulled her close, hugged her to his chest as quiet sobs racked her. Gunner hated that Landon tried the same psychological bullshit that he'd used so effectively on him.

He hated that it had worked.

"I should've told you earlier," she murmured when her breathing had calmed down, but she still wasn't looking at him.

"There's nothing we could've done without more information. And you don't even know what he was showing you."

"It was a cargo dispatch. I know what they look like."

He tugged gently, forced her to look at him. "You've let Landon wrap you up in this. You're not responsible for what the traffickers are doing."

She shrugged, moved back to the pillow. He ran a hand through his hair. "I know you're worried about me. But we have to stop keeping secrets. I started that, I realize, but I thought we agreed, secrets will kill us."

She curled up around the pillow, looking so pretty and so vulnerable. He knew that was all a smokescreen, that underneath it all, Avery had more strength than any of them. She had more of Darius in her than anyone realized, and that in and of itself could be very good . . . and also, very destructive.

Right now he felt like that sense of justice was killing her. "I understand what you're doing, Avery. I did it myself."

"When you were with Josie," she murmured. "That's why you wanted to go back to Landon."

Why he'd been pissed that Josie saved him.

He blinked again and realized that he was in god-

*damned pain, but there was no smoke or chanting.
He'd made it through, with barely any memories of
what had happened to him. But he had no doubts as to
why he'd been beaten and left for dead in the first
place.*

*His only question was why they didn't finish the
job. It wasn't like Landon to leave things undone.
Landon hated sloppy.*

"Maybe you should've just let me die," he told her.

*"If you mean that, I'll throw your ass out the door
right now." Her eyes snapped fire and no, he didn't
need this shit from some bossy thing.*

*"I'll show myself out." Would've too, if he could
get up off the damned bed. His ribs felt like they were
in goddamned pieces, and every time he tried to move,
fire wrenched through his body.*

*Her hands were on his shoulders, pressing him
down firmly. "Why are you being such an idiot? Most
people are grateful to be saved. Or don't you know
that?"*

*"You have no idea about my life or what I should be
grateful for," he told her. "Where'd you find me?"*

*"You were near the back door, in the grasses. Petey
found you," she told him. Petey, a bloodhound who'd
remained firmly curled at his feet. "You were lucky."*

*"Yeah, lucky," he echoed. Tried to get up from un-
der the heavy quilt. Somehow it was easy enough for
the petite woman to push him back down.*

"Stay."

"I'm not the fucking dog."

"You're acting like an asshole."

He stared at the ceiling, trying to piece together what had happened. The last thing he remembered, was Landon telling him that he was done.

The last thing he'd said to Landon was, "If you ask me to come back, I would."

"Landon brainwashed you," Avery said now.

"You think that all of this is Landon's fault," he started. "You want to believe that I'm a victim, dragged in against my will. But that's only a partial truth. That only applies to this last time, when I went back to Landon to save you and the others."

"So tell me."

"And risk having you never look at me the same way again."

"That could never happen, Gunner. I know who you are. In here." She pressed a hand to his heart. "And here." A hand to the side of his head. "Whatever you did that you think was bad, you've more than made up for it."

"Never." His voice sounded hollow. "I liked working for Landon. Especially at first. He was better than Powell. And I was able to justify what I was doing because we were giving criminals a new life, letting them escape justice. I didn't see their victims. And I got to blow the shit out of human traffickers. I got to save women and children. I was the good guy, and I told myself that the end justified the means."

"I think it probably does," she told him. "That's why I feel like such shit for not being able to see a damned line of numbers. I went through all that torture for nothing. If I'd been able to get those numbers . . . it would've been worth it."

He knew exactly what she was saying. Didn't agree, but understood. He didn't want to tell her, didn't even want to think about it. But he had to. Talking about it, remembering it was the only way to make sure he wasn't doomed to repeat the same mistakes.

He'd been so damned young that first time he'd taken down a trafficker. For two years, he'd roamed the goddamned globe, pulling off smaller jobs, helping Landon's merc for hire, Declan Moore. Dec was a good mentor, was in it for the money and the explosions.

"You're taking down bad men," he'd told Gunner.

"And leading others across the border."

Declan shrugged. "Karma. Give a little, take a little."

Declan was killed the week before the transfer. Gunner swore to Landon that he was ready, that he wouldn't fuck anything up.

But he'd fucked up big-time. Gotten the client arrested and nearly gotten himself killed in the process. By the time he'd made it back to Landon's three weeks later, after hiding out in random safe houses, his name was mud and Landon was furious.

"But he called you back," she said. "Is that when you tattooed him?"

He went cold. "I never tattooed him."

"Good."

"Why'd you think that?"

"I needed something to focus on. He had the tribal sun on his shoulder . . ."

Gunner stood, took two steps back as if someone had physically pushed him. "Was it a new tattoo?"

"No. It was actually faded. Looked like it needed a touch-up. Gunner, you're so pale—what's wrong?"

"Landon doesn't have any tattoos."

As soon as Avery told him about the sun tattoo, Gunner was up, grabbing for his laptop, pulling up a picture of Landon. "Was this him?"

"Yes, it was him. The guy from that picture's the guy who hurt me. I'm sure of it," Avery insisted.

"I believe you." He got up and called into the living room for Jem, keeping his voice low. He wasn't ready to let the others in on anything. Not until the three of them dealt with this new information.

"Dude, what's up?" Jem asked, his voice rough from sleep.

"Come in here."

Jem did and Gunner motioned for him to close the door. Since he held the small surveillance camera in his hand, he did so. Placed it where they could all see it but remained standing.

"Landon's brother—any way he could be a twin? Identical twin?" Gunner asked, and Jem froze.

"Fuck me," he said finally, and Avery covered her mouth with her hand. "You think he's pretending to be Landon?"

"I think he's been around, watching me for a lot longer than I realized," Gunner said grimly. "Drew Landon's a bastard, but he's not a liar."

"The question is, if Donal's pretending to be Drew . . . where is Drew?" Jem asked.

"Last I saw him was right before you grabbed me in Bali," Gunner told him. "I saw him hours before. No tattoo. He was heading back to his island."

"So wait, did Donal order the beating?" Avery asked. "Because . . . would Drew's guards take orders from Donal?"

"No, they wouldn't have," Gunner said, looked slightly sheepish. "I might've mouthed off."

"To four men with weapons? And they say I'm the crazy one," Jem muttered.

"None of them really talked to me," Gunner said. "I was the favorite. They all resented the shit out of me, mainly because I could beat the shit out of them."

"And Donal got kicked off the island when you arrived," Jem reminded him. "That's a damned good reason to resent you. You cost him the family fortune."

"How do you know he didn't have money of his own? A business of his own?" Gunner asked. And then he froze in place.

"Gun? Shit, Gunner, what the hell?" Jem shook him and Avery was grabbing his hand as he nearly fell over as the memories hit him.

"The sun," he whispered. "It was him. It was Donal the whole fucking time."

Jem and Avery just sat next to him patiently as the slices of memory crowded his brain like a fast-moving slide show, all the pieces falling into place like so many clicks.

"He . . . When I found her . . . Shit . . ." He rubbed his forearm. "It was carved into her arm. The tribal sun. I didn't even . . . Fuck. I guess I assumed maybe she'd been tattooing herself or . . ."

"Or there was so much going on that night, you didn't even give it a second thought," Avery told him firmly. "Donal had to have gone back working for Drew. Got pissed that Drew gave you a second chance and made sure Josie paid for it."

"He also fucked the job up so badly," Gunner said slowly.

"Ensuring Landon's being pissed at you. He figured you'd stay away from Drew because of Josie and because of the fuckup," Jem finished.

"Strange fucking bedfellows," Jem muttered.

"So we find Drew or Donal or both. And they both go down," Avery said decisively.

Gunner nodded. "It's time to bring this to the group."

Chapter Twenty-three

They'd been circling one another for the week, not wanting to rile anything up. Gunner refused to leave Avery's side and, for her sake, peace was kept. That was mainly thanks to Grace, who kept Dare as calm as possible.

"We keep this about Avery for now," Jem told all of them quietly that first night. Gunner and Dare shook on that.

But now things were coming to a critical point. With Avery resting in the other room with Drea, and the door partially open, the other members of S8 sat at the table and listened to the story Gunner and Jem laid out.

Gunner felt like he was in front of the firing squad—would've been, if Jem hadn't sat next to him, as if ready to defend him.

Crazy, but loyal to a fault. Even when Gunner couldn't have blamed him if he wasn't.

So he laid out what happened to Dare, Grace and Key, pausing in places to keep himself together, especially when he spoke about Avery's attack. "I shouldn't have left her alone like that. But I'd always been safe there. No one followed us. I don't know how in the hell Landon knew about that place."

Dare was struggling with what had happened to Avery. This was his flesh and blood, his responsibility. She'd been brought into this through no fault of her own.

He stared into the man's eyes now. "Dare, I'm sorry."

"And you didn't call us immediately after Avery and Jem brought you back *why*?" Dare demanded. Grace put a hand on his arm, her face drawn tight. Then she got up and left the kitchen, the door swinging behind her.

Dare watched her leave, then stood and faced away from the group. Several long moments later, he sat back down, his eyes red rimmed. "She'll be okay," he said firmly.

"She will," Jem echoed, and Gunner knew they were somehow talking about both Grace and Avery. Key was sitting there silently, staring at his hands.

This group had already seen enough for a thousand lifetimes, and somehow Gunner had caused the worst of it all.

"It's my fault," he said hoarsely.

"And it's mine too," Dare cut him off before he could say anything else.

"Fuck, Dare. I never thought . . ." He pulled himself together. "I love your sister."

"I know. She loves you too. But the future of this team . . . fuck, this isn't going to work. Not with what happened to Avery," Dare told them all.

"I agree," Gunner said quietly. Jem sat back in his chair, arms crossed, not meeting anyone's eyes, but Key . . . Key was staring at all of them, his expression tight.

"You can't take that away from her," Key said in a low, forceful *cut this shit* tone. "If that's the decision she makes, fine. But this is up to her. She *is* the team. Stop treating her like she didn't know what she was getting into. Give her some goddamned credit."

"It's not that easy, Key," Dare started, but Grace's voice cut him off. Gunner didn't know when she'd come back into the room, but it didn't matter, not when she echoed Key's sentiments.

"It might not be easy, but it has to be that easy."

"Avery's the reason S8 came together. She's the reason we all pulled together. She's the goddamned glue of this team, and she dealt with all of our shit and forced us to pull it together," Jem concurred. "We can't let her down now."

"Give her a chance to heal, Gunner." Grace's hands were on his shoulders. "Stop blaming yourself. She won't be able to heal if she knows you're doing that."

Gunner knew she was right, but it was so much easier said than done. For a long while, there was silence in the kitchen. Grace went about making coffee quietly, put the first cup down in front of Dare. When she caught his eye, she smiled and Gunner watched the man's face light up.

Dare smiled at Grace and said, "Avery brought me back from the edge. If it hadn't been for her, I don't know what would've happened when I met Grace. I was angry. Unpredictable. Living in solitude and she woke me up." Dare sounded broken.

Grace put her arms around him, stared at Gunner and asked, "How are we going to take Landon down? Because if we have a plan in place to present to Avery, I think she'll feel less like we're doing this for her."

"I have a copy of Landon's file from the CIA." Jem left the room and came back just as quickly, placing the CIA confidential folder on the table between them. "It's mainly about Gunner— James, actually—his jobs from the past six months. I don't think there's anything in there that ties him to Landon."

"Let me look," Gunner said quietly. He didn't want to. Knowing he'd done all the things written on paper was bad enough, but to have to revisit them in black and white . . .

For Avery, he would. He sat and opened the

file. Pushed his anger back and he read until his eyes blurred, until he'd gone over each and every detail of his missions in living, breathing color. He could still smell the blood, taste the fear of the men he'd taken down. He knew every single reason why he'd done these jobs.

None of that made it right.

"Anything?" Dare asked. He'd been pacing until Grace led him gently to one of the couches. Gunner had been so engrossed he hadn't realized that they'd all been staring at him. Waiting.

He looked back down at the two pages he'd pulled. They didn't have much more detail than the others, but they had location points he hadn't noticed before.

He flipped the page so the others crowding the table could see it. Jem had a map out, pointed to the coordinates. Gunner nodded. "We start here."

"Where's that?"

Avery's voice.

"What the hell is it with women and sneaking up?" Jem demanded. "If we can't tell Grace or Avery's coming, maybe it is time we all retired."

"Or maybe we're that good," Grace told him, and Jem snorted.

Gunner had already gotten out of his seat to help Avery. "You shouldn't be up."

"You're all making plans without me," she said.

"We're making plans that include you," Gunner corrected.

"Landon's mine," she told them all, and Gunner felt the anger coming off her in waves.

"Why not let us help, Avery? It's what we do," Key reminded her.

"And you should've called before this," Dare added, but gently. "Fuck, don't ever do that again to me, sis."

Avery smiled at her brother. She was leaning heavily on Gunner and he looked toward Drea, who shrugged and mouthed, *Couldn't stop her.*

There was too much truth behind that statement.

"We had months to decide. I wasn't going to pull you all back for this. You had to make your decisions without duress. I couldn't do to you what we ended up doing unwittingly to Gunner," Avery told them all.

Dare flinched. It was apparent he felt as guilty as Avery did about that.

"I'm in," Key said.

"You already know my answer," Jem added.

"Someone's got to keep an eye on all of you." Dare crossed his arms.

"I want you all to know that I'm a better shot than Dare," Grace told them, breaking the tension.

Dare turned to her in mock frustration. "One time. My hands were acting up."

Grace took Dare's hands into hers and rubbed

them. "I want to be involved. You have to let me. Even though it might not be by blood, Gunner's my brother."

"We're all family," Avery said quietly. "And this is what family's supposed to do for one another."

"Section 8's as much about protecting its own as it is about protecting the innocent. We're all legacies. We all deserve to be a part of this," Dare said.

"Let's start thinking of ourselves as lucky to be a part of it instead of cursed," Jem said, throwing a sideways glance at Key. Gunner was sure he'd eventually find out what that was all about. For now, all he needed to know was that they were bound by pain and pride. They would always know one another's deepest, darkest secrets, a fact born of necessity. All secrets weren't uncovered, not yet, but they would need to be put on the table. Because secrets could be used against the team.

Avery looked up when Grace came into the room. Drea had given her another pain pill without Avery having to ask. Now she'd settled back against the pillows, glad she'd forced herself to make the trip into the kitchen. She needed to show them that she was all right. That she would be.

Whether or not she truly felt that way would be her secret for now. Hers and Drea's and

Grace's, since she knew she couldn't pull shit on these women.

"Nice job in there," Grace told her now. She pulled the door closed behind her. "They really needed that."

"They're hurting," Avery said.

"They're better now that they know you're still in," Grace assured her. She sat on the edge of the bed by Avery's feet. Drea was on the other side, curled up on a pillow, her tattooed arm resting lazily above her head. Avery leaned back against the pillows as the pill began to work. The throbbing pain receded, replaced by a low-level ache she could most definitely handle.

"Do you guys want to be alone?" Drea asked.

Grace shook her head. "You seem to be in as deeply as we are," she told Drea, before turning her attention back to Avery. "I didn't know if I should give you these or not."

For the first time, Avery noticed Grace had something tucked under her arm. She was holding three of the journals that Avery instantly recognized as part of Adele's set. The woman had liked writing in a certain type of journal, with a certain pen, and she seemed to have never wavered from that. That in and of itself comforted Avery. It had probably comforted Adele too—it was something that never changed in what had to have been a tumultuous existence.

"Why not?"

"These should've gone before the others," Grace admitted.

"I thought there was . . . something missing." There had been, physically, a full year in which Adele hadn't written anything. Avery thought a lot about what could've happened during that missing year. "I'd hoped she'd fallen in love."

"She did. But something else happened to her too." Grace held the journals tight against her body, still unwilling—seemingly unable—to part with them. "I didn't want to scare you."

And just then, Avery knew exactly what had happened to Adele. Drea seemed to know too, even though she didn't know who Adele was. The room stilled and Avery reached out for the journals. Slowly, Grace relinquished them.

Avery put them in her lap, traced the leather bindings with her fingers. "Was she raped on a job?"

"Yes."

"And the men knew?"

"She only told Darius. A year later," Grace said.

Drea gave a low whistle under her breath, then said, "Tough broad."

"She was," Avery agreed, making a note to let Drea read some of the journals. She didn't know exactly what the doctor's deal was, but suspected Jem would, soon enough. The very fact that she'd basically saved Avery's ass was enough to win her Avery's devotion.

"I didn't . . . Dare didn't tell you because I didn't want him to. I wasn't sure I was ever going to tell you what happened to me," Grace started.

"Grace, no . . ." Avery breathed.

"Dare didn't tell you everything. He kept a big part of it private. You all knew how bad my time with Rip was, but . . ." She paused. "It was Rip's men," she explained. Avery knew Grace's stepfather—and Gunner's father—had locked her in the basement rooms of the mansion and tortured her for a year, but she hadn't thought that he'd be capable of having his own step-daughter raped. "It happened a lot that year. And it still comes up to bite me in the ass, and I hate it. And I know Landon didn't rape you, but he still took something from you. I just want you to know, when I say I understand, it's not just lip service."

Avery grabbed her hand, squeezed it hard.

"I'm not saying I'm fine. I'd be lying," Grace continued. "But I needed you to know I've been there. I know what you're feeling. We're all sticking together, but you and me, we need to rely on each other during the tough times. Because we'll each have them."

"Every time I close my eyes," Avery started, was unable to finish. "It's nothing compared to what you went through."

"Do not even go there, my love. What we both went through was horrible."

"Do you have nightmares?"

"Yes."

"Gunner does too. But I don't think they're all from me. I think . . ."

"Living with Rip is enough to do that to anyone," Grace whispered.

"I guess we've got our very own support group," Drea said softly.

"Ah, dammit." Grace took the doctor's hand in hers. "The Fates have a way of bringing those we need right to our door."

"Or they have Jem do it," Drea said, and that got a laugh from all of them. "My ex is abusive, just like my parents. You'd think I'd have learned to avoid the wrong kind of people."

"I think maybe you've finally found the right kind of people," Grace told her. Avery noticed that she sounded so sure of herself, wondered if Grace's sixth sense was kicking in something fierce about Drea, or if, like Avery, she just sensed that the doctor needed them.

Either way, it didn't matter. For the moment, they had one another.

Chapter Twenty-four

Jem made a few calls and the next morning, he got an e-mail file he printed out for Gunner to see.

"These are Maria Landon's hospital records from the night she gave birth," Jem told him.

Gunner took the seat next to him. "I hope you don't run out of favors anytime soon."

"No chance of that," Jem assured him. "Doctor's notes indicate that the second birth was a surprise."

"How the hell can you read that chicken scratch?" Gunner asked.

"Been reading hospital records my whole damned life, Gun." Jem ran his finger along the lines of scrawl. "Okay, yeah, so second baby came five minutes later. Doc was delivering the placenta when Mom started yelling and contractions started again. Said baby was blue when first delivered but roused quickly. No permanent damage."

"Yeah, right," Gunner muttered. "How would we know if they're identical or not?"

"Look, DNA testing wasn't done back then. Obviously, there wasn't an ultrasound or no one would've been surprised. Doc notes that twins shared the same placenta, but that's not always an indicator of anything. Nurse noted that footprints looked alike."

Gunner leafed through the file and pulled out the inked markings from the two boys and held them up, side by side.

"Why the hell wouldn't Landon have mentioned the fact that he's a twin to you?" Jem asked. "I mean, an identical twin's not exactly run-of-the-mill."

"I guess he never thought the guy would try to impersonate him." Gunner thought back to what Landon used to say about family. From his first moments on the island, when Gunner stood stiffly in Drew's office, not sure what the hell to do, Landon had gone out of his way to be kind.

"Your father didn't have to do this," Landon told him. "I never asked him to."

"But he did," Gunner bit out. Wondered why it was so important that Landon tell him all of this.

"Sometimes family has their reasons." Landon motioned to the helo that was waiting on the lawn. It arrived after Powell's had left, and now Gunner watched a man walking toward it, carrying a bag

slung over his shoulder. The man never looked back, but Landon had looked so damned sad.

"I asked my brother to leave," he said.

"So maybe you don't give a shit about family either," Gunner told him, waited for the slap or maybe he'd been secretly hoping Landon kicked him off the island too.

Instead, the man looked at him with a sad look. "James, I care too much about family. Maybe someday you'll understand, maybe you won't. But our family can be the most fucked-up part of our lives. If we're not careful, they can ruin us."

"I thought he was trying to tell me he understood about my father being the biggest prick on the planet," Gunner said.

"And here I always thought my pops won. But hell, yours does have him beat by a mile," Jem said, and Key clinked his beer to Gunner's, said, "Hear, hear!"

Gunner shook his head. "So glad to win this round of 'my family's got the biggest asshole.'"

Jem shrugged. "Safe to say none of our childhoods were peaches and cream."

"Except Avery's seems like it was pretty damned sweet," Key said, then turned to Gunner and added, "Yours too, until your mom died."

"Both our parents were poster children for *don't spawn*," Jem added.

"My mother could earn a spot on that poster,"

Drea said quietly. Gunner had seen her come to the doorway a few minutes earlier, was sure the brothers had noticed it too. But rather than scare her or go silent, they'd continued talking in the hopes that she'd be comfortable enough to join in.

"Come have a beer, *chère*." Jem grabbed one from the fridge without leaving his chair. She only hesitated for a moment before joining them, taking the vacant chair next to Jem. She took a long sip and then said, "So, is the prerequisite for being a supersoldier—"

"I was a sailor," Gunner pointed out, but she continued. "—a shitty childhood?"

"Most of the time, yes." That was Dare, coming in from his run. He gave Drea a small smile. "What doesn't kill us, right, Doc?"

"So far, that's been right," she told him. "I'll let you guys get back to your work."

When she left the kitchen, Gunner filled Dare and Key in on what else they'd discovered.

"We've got to protect Gunner from the CIA," Dare said.

"In all of this, the CIA's the least of our problems," Jem told him. "Landon's got a hell of a lot of protectors. They'll all turn on Gunner, because if Donal's killed Drew and he's impersonating him, they probably have no idea."

"There's one other scenario," Gunner told them. "What if Drew and Donal have been in on this from the start?"

"Guess there's only one way to find out," Jem said. "I'll go through the bank accounts."

Gunner's phone buzzed on the table. He glanced at the number. "It's Landon."

Jem hooked it into the computer so they could trace it and nodded. Gunner pressed TALK and said, "What do you want, Landon?"

"You."

Avery knew something was wrong. She'd always been intuitive, but after working with Dare and Jem and the others, her instincts had gone into overdrive. She'd hauled herself out of bed and limped toward the kitchen, holding her side.

The men were so focused they didn't hear her. If they had, she didn't doubt that one of them would've carried her away from here.

Landon's voice was in the room. She clutched the doorjamb as a wave of panic hit her. She knew he was on the phone, not there in person, but she hadn't realized that his voice alone would have such an effect on her.

And if he was in front of you, how effectively could you hurt him then? a small voice inside her asked harshly. *You have to handle this.*

"You're not getting me, Landon. You broke too many goddamned promises," Gunner was saying, his voice calm and controlled. She knew by the set of his shoulders he was anything but.

"I'm guessing you don't want your friends safe?" Landon asked.

"Oh, I do. But that's not going to happen by doing anything for you," Gunner told him. "Hear this—we are coming for you. As of now, you're the one who's being hunted. I'd make sure I kept looking over my shoulder if I were you. One of these times, you're going to see me. And I'll be the last thing you do see before you hit the ground."

Gunner reached out, severed the connection, and there was dead silence in the room. She wanted to back away, but she couldn't be quick enough about it.

"He will never hurt you again, Avery," Gunner said then. "Do you hear me?"

He'd known she was there the whole time. "I do."

As she'd spoken the words, the house began to rumble under her feet. She didn't know exactly what was happening, but she saw the war in all the men's eyes, and then they were moving fast.

Later, she'd look back and not understand how they'd managed to escape so efficiently. She didn't know that Jem, Dare, Gunner and Key had an emergency plan in place, that they had supplies in the cars they kept in a garage around the corner. That they didn't leave anything in this house they weren't prepared to lose, information-wise.

Now all she knew was that someone grabbed her and they were running. She bit the inside of her cheek to keep from screaming, from fear and pain, and whoever carried her knew that. Because as soon as he put her down, Drea was next to her, injecting her with a mild pain med—that's what she told Avery. And then the truck was moving, fast.

She heard the explosion—it rattled the car windows, shook the road beneath the truck. Saw the fire reflected in the back window.

"Please . . . did everyone . . ."

"Everyone's out," Jem said. "Gunner's in the other car with Dare and Grace. You've got me and Key here, with Drea. We're all safe, Avery."

As he said that, the sound of the chopper's whirring blades grew clearer.

No, they weren't safe at all.

It had always been part of the plan to separate Gunner from Avery if something went down. Although Gunner wasn't happy about it, he understood the reason for it.

Now, as the dark trucks with the tinted windows tore down the road toward the highway, Gunner glanced back and watched the chopper hover over the house.

They'd gotten away—that was the most important thing.

"How did they find us?" Dare demanded, and that was the second most important thing, because hell, if Landon found them this many times, this easily, it was no coincidence.

"Gunner's phone's clean," Jem said over the speaker of Dare's phone. "We only forwarded the number, but it's a new everything else."

"Can't he ping the number?" Key asked.

"Not the way I have it set up," Jem said.

"They're still coming," Grace said. The *whoompa* of the helo's blades was relentless in the night. Even driving without their headlights on, the helo was tracking them.

He heard Key's voice. "Gunner, pull away from us. See which way the helo goes."

Gunner did, taking the corner fast, the truck shaking. He flew down the highway, mixing in with other cars in the hopes that Landon wouldn't be taking out everyone on the highway.

His worst fears were confirmed. The helo was following the truck Avery was in with Jem and Drea.

Avery heard the chopper's blades follow their truck, not the one Gunner was in, and she knew they were in trouble. "It's got to be me," she said.

"How the hell are they finding you?" Jem asked.

"It's not possible," Avery said. "I have nothing left from before. Everything's new."

Drea was staring at her. "Tell me about the stitches under your right arm."

"What stitches? The ones you gave me?"

"Doc, no offense but—" Jem started but Drea waved him off. She moved Avery's short sleeve up and pointed to a row of black heavy stitching.

"I didn't stitch that," she told Avery. "I saw it, figured you guys were in a dangerous business, so I didn't think to mention it."

"Why would Landon slice her and then stitch that one spot?" Key asked. "Unless he planted something in there."

"No fucking way," Jem muttered. The chopper was closer now, and Jem swerved off road into a wooded area to try to slow them down.

Drea was probing Avery's arm with her fingers, lightly at first and then harder, a frown on her face. "I can't feel anything. He could've put it in deep enough so a doctor wouldn't."

"And he counted on her having so many cuts she wouldn't notice one extra. He was hoping the doc who helped her wouldn't notice," Jem said, and Drea let out a nice long string of curses that Avery knew were directed at Landon.

"Motherfucker didn't know who he was dealing with," Drea muttered as she rifled through her bag. She held up a syringe and a scalpel. "You ready?"

"Get it out," she told Drea.

Key climbed over the seat to help them. Both he and Drea gloved up after Drea numbed the area.

"It's still going to hurt," she warned Avery.

"Doesn't matter," Avery told her, and Drea didn't hesitate with the scalpel. With the car jostling, which couldn't be helped, her concentration had a razor focus.

Key was holding a pressure bandage at the ready and Avery hissed as she felt the probing of Drea's fingers. The car shimmied hard and Drea pulled away.

"Jem, you have to stop. For just a few seconds," Drea said. "I don't want to damage anything by mistake."

Jem cursed and braked hard. Drea didn't hesitate. Avery concentrated on Drea's face instead of the pain, and Drea's eyes widened.

She nodded, talked to herself under her breath as she gently moved her fingers around in the underside of Avery's arm. In the next ten seconds, she pulled out completely, handed the chip to Key and held the pressure bandage to Avery's arm.

"We got it," Key said.

The truck began to move again, fast, and Jem said, "And I know just the place to put it for the perfect distraction."

The truck bounced along the ruts and Drea just held her arm as both women had their eyes on the ceiling, as if they expected the chopper to come through the roof of the truck at any moment.

Key was wrapping the chip to the side of a gun; then he moved to the window, opened it and waited until Jem said, "Now, Key."

Avery propped herself up to see what was happening, but it was so dark she couldn't.

"There's a river," Drea told her. "We're driving right alongside it."

"It'll keep the chip moving," Avery said with a nod. The truck continued at its frantic pace, but the sound of the chopper got fainter.

"It's following the chip." Jem sounded relieved, and Avery figured he was talking to the other car. "She's okay."

"I'm okay," she called. Because she was. The fight inside her had been renewed even as her head spun with the knowledge that Landon had known where she was the entire time.

Chapter Twenty-five

Staying together might be the worst idea ever, but now that none of them was carrying a GPS chip inside their body, no one thought to voice a difference of opinion.

Avery didn't even know what time it was when the truck stopped moving and Jem helped her into a new safe house. Later, she'd ask what state and city they were in, but for now, she went into the bathroom and let Drea stitch her up.

Gunner stood in the doorway, watching, until Drea asked for his help. He caught Avery's eye, waited until she nodded before coming forward to assist.

Within half an hour, Avery had a new bandage, some more pain medicine and a newfound sense of teamwork, especially when Gunner said, "We need to meet now. Whether you're up for it or not."

Good. He wasn't treating her like glass. "I'm definitely up for it."

"Drea, you can join us," Gunner told the doctor. "You deserve to know what's happening before we go farther. And if you want out, as in away from us, no one will blame you."

Drea nodded, stripped her gloves. "I'll be right there."

Avery let Gunner guide her into the kitchen, where everyone else was sitting around the table. Grace had made some eggs and bacon and toast. She pushed coffee in front of Avery when she sat, and Avery drank it gratefully.

Despite what they'd been through that night, coming out safe on the other side always made for more of a happy atmosphere, no matter how bad the danger still was. This time, there was no immediate danger, but it was imminent just the same.

"Where do we start?" she asked quietly, as if she was waiting for any of them to tell her she wasn't ready for this.

But no one did. Gunner was sitting next to her, but he turned and spoke directly to her. "We don't know if Donal's killed Drew and is impersonating him, or if the men are working together. It doesn't matter, because the plan's the same. Rather than going directly after Landon, our best bet it to start by taking out his customers. Then his suppliers. Hit him where it hurts, which makes things safer for us."

"We'll have to do it fast," Key said.

"Set up on different sides and blow them all at

once," Jem agreed. "As dangerous as being separate is, staying together is worse."

"Avery and Gunner shouldn't be together," Dare said.

"Landon will expect that," Avery said. "Which is exactly why I'm not letting Gunner out of my sight."

"Way to take his manhood," Jem said. "You've got to let him say that about you."

"If that's the way it's supposed to be, forget it."

"Guess I have a bodyguard," Gunner said, a small smile on his face. "That plan works for me."

"So we blow things up and then what?" Grace asked. "Go right after him?"

"I don't think so," Dare said slowly. "Let him stew. Let him reach out to other contacts."

"Contacts that we'll infiltrate," Key added.

"It's a semi-long-term approach. Six months of planning," Gunner said. "Which means we need a place that's secure as shit. Because we need to be together for the planning."

Grace was pacing and then she snapped her fingers.

"Honey?" Dare said.

"I think I know the perfect place," she said.

Dare pressed his lips together grimly before saying, "Absolutely fucking not."

"We all sacrifice," she started.

"And you already have," Dare pointed out.

"Get the feeling we're missing something?" Jem asked.

Grace told them, "Right before Dare and I came back here, I found out that Rip left everything to me."

Avery's eyes widened. "Everything as in . . ."

"The island. The money. Everything. A locked will. The attorney doesn't even know what it says. Just sent me to open a safe-deposit box. Everything was put into my name, although that information is guarded by the banks under a different name. He thought of everything." Grace paused. "We were going to tell you guys right away, but there was so much else to work on. It wasn't an urgent matter, but now . . ."

"We go to the island. Clean it up, security-wise, and it could work," Jem said.

"You don't think Landon will watch the island?" Dare demanded.

"Why? We'd never thought of it," Key said, and Gunner got up so fast his chair slammed against the wall behind him. Avery went to get up, but Grace put a hand on her shoulder.

"I've got this," she told Avery, and Avery knew it was important enough to stay put and let Grace work some magic.

Gunner was in the living room, pacing, when he saw Grace push through the kitchen door. Of all people to send after him now, she would definitely be the most effective.

He wondered if she'd gotten Dare to say yes in that short time. In which case, the guy was definitely whipped.

Like you're not.

"Grace, I appreciate you coming out here, but—"

"You were trying to tell me that you were Rip's son, that night, at Darius's, when I had the fever," Grace said, and no, that wasn't what he had expected.

He thought about the first time he'd met her, how sick she was. How Dare told him about the scars that covered her body.

How Gunner already knew that living with Powell was like a death sentence, with the majority of time served on death row with no hope of actually escaping. "Maybe. I wanted you to know you weren't alone."

But that wasn't the only reason. What good would telling her have done? For her to know that maybe there was someone out there who knew what she'd gone through, because he'd been there. . . .

"There was nothing you could've done. No way you could've known. If anything, my mother and I got you chased out," Grace told him firmly.

"You're a mind reader now?" he asked to try to break the tension.

"I'm good with feeling guilty over things I had

no control over. I recognize that instantly," she shot back.

"It wasn't that. Powell had a business deal gone bad. I was a fair trade."

"I'm sorry. So sorry about what happened to both of us. I know going back to that house will be as hard on you as it will be on me. Maybe I had no right to make that decision before speaking to you."

"Going back there is going backward, Grace. Touching that place . . . it's fucking poison," he told her.

"No place is poison, not if we don't let it be," she said.

"I think we're getting ahead of ourselves," Jem told them. Gunner had seen him come into the room, and Dare probably had too, but suddenly Crazy Man was the voice of reason. Again. "First, we need someone to pose as a job—a criminal who needs to leave the country."

"How about a criminal's wife?" Grace asked. "That would make things less suspicious."

"Woman, you are really pushing things tonight," Dare growled. "You did not just offer yourself for the job, did you?"

"He's never met me in person. He's seen me on the tape with a gag in my mouth," Grace pointed out.

"A guy like Landon can use facial-recognition software," Key reminded them.

"And he already has," Gunner told them.

"How do we know that for sure?" Avery asked.

"Because I was identified." Gunner went into the kitchen, came out and sat on the couch. He typed in the code and then turned the screen outward to face them.

Avery blinked. "It's us."

"Like the fucking Brady Bunch," Jem muttered, and indeed, the screen was split into six boxes, showing Gunner, Dare, Grace, Jem and Key. The last box was blank at the moment, but the shots had been taken from when they'd been on Powell's island.

"Can't we wipe Landon's computers?"

"I already did. Doesn't mean he doesn't have copies. Everyone uses facial-recognition software these days," Gunner said.

"But if we disguise Grace's face, put some fake cheekbones and shit, it'll throw the software off," Jem said. "She's our best shot."

"She'll have to change the way she walks. The best software does more than faces," Gunner said.

"I can change anything if it means getting rid of this guy from our lives," Grace promised.

"Or I could help."

Jem turned at the sound of Drea's voice. She'd remained in the doorway of the kitchen but now moved forward and Jem willed her not to say anything more.

Which obviously didn't work when she said, "The asshole who hurt Avery doesn't know me. I could do it."

"No way," Jem said before Avery could open her mouth.

"Why not?" Dare asked, arms crossed.

"She's not trained, for one," Jem pointed out.

"I can shoot. I can use a knife. Well, a scalpel. Same thing really," Drea said. "And I know how to fight."

"Sweetheart, this fight would be like nothing you could've ever imagined," Jem promised her.

"It's one meeting," Grace pointed out. "She'd pass his scrutiny in a second."

Key nodded and Jem walked toward Drea, hand on her biceps, and tried to steer her out of the room. "What do you think you're doing?"

"Offering to help."

"I already told you, you don't owe us."

"I heard you, Jem. But what if I want to help you?"

"Too dangerous."

"You need me to get to him. I'm your best option. He's suspicious already—you said so yourself."

"We'll just go with our original plan of making his life a living hell," Jem said.

Avery shook her head. "It's going to take too long, Jem."

"Dammit." He was having more of a problem

with the women in his life being in the line of fire
than he'd thought. He'd always been equal opportunity, felt that if women could do the job,
they could have it. And he knew Avery could.
But that didn't stop him from freaking at the
thought of her getting hurt again. Same went for
Grace, and now for Drea.

"This is for Avery. And Grace. And for me,"
Drea told the group, but really, she was speaking
to him. All he could do was nod his acceptance,
even though he wasn't accepting it at all.

Chapter Twenty-six

Goddamn, it had been a long day. All the sitting around and talking rather than getting out there for some action was making the men act like caged lions. Pretty soon, they were going to start wrestling in the middle of the living room to blow off steam.

It was close to three in the morning after Jem had finished doing some research with Key, left his brother still working to relieve Dare and check on Drea.

She was in bed, but reading. Looking wide awake and fucking adorable in his T-shirt and a pair of sweats that were broken in just right.

"Can't sleep?" he asked.

"Lately, it's the last thing on my mind." She accepted the mug of hot chocolate he handed her and tucked herself under the covers. She'd left room for him in the bed and oh yeah, he liked that.

Too much. It was fucking with his game. "Look, I appreciate what you did back there—"

"No, you're pissed about it."

Her honesty disarmed him. She was such a straight shooter. "Yeah, I am. Worried more than pissed but . . . dammit, Drea, you've got to stop putting yourself directly in trouble's way when I'm trying to get you out of it."

"I guess I'm good at finding trouble." She let her gaze fall on him meaningfully.

"Aw, come on, that was too easy."

"You walked into it," she pointed out. "Can you tell me a little more about this Landon guy you're all discussing? What he does for a living?"

"He's a smuggler. He helps criminals leave the country, but he also stops human traffickers. Lots of shades of gray," Jem explained. "We'd have no problem with him if he didn't keep trying to kill us."

"He's the one who hurt Avery?"

"Yes. Now can you understand why I don't want you anywhere near him?"

She nodded. "But Grace can't do it. And you don't have anyone else."

"We'll find another way. There's always another way." Only this time, there really wasn't, and Drea knew that as much as he did. As much as they all did.

Avery dreaded reading Adele's missing journals, but once she'd forced herself to start, she was angry she hadn't done so earlier.

It's the worst thing that could ever happen to a woman, and they know that. It's why it's their best weapon. But after months of healing physically, I'm going to accept that I'll never be the same. That's all right. I'm still strong. I'm just different. And to change is to live. To survive.

She was a survivor.

"It's a shame she never had kids," she'd told Grace after she'd finished the first journal. "She would've been the best mom."

"She was," Grace said, hugging her arms around herself.

It was then Avery remembered how much they'd all lost. If they hadn't been broken by now, she had to assume they never would. "I forgot how long you spent with her."

"I didn't read these journals until she'd left. But then I understood why she got me—didn't yell at me about being promiscuous. She understood it was my way of taking back my power," Grace said.

The planning was happening around her. Gunner briefed her at night, and sometimes she fell asleep while he was talking. That was all right—it was as if what he said was solidifying in her brain, adding fuel to the fire. And every day, the need for strict vengeance wore a little thinner. The need for justice grew stronger. It was a much better balance.

After a month, they moved locations. A different state, a better safe house that Jem and Key vetted for a week before they allowed the others to move here.

It was all temporary, Avery knew. Her ultimate goal was to get Gunner back to his tattoo shop. Back to at least drawing, which she hadn't seen him do once.

She'd forced herself to look in the full-length mirror daily since Drea took the bandages off. Wanted to know exactly what Landon had done, wanted to watch the black stitches dissolve and the bright red scars fade to pink and then eventually white, knowing her anger wouldn't fade as quickly. Not until Landon paid, and paid dearly.

He didn't have family. No one close to him that she could hurt him with, beyond Gunner. Even if there were, she didn't think she could do that.

But not having anyone to care about was how the man stayed on top for so long. You couldn't care about anyone or anything that could be used against you. And that was S8's fatal flaw. She couldn't see that changing any time soon. It was the only way to keep their consciences in check, the only way they'd ever be able to love.

"We could retire to an island. Work enough to live and then just hang out," Jem had suggested yesterday.

"You? Hanging out? Doing what, lying in the sun? I give it less than an hour," she'd scoffed.

"Maybe I'd love it."

She knew she wouldn't.

She traced the scars now, her fingers trailing as her eyes never left the mirror.

Every night, she curled up next to Gunner, fully clothed. And every night, he'd held her through nightmares that went from multiple ones nightly to one per night and then a few times a week. Body and mind seemed to heal at the same time. Having Grace and Dare and Key there helped. She could concentrate on healing, without worrying that everyone was in danger.

There were thirteen scars in all. Different sizes, some vertical, some horizontal, done purposely to scar. The biggest one bisected her tattoo and she traced the X that marked her beautiful flowers.

Gunner would work miracles on this. She knew that. But she hadn't wanted him to see her naked yet, because she was more worried about how these scars would affect him than anything.

She drew a bath, sank into the bubbles and tried to relax. Time was passing. Plans were being made. Soon, it would be time to put up or shut up.

She would make Landon pay for everything he'd ever done to her family.

Chapter Twenty-seven

It had been seven days since they'd moved to this house, and the closer they got to firming up plans to take Landon down, the harder Avery had been pulling away from him.

She'd been in planning mode. She was healing. Stronger. Sharp too, but that didn't mean she was totally ready for this. None of them were.

Gunner glanced into the kitchen and found the others there, except for Avery.

"Thought she was with you," Jem said.

"She's taking a bath," Grace told him. "I just checked on her."

And now he was going to. She'd been avoiding him and he wouldn't let that happen. He burst into the bathroom and found her soaking in the tub, up to her neck in bubbles.

"Can't a girl have any privacy?" she asked.

"No. None. You're not leaving my side." Jesus, he might as well have simply said, *Me caveman, you woman.*

She blinked, stared down at the bubbles. "Can you at least wait outside the door?"

"I won't leave you alone inside a room with a window."

"I'm below the window."

He wanted to tell her that a sniper wasn't the only way Landon could try to get to her, but instead he told her, "You need to get out."

"Is it me or Landon you're worried about?"

"Both. Now up," he said firmly, held up a towel.

"I'm all soapy. I have to rinse off."

He sighed, moved to the window and said, "Go ahead."

"Can't you at least look away?"

"No." Why was she being so stubborn? He'd seen her naked, made love to her. Now wasn't the time for false modesty. "And if you don't move soon, I'm hauling you out of there myself."

"Fine." With a determined set to her jaw, she let the water out of the tub and stayed seated and used the handheld showerhead to wash off for a while. And then she finally stood, her taut body naked and dripping wet.

He stared as something caught his eye. She stilled, because she knew.

She'd hidden the scars from him. Jem had helped her. He'd assumed the bandages she'd worn for weeks had been because of broken ribs.

He'd been so very wrong. There were deep

cuts through her beautiful tattoo. And the initials DL carved into a heart. Slashes on her breasts that were on their way to healing still looked angry. They'd never fully fade.

"Not as pretty as tattoos," she said tightly.

"You'll always be beautiful to me, Avery."

"Dammit, Gunner, I didn't want you to find out about them like this."

"Come on." He wrapped her in the towel because she'd started to shiver.

"I don't have regrets."

"I do, Avery. It's my fault you sank deeper into this world."

"I would've been here sooner or later. It's my legacy, remember?" she said almost defiantly as she stepped out of the tub and walked into the adjoining bedroom, holding the towel around her.

Gunner started after her. She was still in pain, and pretending everything was fine when it goddamn wasn't. So what was this all about? Revenge? Redemption? Or more than a generous helping of both?

He followed her now, found her sitting on the bed, holding a sketch pad. It was brand-new, and there were pencils there too. She must've asked someone to pick them up on one of their runs into town.

"Draw me," she told him.

The seeds for his revenge against Landon had been planted when he'd found Josie on the floor. He just hadn't seen a way out that didn't involve him losing what little he had left. And when his art had soothed him, he'd clung to that, because he didn't want to lose it again.

The art—the tattooing—was to honor Josie and what she'd done for him. But she'd always known that his art was important to him.

Avery wasn't going to let him forget that. She dropped the towel. "Do it. Scars and all." And just like that, she fucking posed for him. "Plan what other tattoos you'll do after that."

Those he would draw right on her body, just so he could get the curves right. For now, he concentrated on sketching the warrior he saw in front of him. Because he didn't see the scars, not the way she'd thought he would. "I'm drawing you exactly as I see you."

"Tell me what you see," she said.

"You. Beautiful survivor. Map of where you've been, how far you've come." He looked up.

"The scar over your heart . . ." He paused, then bent down to sketch again. "Means you've been given more room to let people in. More room for me and all my mistakes."

"Not so many mistakes," she said softly. He heard the smile in her voice as he traced a breast on paper with the edge of the pencil.

"Scars make you stronger."

"Until I had them, I never understood what people meant when they said that."

"But now you do."

"Yes."

"When I look at you, I don't see scars, though. I see . . . you."

"And places you want to tattoo."

"That too." He stood, moved closer. Traced the pencil's eraser over the lines on her breasts. "I've got plans. Short-term and long-term."

"Does short-term involve you in my bed?"

"Definitely."

Gunner's hand wound around the back of her neck as he spoke. He dropped the sketchbook onto the night table as she stood, pressed her naked body against his clothed one.

Her heart was beating so loudly she was sure he could hear it. But she'd never felt more strong and sure in her life.

"Don't be gentle with me. Don't you dare," she told him. Something glinted in his eyes and he swooped her up and brought her over to the bed. But instead of covering her body with his, he rolled them so she was on top of him. She stared down at him, wondering how he could know so much, how he could just know what she needed.

"Go ahead, woman. Have your way with me,"

he murmured. He wound his hands around the metal bar across the headboard. "Use my T-shirt. Cuffs. Whatever you've got."

"I want you to touch me," she said, even though she knew he was right, that she wouldn't handle that well.

Reluctantly, she used the handcuffs from Gunner's bag, because she knew he would have a tougher time getting out of those. Hated that Landon had done this to her and then realized that she never, ever wanted Landon in her mind, in her bed ever again. That would mean he won, and she couldn't let that happen.

She kissed him. He kissed her back but let her set the rhythm. She gripped his hair, kissed him like there was no tomorrow as the familiar passion filled her. She was wet between her legs, her nipples hard.

Her body still worked. Maybe scars really did make you stronger.

His cock was hard against her sex. And although she wanted him inside her, this felt too good to stop. It had been too long, and before she could think about it, her belly clenched with pleasure. "Gunner."

She heard the surprise in her own voice.

"Yeah, baby. Just like that. Keep looking at me. You're with me, and you're safe. And you're so fucking beautiful, I can't stand it."

She rubbed against him until the orgasm burst

through her. She saw stars, held on to his shoulders.

And then she wept. When she was able to stop, she wiped her eyes, looked at him and then at the sketchbook.

He'd drawn her with no scars at all.

I drew you exactly the way I see you.

Chapter Twenty-eight

Nearly four months had passed since Landon tried to firebomb them. He hadn't called, and things had been quiet on that front. Not so much with Landon's business, which Jem helped Gunner trace.

Landon—Drew, Donal or both—was still active. And so their plan to have Drea pose as the wife of a recently indicted businessman was moving forward full steam.

And Jem wasn't happy about it at all. He'd voiced his unhappiness in every way, shape or form he could think of.

"It's not them. It's us," Gunner had muttered just last night, and Key nodded in agreement.

"And we'll drive ourselves and them crazy if we keep focusing on it," Jem had added.

"You were already there," Key pointed out.

Now Jem concentrated on putting a microphone and camera buttons in some of the high fashion bags and accessories Drea would wear when she met with Landon. Grace had taken her shopping, with Dare as their escort.

He'd grumbled something about it being horrible, but he'd come home with new clothes, Jem noted.

But the transformation hadn't stopped with clothing. Drea spent part of the day at some kind of spa—and Dare got a manicure, Grace was quick to point out—and when she came home, she looked beautiful, but different. She looked high society. The right makeup and hairstyle, the right dress and jewelry and suddenly Drea was Andrea, pronounced with an O sound.

Drea was used to dealing with deadly maniacs. She'd been threatened for so long, standing in a room with men of Landon's caliber wasn't going to throw her.

That didn't mean that Jem was ready to let her do it. And the fact that he'd bucked the idea so hard let him know that he had feelings for Drea. Real goddamned feelings, and he'd somehow let that happen when he'd promised himself he never, ever would.

She stood in front of him almost shyly, the expensive fabric of the well-cut dress draping over her perfectly. Her legs were long and lean and finely muscled and the heels she wore emphasized that.

He'd forced himself to stop sleeping in her bed weeks ago, when the planning intensified. They hadn't done much more than kiss, even though he wanted much more.

"You look fucking fantastic," he told her, and she blushed.

"Jem, come on. I don't look like me."

"No, you don't. And when you're done, I'm going to help you wash it all off," he promised.

Her blush deepened. "Stop. I'm already nervous. I've never dressed like this. I feel . . ."

"Hot?"

"Silly," she countered. "Why do women feel like they need all of this?"

He shrugged. "Armor. I carry my gun, a woman shields herself with makeup and earrings and bags."

The meeting was set up for two o'clock. Drea had perfect identification—Jem saw to it that there were no mistakes. The real wife was in federal custody—Landon wouldn't know that. For all intents and purposes, S8 made it look as though the feds leaked that she was still missing, that they were searching for her. The situation played right into their laps.

Except Jem would have to let Drea out of reach to pull this off. Landon insisted on sending a car for her. Jem would wait at the second safe house with her, but after she got into the car, she was on her own.

He'd spent the better part of the month making her brush up on her self-defense skills. She went to the shooting range. He gave her knives that were sewn into strategic places in her dress, ceramic ones that wouldn't set off any metal detectors. She had pills she could dissolve into people's drinks, if things got bad.

"It's just a meeting, Jem. She'll pull it off and be right back to us," Gunner said, but his voice was tight too.

Everything they'd done over the past months had led up to this. Key and Dare, and sometimes Jem, had spent the time traveling to various ports and thwarting cargo ships filled with women and children. Gunner had the edge, knowing Landon so well, and although Landon might suspect Gunner was behind it, he had way too many fires to put out and his resources were stretched thin trying to plug the holes in his business. Because Gunner also stopped two major criminals from leaving the country with Landon's men. It was all taking a chance, but that's what they were all about.

Word was beginning to leak out that Landon's business was suffering. Add to that the other men that S8 put out of business, traffickers and other businessmen who would normally support Landon, and Jem knew the walls had begun to close in on Landon.

He leaned back and snapped a picture of Drea, the way he'd been doing over the past months. And he fed it into the facial-recognition software.

They'd run tests on Drea for weeks now, with all different programs, and there had never been a hit.

Until now.

When the computer started beeping, he stared at it in surprise. Thankfully, Avery had called Drea away, so she hadn't noticed, but Key had. Stared over Jem's shoulder.

"The feds are after her," Jem told his brother, who gave a low whistle.

"She ever tell you anything about that?"

"No. Don't know if she even knows," Jem said. "She's been honest about everything else and it's the first time she's come up in the system. Maybe that asshole ex is using her for an immunity plea?"

"Either way, they're gonna force her to testify."

"Dammit." Jem sighed, because she was definitely a fugitive. It was one thing to have her hiding out from the OA. But the feds were a whole other story, and once they got their hooks into S8 . . .

"She'll compromise us, yes. But Avery's not going to care."

"Avery's not the only one on the team."

"Jem, did you stop to think this could actually work in our favor? The guy's wife is wanted by the feds. If Drea's face shows up as wanted . . . can't we just change the information on her?"

Jem could easily change Drea's name and

other details, and he would, but that didn't change the fact that he hated this plan. "She has a right to know."

"Agreed. You tell her, and I'll share with the rest of the group." Key patted Jem on the back as he walked away, calling, "Hey Drea, Jem needs to talk to you."

Drea came over to him. She'd taken off the heels since this was only a dress rehearsal for next week. She was already tugging at the dress and he knew she'd be back in her jeans as soon as they'd let her.

For now, Avery was busy taking pictures, building up a portfolio of a life Drea didn't have.

"What's wrong?"

"Your face came up on the recognition software."

"What does that mean, exactly?"

"It means someone put you into the system as wanted." He pointed to the computer and let the screen do the talking.

"The FBI?" she asked.

"And they don't see the picture I scanned of you—I made sure of that. You haven't been caught, but they want you."

"What did they say I did?" she asked, her eyes wide. "Wait. I know. Dammit."

Her eyes were troubled. He didn't push her, thought about how he couldn't wait until she showered and got all that shit off her face. She'd drop her towel and pull on a T-shirt to sleep in. Then she'd run her hands through her long hair—that was the extent of her beauty routine and she always ended up with hair that looked like something out of a magazine. It amazed him every time that she was so carelessly beautiful.

He'd fallen in love with her, maybe from the second he'd seen her helping a woman most doctors would've gone out of their way to avoid. In that split second, he'd known everything he needed to know.

Seemed maybe he didn't know *everything*.

Finally, she told him, "It's the drugs. Morphine mainly. Some Oxy. I never gave it to them—I told Danny they'd take my medical license. But I know the clinic was robbed a few times."

"So Danny told them they got the drugs from you?" Jem asked.

"He'd do anything to get his ass out of a sling. Especially if it means I sit in jail next to him so he can keep an eye on me."

"What's their main source of income?"

She shrugged. "I didn't get involved in that. I know they did some gun runs. Some drugs, obviously. Maybe some prostitution, but nothing I have any evidence of. Danny made sure I knew just enough to keep me in line and not enough to ever get the club in trouble."

"I'll figure something out."

"In all your spare time?"

"Drea—"

"Jem, you're going to have to let me go hide somewhere. I mean, this tour of the world's been great, but sooner or later, you're all going back to your home base. I can't compromise what you do."

And she'd put it together faster than he thought she'd be able to. "Maybe turning myself over to them's for the best. They can put you in protection."

"You do not trust that shit, Drea. Trust me—you cannot trust them worth a damn. They will fuck you over to make their case. Use you and spit you out." He heard his own voice shake with anger. "I've seen it. Not pretty. I won't let that happen to you."

"Then what, Jem?"

"How about we finish off Landon first, and then we figure out you, okay, baby?"

She nodded, because there wasn't much choice. They were too far into this to stop now. Landon had more heat on him with each day that passed. His contacts were slowly turning on him. It satisfied S8's need to help people along with scaring the shit out of Landon. Much more satisfying than a slow kill.

If Landon was trying to send men after them, they weren't showing up on anyone's radar.

Chapter Twenty-nine

It would take everything Avery had to stand in front of the computer screen and see Landon again, hear his voice, watch him shake hands with Drea. But for the woman who'd risked so much to help her, she would absolutely do so, despite the fact that Drea herself didn't want her to.

"Avery, it's too much, too soon. Let Jem and Gunner watch. You don't need to do this," Drea had told her only hours before Jem took her to the meeting place three towns over.

"I'm there. Just remember that while you're with that bastard. I'm there. We all are," Avery told her.

Now she watched Jem return, his face grim. He'd had to leave Drea alone in the house—it was too risky otherwise.

"She's still alone," Gunner told him. Jem nodded, his face expressionless as he sat down next to Gunner. Grace stood next to Avery behind them. Gunner had left a seat for her, but she didn't want to distract him or Jem. This was too important. No matter how scared she might be, Landon was on the other end of a computer. Drea was the one dealing with him face-to-face.

"You're sure he'll come to the meeting?" Dare asked.

"He always takes the meetings. Always. It's his MO," Gunner said. "If he doesn't, we know we're made."

And Drea had a contingency plan for that. All she had to do was hit a button and the entire house would fill with gas. It would knock her out along with Landon and his crew, but it wouldn't be enough to hurt them. It would give Jem enough time to get back to her.

"Why the hell don't we just gas and kill them?" Jem asked for the thousandth time, even though he knew the reason well: In case the part of Landon was really being played by two men instead of one.

No one answered Jem, but Key squeezed his brother's shoulder.

And then the doorbell in Drea's safe house rang. She went to it and answered the door, looking stylish, but nothing like the pictures they'd taken of her. If she was really a woman on the run, she wouldn't be dressed to the nines and calling attention to herself.

But Avery knew that rich women always

looked elegant, no matter what they were wearing. Drea fit that bill. They'd spent an hour covering up her tattoo sleeve with special makeup, but it was worth it for all of their peace of mind.

She held her breath when she heard Landon's voice. Her fists clenched when he ordered his men to search the house, and told another one to hold her still for the photo. The man grabbed Drea's arms and pulled them behind her back and Landon snapped a picture.

"We're on," Gunner muttered, and Jem started typing furiously. He inserted the corrected information into Drea's federal profile, information that would only remain for sixty seconds.

It would hopefully be all they needed.

"He's got his hit," Jem said, his voice raw.

"You're a wanted woman," Landon said with an approving smile.

For once the feds had worked in their favor, and they all breathed a sigh of relief. Jem lit a cigarette as they watched Drea hand Landon the money he'd requested. Only then did Landon sit her down to go over the final plans with him about smuggling her out of the country.

She asked the right questions—where would he put her and why? How would she get new identification? How soon would he be able to get her husband out of custody?

In the good old days, before S8 started fucking with him, Landon would've had the power to do that. As of now, Gunner made sure he wouldn't be able to deliver on that promise, but Landon had no way of knowing Drea knew too.

The idea was to get Landon working on a high-profile job that Drew could've pulled off in his sleep. Donal didn't have a quarter of the experience or the finesse, and all his time would be put into this dream job. His attention would be divided and that's when Gunner and S8 would strike at him on the island, on his turf.

Only then would Gunner know the truth about Drew. And everything was going fine until Landon said, "I hope you have a bag packed."

"I do, but you said this would happen next week."

"I said your move to your permanent new country of residence would happen next week. Today, you'll fly out of here with me. Trust me, it's much safer this way. I don't like having federal agents circling my clients."

Drea paused. "I don't think I'm ready to leave."

"You have to be. Cutting ties is the hardest part, and the most important. Best to make it like ripping off a Band-Aid. We go now," Landon said, and Jem cursed under his breath.

"I have personal belongings that will get lost if I don't collect them."

"It's either you come with us now and we

leave in the morning or we don't have a deal. I'm sure your life is more important than your belongings, no?"

"I know what's important," Drea said, and that was completely for their benefit. She stood, went into the bedroom and wheeled out the luggage she'd packed. One of Landon's men took it, to search it, no doubt, and then without a final look back, Drea was gone.

There was dead silence in the room as Jem continued to stare at the empty screen. Drea had a choice and she made it, and goddamn her for risking her life.

For your family.

"We go in now," he said. No one argued. Not right away, anyway. After a few minutes had passed and Jem was able to make sure the tracking for Drea was working, Key started in.

"Bro, we've got to give this a day to work."

"She doesn't have a day," Jem told him fiercely.

"I think Landon's bringing her to the island because of everything we've been doing," Gunner broke in. "He's extra paranoid. That's good for us."

"Suppose he doesn't bring her where he says he's going to? Suppose he made her?" Jem demanded.

"Twenty-four hours, Jem," Key repeated. "We

can get close. But if we don't wait, we could be risking Drea's life too."

Jem knew that. Rubbed his temples and fought the urge to slam his fist through the wall.

It was going to be the longest twenty-four hours of his life.

Chapter Thirty

The island was more heavily guarded than it had ever been. Gunner used the rubber Kodiak to take them in, letting the tide and their manpower do the work to get them to shore. Grace was waiting on the bigger boat two miles out—she was armed and ready for trouble but knew that those on the boat were headed to the biggest trouble.

Gunner dragged the boat to the sand, helped Avery out. He stored the boat by the other boats used to access visiting yachts and the like—it would go unnoticed for the most part. They would as well until they got within twenty feet of the main house.

The guards circled Landon's house. The last takedown of traffickers that Key and Jem had scored had sent two different teams of men here, all looking to kill Landon. Word was that Landon had escaped, but a lot of his men hadn't.

Which meant many of these guards were new enough not to recognize Gunner on sight. Unless

Landon had been smart enough to post his picture—all their pictures.

None of that really mattered. They were heavily armed, ready to take back Drea and take down the man, or men, who had hurt them all.

"Company," Key said softly, and Gunner saw Jem smile and make fists. The man was so ready to take someone—anyone—out, and Gunner motioned to him. "Have at it."

Jem ran into the crowd of men and threw himself at them like he was a bowling ball and they were the pins. His body actually went sideways and he took down five of the six men, forced the sixth to trip a little.

"So's that a spare?" Key asked before he dove into the fray. Gunner followed, his AK-47 held out in front of him.

"Gentlemen, let's talk," he said, and the big guard he'd beaten down months ago stared at him.

"You—we have orders to bring you in alive. Landon's going to have fun with you," he told Gunner, just as Jem came up behind him and put him in a headlock.

"Where's the woman?" he growled.

"Fuck you," the guard spat, and then he stopped, because Jem was cutting off his air.

"Jem, hold up," Gunner said, then spoke directly to the guard, the only one near them who hadn't been knocked out. "The man you've been taking orders from isn't Drew. You've been taking orders from Donal, the man who killed your boss."

He waited to see if the guard would contradict him, say that both Drew and Donal were working together. Instead, the man looked confused but didn't say anything.

He had no real reason to believe Gunner, but he pulled out a picture of Donal and Drew and showed it to the man still in the headlock.

One of the guards on the ground had woken up, was listening. He was handcuffed and his ankles were tied, and Gunner showed him the picture too.

"You never wanted to be back," he sneered. "Now we're supposed to believe you've got Drew's best interests at heart?"

"I don't give a shit what you believe, but if Drew's still alive, I'm betting he won't be for long." Gunner dropped the photos on the ground. "This happened about two months ago. Maybe a little bit before. Probably around the time I left to do the last job. Anything strange happen around that time?"

One of the other guards started to speak, but the big one barked at him to shut the fuck up.

Jem knocked out the big one. "Say what you were going to say."

"Just around the time you left . . . Drew said that we needed to tighten security. That no one was to come on the island unless he gave the okay in person. Didn't matter who they were. We weren't even supposed to let boats inside a two-mile perimeter."

Gunner looked at Jem. "Landon knew Donal was coming for him. Had to be because I came back to work for Drew."

"Sounds that way."

"Tie them up good. Give them the shots and let's go find Dare and Avery," Gunner said. Jem and Key used the sedatives Drea had prepared. But first, Jem took the guard he'd nearly killed aside and Gunner heard him ask about Drea. Again.

"If you tell me, you can keep your balls."

"Go ahead and kill me," the guard said.

"I'm not going to kill you. I'm going to castrate you and let you live," Jem explained patiently. "And I'm not going to use anesthesia. I'll stitch you up myself to make sure you live, you ball-less fuck."

The guard went white. "She's in the tower. Landon wanted us to keep her here. Said her husband would pay good money for her."

"Did you hurt her?"

"No," the guard said. "Can't say the same about Landon."

It was Jem's turn to go white.

"Take Key and go find her. I'll go after Avery and Dare," Gunner told him. As soon as the men were unconscious, they went their separate ways, Gunner praying the entire time that Drea was all right.

*　　*　　*

Jem ran the tower steps two at a time. Key went slower behind him, backward, watching their six just in case the other guards were alerted.

If I'm too late . . .

No, he wouldn't think like that. Never dealt in the negative.

He didn't want to call out to her and alert any guard who might be with her. Instead, he moved quietly once he got to the last twenty steps. Key did the same.

He peeked into the tower and saw her, sitting so still on a chair in the middle of the circular room.

"Drea, it's Jem," he said quietly.

She didn't move. He held his breath as he walked around her slowly, and when he met her eyes, he saw why she wasn't moving.

The bomb's trigger was attached to her chest. If she spoke, even breathed heavily, it would set off the bomb.

"It's okay, baby—we're here. Not a problem," he told her. "You just keep holding it together. Everyone's okay. And now you are too."

She stared at him. She looked exhausted, relieved and scared to death all at the same time.

Avery and Dare took the building while Gunner, Key and Jem subdued the main guards. Dare entered the house first, took down three beefy guards who came at them. He'd used a silencer but they'd kept moving anyway, clearing the first floor.

Avery locked the kitchen staff into a closet after tying them up and taking their phones. They looked scared and might be innocent, but she didn't trust anyone associated with the Landons.

The second floor was empty. She looked out the window and it was all quiet. Maybe too quiet.

"Clear," Dare told her, and, weapon drawn, she went up the third flight of stairs. It was deadly quiet up here now that Dare had cut the alarm.

She listened for Dare's footsteps behind her. He'd been on her six the whole time, but she was alone. She was on the landing of the third floor, was about to turn back to find him when an electrical current tore through her body. She would've toppled back down the stairs if Donal Landon hadn't yanked her forward.

She landed on her side on the hard, cold marble floor, unable to do anything but convulse from the Taser. He was keeping it on her, keeping her helpless, unable to cry out for help or defend herself.

Not again.

When he moved the current from her body, he asked, "Back for more?"

She blinked, stared up at Donal Landon. He held a Taser in one hand and a knife in the other. "Trying again, you chickenshit?" she managed, and he slapped her hard across the face. Her cheek stung, her lip split against her teeth, but she didn't stop.

She rolled before another slap could come, but he caught her with the Taser and her muscles contracted involuntarily for several long moments as he held her caught in its electrical current. Her only comfort was that he couldn't do much to her while her body jolted. He could just kill her this way.

Finally, he pulled the current away and her body went slack. She could move, but she'd paid a price from too many of the Taser's shocks in such a short period of time.

"You're mine, bitch."

"You've got that backward—you're my bitch," she told him before she kicked him hard in the side of the neck. He lost his balance, Taser and knife went flying and she was up and on him in seconds. She wouldn't waste this opportunity, so she dove on him, scratching and punching, looking to maim, disable . . . and then she would kill him.

They rolled together, her hand on his Adam's apple, his hand on her wrist, stopping her from crushing his trachea.

"You'll never be able to forget me," he croaked.

"That's where you're wrong, Donal. As soon as I kill you, you'll be completely forgotten."

He smiled quickly to cover his look of surprise at hearing his real name, then kicked. It caught her on the side of her head and she went down, still holding on to him. That put her in the worst position possible—underneath him.

He had the knife above her throat and she couldn't move. Fear flooded her and she pushed it back. "What did Drew do to you that made you hate him so much?"

Donal considered that for a long moment, never moving the knife. "He was born with a conscience. I wasn't. That always seemed to put us on different sides of the fence. Drew always felt too much. His emotions seemed strange to me, and at first, I tried to copy them, but then I gave up. When Father was alive it didn't matter as much, but once Drew was put in charge, he made it his mission to go after the traffickers."

"And you didn't want to."

"Avery, I didn't know you cared."

"Last chance to tell your story."

"Always the optimist." The knife's blade was cold on her skin as he continued. "I wanted to get in with the traffickers. That's where the real money was. But Drew couldn't get past what happened to Mother and Julia."

"And you could?"

"Easily. Father fucked up and we paid the price. End of story. And if Father had simply done what the trafficker had asked—move some of his merchandise to make up for the loss—none of it would've happened. Stupid pride, all over people we don't know, people I certainly don't give a shit about."

"Innocent women and children."

"Nobody's innocent, Avery. I thought you of all people would understand that. You're the young one in your family. The one no one told anything to. I was younger by four minutes, but somehow, in this family, that was a lifetime."

He ripped her shirt open and the look on his face was pure gloat. "It looks perfect. I was hoping you'd have someone decent stitch them up. I tried to be precise in my cuts—I was premed, you know."

"You're all asshole. Don't worry—Gunner will cover those up. His tattoos will be on top of them. He'll win. He's always going to win," she told him.

"That's what you think."

"That's what I know," she told him, just as Gunner came up behind Donal and grabbed him around the neck, a knife held to his carotid.

"Up, slowly, Donal," Gunner growled. She swallowed as Donal didn't move the knife from her throat, not at first, and then he did, dropped it by her side.

As soon as he was halfway off her, she scrambled backward, grabbed the knife and lunged for the Taser too, just in case.

But Gunner had him in a grip. Told her, "You should go."

"No way. I'm not leaving until he's dead."

She met Gunner's eyes and saw the understanding there, the way she always did.

Chapter Thirty-one

Gunner's satisfaction in getting Donal before he could do any more damage to Avery was short-lived when several men came up the stairs, all of them holding automatic weapons.

They weren't Landon's men, which could be good, or really fucking bad. Gunner backed up with Landon, and Avery went to his side, slightly behind him. "Who the hell are you?" Gunner demanded.

"I'm Juan Carlos," the man in the expensive-looking suit said. He didn't have a weapon, but his men did, and they surrounded Gunner and Avery. "We've spoken before."

They had. Juan Carlos was a businessman in Drew's circles—he wasn't a trafficker, but Gunner knew he often helped Drew's clients with their financial needs once they'd successfully been relocated. Gunner had placed many calls to Juan Carlos over the years, although he remained a mysterious figure. "What are you doing here?"

"I haven't heard from Drew. That is . . . un-usual. I grew worried. I see I was right to be." Juan Carlos was staring hard at Donal now. "My friend, I'll take care of this."

Donal nodded, tried to jerk away from Gunner, but Gunner refused to let him go. He told Juan Carlos, "This isn't Drew."

"Don't listen to him," Donal spat.

Again, Juan Carlos looked hard at Donal. After a pause, he glanced up at Gunner, looking troubled. "And why would I believe you? Aren't you a disgruntled former employee?" Juan Carlos made a motion and one of his men moved forward, a gun pointed at Avery. "Let him go and she'll be unharmed."

Gunner let him go and Donal preened smugly. "Juan Carlos, I apologize. I gave James a chance when I shouldn't have."

Gunner stared at Donal for a second, then grabbed the man's arm. Donal tried to pull back, but Gunner kept the death grip on him, put Landon's hand over his crotch.

The man hissed and pulled back like a demon that'd been burned with holy water. And Gunner smiled.

"What the hell's going on, James?" Donal bit out.

"Drew Landon would've given his fortune if I'd touched his cock," Gunner said, and Juan Carlos was studying them intently.

"I'm not gay," Donal spat out.

"No?" Juan Carlos asked, as if he'd been waiting for this moment, and suddenly the air around them seemed to shift dramatically. Donal remained frozen in place as Juan approached him. He reached up and stroked hair off Donal's face and Donal moved to rebuff the gentle gesture. "Do you remember the last time I saw you?"

"Yes. We had a meeting in Cairo," Donal said confidently.

"Yes, a meeting," he repeated. "And you missed another one—what happened?"

Donal frowned. "There was nothing in the appointment book, Juan Carlos. I'm so sorry—it won't happen again."

"No, it won't." Juan Carlos had his hand wrapped around Donal's neck before anyone could blink.

Gunner saw Juan Carlos's men shift their weapons toward Donal, and Gunner pulled Avery closer to him.

"It was an honest mistake—James has been fucking with my business," Donal told him.

"The meeting you missed would never have been in any appointment book of Drew's," Juan Carlos told him in a fierce voice. "It was a standing appointment. Every three months. And Drew never, ever forgot. Not once in ten years."

Donal struggled a little, but the bigger man's grip was tight. Juan Carlos turned to Gunner.

"He flirted. I know that. But Drew Landon was mine."

He turned back to Donal, loosened his grip slightly when he asked, "Where is he?"

"I didn't know my brother . . . was a fucking faggot," Donal spat, and in a fast move, he kicked Juan Carlos's knees out from under him and moved back.

"Don't shoot him," Juan Carlos told his men as Gunner advanced on Donal. At that moment, Gunner began to fight like it was for his life. It was for all those times he was made to fight Drew Landon's guards, all those times he'd been made to do things he hadn't wanted to. For all those things he'd done willingly too. All his demons were taking themselves out on Donal.

Finally, he pulled back. "Where is Drew?"

Donal laughed, his mouth bloody, teeth broken. "Why? You miss him? Gonna cry at his funeral?"

"I don't believe he's dead," Gunner said through gritted teeth. "You'd have been bragging by now."

"I don't remember." Donal was choking on his own blood. "I do . . . remember . . . killing . . . your . . . bitch. She . . . begged. Called . . . for . . . you."

Gunner drew his hand that held his weapon back, but Avery caught it, stopped him. "Don't, Gunner. Please."

"Let me go, Avery."

"I won't. He doesn't deserve to win this. Please."

It was her *please* that got him. He looked up at her. "We can't let them win. We may hate them, but we can't let them win by bringing us to their level."

Gunner looked down at Donal, told him, "You're useless." When he pushed up off Donal, he saw Avery staring at Donal. Juan Carlos was staring at her.

"This man hurt you?" Juan Carlos asked her.

"Yes."

"And you won't let your boyfriend kill him."

"We've done what we needed to. I won't put another death on his conscience. I don't care how justified it is."

Juan Carlos studied her, and then looked at Gunner. "Drew always liked you. You have to know that."

"I do," Gunner said.

"Donal's the type who would keep Drew alive and suffering," Juan Carlos said grimly. "Please, go find him. I will deal with this, the way Drew would want me to. I begged him to stop Donal years ago. But he had a soft spot for family."

"I'm sorry," Avery told him. Juan Carlos nodded, aimed his weapon at Donal's head, and Gunner grabbed her hand and headed down the stairs as the first of the shots was fired.

"Any idea where Drew might be? We searched all the floors," she told Gunner.

"Did you go to the guesthouse?" he asked.

"No. We didn't see one," she said. They raced down the stairs, where Dare was on the second floor, just escaping the bindings Juan Carlos and his men no doubt put on him.

"Thank God." He let Gunner help him out of the last of the cuffs, and then Gunner led them both across the grass toward the guesthouse.

"Where're Jem and Key?" Dare called.

"Looking for Drea," he called over his shoulder. "I've got this—go help them."

He watched Dare break away, but Avery remained with him. He slammed into the guesthouse and found it empty on first look. Together, he and Avery searched every inch of the place and found nothing.

As he looked around, his phone beeped. He looked at the text message from Jem.

Place is set to blow. Drea's the trigger.

"What is it?" Avery asked. He showed her the message and she grimaced. "Can they defuse it?"

"I'm sure they're trying. The faster we can find Drew, the better. We have to know if he's still going to be out there after all of this."

"Where else could he be? Is there a basement, like in Powell's house?" she asked.

He stopped cold, a sudden memory flashing.

"No, there's no basement. But there's someplace else. Come on."

He grabbed her hand, pulled her along the lawn, looking for the small statue that was nothing more than a square monument that listed the name of the house and the date it was built. Innocuous, but in an odd spot. One night, Gunner had figured out why.

Now he yanked on the rock, pushed and pulled and heard the mechanism under the grass begin to move. Slowly, he rolled back the Astro-Turf to reveal the opening. Then he went down first, with Avery following close behind.

The catacomb tunnels were narrow, claustrophobic. It was damp down here, and Gunner was almost certain it flooded during high tide. The lapping of the water along the floor as they rounded the corner told him he was right. Both their boots sloshed in the water that grew progressively deeper as they approached a hallway with several closed, locked doors.

Gunner kicked open each and every one of them, Avery holding her weapon, covering him. When they got to the last door, he kicked and saw the body lying in the water on the floor.

The man's skin was deathly pale. There was blood coming from his nose and his ears. But still, Drew Landon had the strength to turn his head to look at him.

*   *   *

Key was next to Jem and both men got as close as they could to check out the mechanism.

"Gotta be attached to the main house in several places," Key said quietly. There was no way to not let Drea know what was happening, and hell, they were certainly in this together.

"I'm not leaving you, Drea," Jem told her. "Not leaving you here."

He turned back to Key. "Is it timed as well as triggered?"

"Yes. Near as I can tell, we've got about four minutes left before it blows. The weight of the stone means it's not going to go down all that fast. We can get out. But it's going to be tricky."

Is she wired to blow? he mouthed, and Key's expression tightened. He nodded, pointed a finger at the red and green and yellow wires that snaked into her shirt.

"If we cut them?"

"The main bomb goes."

Jem cursed and texted Gunner as Dare yelled for them before he came into the room.

"Where's Gunner?" Jem asked.

"Looking for Drew."

"He's not answering my texts."

"We've got to cut the wires, Jem," Key told him. "Waiting's not going to save anyone. They'll have time to get out."

Jem took the cutters from Key and nodded. "Go, brother—you and Dare, get a head start."

"No fucking way, Jem."

He looked up and Dare shook his head. He cursed, then smiled at Drea. "Once you're free, I'm going to carry you out of here. I'm going to run like the wind, baby, so you just hang on as best you can and know I'm not letting you go."

And then he held his breath and cut the yellow and the green wires, effectively stopping the trigger that would cause the bomb attached directly to her to explode.

Things happened so fast after that. The rumble started under their feet as the explosions went off in a series, rather than all at once. He cut her loose and put her over his shoulder. With Key in front and Dare behind, the men flew down the steps as fast as they could, bricks and stones slamming around them down the narrow passageway. The floor was shaking under their feet and they had to get to solid ground.

When a column fell in front of them, nearly trapping them on the stairs, Key managed to shove himself through.

"Hand her to me, Jem," Key said, and Jem did so. She was so cold and pale, but thankfully she was malleable enough for him to get her through the small space. He crawled forward, Dare right behind him. Jem put Drea over his shoulder again and as they landed on the last step, the stairway collapsed with a loud boom behind them, the air in front of them a dustbowl they could barely see through.

"Keep moving forward," Key shouted. Jem hooked a hand onto his brother's shoulder, and Dare did the same for him.

"I have her mouth and nose covered," Dare told him after he let go of Jem for a second. As he followed Key, he realized that this was exactly what they meant by blind faith.

The sound of the explosion was magnified down in the catacombs. Avery grabbed Gunner's arm and they both looked down the hall. The main doorway wasn't blocked. Yet. But the way the rumble sounded, it wouldn't be long.

Gunner went to Landon, a hand on his chest.

"Donal . . . never right," Landon managed. "I tried. Always . . . got burned."

"I know he killed Josie."

Landon's eyes fluttered. "Never . . . believed me."

"I didn't. Not until now."

"Tried . . . to make you . . . feel like family."

Gunner couldn't tell him he didn't want to be a part of Landon's fucking family, but would never do that to a dying man. A dying man who'd done his best to help Gunner in his own sick way.

Drew gasped; then his eyes closed.

"Is he dead?"

"No, he's still alive." Gunner felt the weak pulse and raised the man's eyelids. "Barely."

He sat back on his heels as the walls started to crumple around him, stared at the man who would no doubt rather be dead than paralyzed. His entire business was ruined, an empire brought to its knees by careful, vicious planning.

S8 had made a name for itself over the past months by taking down everything Drew Landon had worked so hard to build, and all because he couldn't extricate himself from his family.

Leaving him here might be the kindest thing Gunner could do for him.

"Gunner, we have to go. Now." Avery touched his shoulder. "Do you want to take him with us?"

So much fucking understanding in her voice. He stood, took her hands. "I love you, Avery. Have from the first second I saw you."

"I love you too, Gunner. Always will," she murmured, and they stared at each other, even as the walls began to crack around them.

"We'll leave him. He always said he wanted to be buried here. Should get his wish. And we leave him behind. We start new."

When he looked back at Landon again, the man had passed. Gunner didn't know how he knew, but he just did. And the cycle was broken, just like that.

Chapter Thirty-two

Jem made it out of the building with Drea, Dare and Key just in time to watch the tower where Drea had been for the last day and a half crumple. He glanced behind him and kept running until they were at a safer distance, knowing that Dare and Key had broken off to run back toward the collapsing mansion.

"Drea, honey." He put her on the ground, brushed the hair from her face. She was pale. Barely breathing. In shock for sure. He'd suspected as much in the tower, but didn't want to risk breaking her out of it and having her possibly panic and flail and set the bombs off.

But now . . . "Come on, you're okay. You made it. So fucking brave."

He rubbed her arms, her face, rough touches meant to bring her back, but she sat like a stone. He took off his jacket that had all the ammo and weaponry in it, wrapped it around her, but she still shivered, even under the warm sun. Not a good sign.

He looked back and saw no one coming toward them. Grace was texting him, asking for an update.

He had nothing to tell her. Dare must've texted her as they'd gotten free from the building so she wouldn't worry. At least not any more than what they'd already put her through.

All he could do was hold Drea, tell her it was okay, over and over, and pray he was right. And finally—fucking finally—the rest of his team appeared. They were running from the building that was leaving a thick cloud of dust in its wake and Jem picked Drea up and began to run toward where they'd left the boat.

"He wired the ground!" Key was yelling as they all ran, got into the water as Gunner dragged the boat. They were floating maybe ten feet from shore as they watched the grass they'd just run on go up in flames.

"Jem, lay her down—raise her feet above her heart," Gunner was saying. Jem grabbed some of the cushions from the seats, threw them on the floor as he lowered her. Avery came over and held up Drea's legs, as Gunner instructed.

"Check her, Gun—make sure," he said as Avery held on to him. "Did you get them?"

"They're both dead," she confirmed. "Drew wasn't in on it."

"Still deserved what he got," Jem said, and Gunner nodded. "You're free, Gun. Finally free."

Gunner put a hand on Drea's forehead. "At what cost?"

"She'll be okay. She has to be," Jem said fiercely, because he couldn't believe anything else. And when they pulled up to the boat, Grace was waiting for them.

"Coast Guard's been called. We're going to have to get ahead of them," she said.

"I'll do it," Key said, and Dare followed him. The boat started moving as soon as Jem boarded, as he was the last one on. Gunner already had taken Drea downstairs, and he joined them and Avery and Grace as Gunner ran IVs and tried to get her stabilized.

"She's been in shock for a while . . . maybe since he wired her," Gunner said.

"It's a wait-and-see, Jem. There's nothing more a hospital could really do for her, but we can get her to one. I'll flag down the Coast Guard," Gunner said.

"And get caught?"

"I don't care," Gunner said.

"Gunner, there were safety measures Landon put in place if he died. Pictures of you, proof of your jobs were going to be sent to the CIA," Jem reminded him.

"We don't know if that's true," Gunner said. "And even if it is, I've disappeared before."

Avery nodded her approval, even as she held on to Drea's hand, brushed her hand over the doctor's forehead, her lips moving in a silent prayer.

"It's a waiting game, Gun. You and I both know that. The hospital won't do anything more than you can. But thank you," Jem told him. They all knew he was right.

Her heart rate was still tachy. Her eyes were unblinking. She wasn't in pain.

"Shock's the body's way of protecting itself— the mind shuts down when it knows you can't handle it. This saved her, Jem," Gunner told him. "She's going to come out of it."

But no one could know that for sure.

Avery found Gunner on the deck, facing the bow. The boat cut through the water at a fast speed, Key behind the wheel and Dare directing him in the dark that had descended.

They'd made the decision to stay on the water close to shore; that way they could get Drea to a hospital if things worsened.

They hadn't. But they hadn't improved either.

Jem wouldn't leave her side. Insisted Avery go check on Gunner.

Grace grabbed her on the way up, handed her some sandwiches to bring to Gunner and then went to bring some down to Jem.

"She's got to be okay, Grace," Avery said.

"I know. God, this is so unfair." Grace looked angry. In the time Avery had known her, she hadn't really seen that emotion come through. But Avery agreed with the sentiment one hundred percent. "I still want to do Section 8. Just know that—now more than ever."

"Me too." She smiled for a second as she thought about Adele. "Adele would've been proud of us, I think."

"I know she *is* proud of us. She's like our fairy godmother, except she'd kill me for calling her that. Probably literally." Grace gave her a quick hug. "Go to Gunner. Feed him."

Avery did as she was told, looked forward to some quiet time with him, even if it would only be for a few minutes. "Hey, Grace made some food."

"Thanks, *chère*." He took one of the sandwiches, ate it quickly, then devoured another one. She nibbled on one too as she stared up at the stars.

When he'd finished the sandwiches, he drank down the soda too, and then she put all of that aside. She ran her hands over his shoulders, massaged them for a few minutes. He dropped his head forward and she heard the groan of appreciation.

"If you sit, I can do a better job, Tall Boy," she told him.

He glanced over his shoulder. "Tall Boy?"

"It's a nickname I'm trying out. I could call you G if you like that better."

"Don't you dare," he warned, and then he sat on one of the deck chairs and leaned forward, forearms on his thighs. She moved behind him again and proceeded to work the kinks out of his shoulders and neck, kneading and caressing until his body was relaxed. As relaxed as it could be under the circumstances.

It had been forty-eight hours with no changes in Drea's situation. Forty-eight hours on the boat, with one stop to refuel. From Drea's side, Jem had been monitoring the situation, checking for blowback on S8 and Gunner especially. So far, it was all quiet. But that didn't help them in their decision-making process.

The most important thing was that they were together. Safe. Grace and Dare had put Powell's money in a separate account, kept it offshore. Even though it was blood money, they planned on doing some good with it. So money wasn't the issue. They could all disappear if need be.

But none of them really wanted to. Not now. New Orleans held a special spot in their hearts.

"She's awake!" Grace called to them, and she and Gunner went down to the bunk where Drea had been recovering.

They crowded into the room and Drea blinked at all of them, like someone waking up from a long nap. She looked disoriented. A little pale still, but she appeared to have all her faculties.

Jem had been talking to Drea nonstop, murmuring softly, telling her she was fine, safe, that he would make sure nothing bad happened to her. That it was okay to wake up.

He told her jokes and stories. He played her music. He slept next to her, when he did allow himself to sleep. Most of the time, he was too busy watching her and monitoring comms to do so.

When she'd blinked normally the first few times, he'd pretty much held his breath. The monitor showed her heart rate returning to normal, and he took the nasal cannula of oxygen from her and watched her levels.

Fine. She was fine. She swallowed. Coughed. He handed her water, and her arm went up. She uncapped the bottle and brought it to her mouth and drank. She was a little shaky but overall, co-ordinated. There was no apparent damage, apart from what she'd been through.

He called for Grace softly, and she poked her head in. Must've called for Gunner and Avery, because they were there in a few moments.

"Drea, honey, welcome back."

She tried to get up but couldn't. When he moved closer, she put her hands out. "Who the hell are you?"

His heart squeezed. "My name's Jem. You were hurt. I'm helping you."

She nodded, still looking suspicious. She glanced around at everyone. "Who are they?"

"These are my friends. They helped you too," Jem told her.

She stared at him, her head tilted. "You've been here talking to me."

"Yeah, the whole time. I never left you."

"I don't . . . Where are we?" She looked around the small cabin.

"We're on a boat in the middle of the ocean," he told her. Everyone else was quietly watching her, the expectation level high. "The mission's over."

"The mission?" she asked.

"Maybe too soon," Gunner said, and Jem nodded.

"Doesn't matter, Drea. You're safe, okay?"

"Okay. But I don't . . ." She shook her head a little, stared around the room. "I'm okay."

She seemed to be saying that to reassure herself more than them. She took more water, smiled a little.

And then she ripped the rug out from under him by asking, "Did Danny send you? Is he here? He must be worried if something happened to me."

Danny. Her Outlaw Angel ex.

He recalled his psych days, watching the doctors dealing with amnesia patients, had known it could happen to Drea. Had prayed it wouldn't.

"Sometimes the mind takes us back to a place in time when we last felt safe," one of the doctors told him when he'd asked about the causes of amnesia.

Had Drea never felt safe with him at all? Or had it just not been a long enough time yet to compete with the memory of Danny taking her out of her house and away from all the abuse she suffered at the hands of her parents?

"Just go with the Danny thing for now," Gunner murmured. "Don't freak her out any more."

Grace moved over to Drea, said, "Honey, let's get you to the bathroom, okay? And then we can talk about Danny."

"Yes, that'll be good," Drea agreed, and Jem let her go. Turned to Gunner and Avery, not knowing what the fuck to say.

"She wants to go back to Danny. To the OA," Avery said, her voice low but urgent. "We can't let that happen."

"What do we do—kidnap her again?" Jem asked.

"It's for her own good," Gunner said, and Jem sagged against the wall.

"Returning her to Danny would get the feds off her case," Jem said. "Danny would rescind his testimony."

"You can't be serious about letting her go back to him," Avery said.

"Keeping her away from him might fuck her up more," Jem said. "Trust me, Avery—I know about this shit. Seen it firsthand."

He stared at the closed bathroom door and wished to hell he knew how to fix this.

Chapter Thirty-three

Two months later

Avery lay down on the table in Gunner's shop. It had been damaged from the bomb, with the shop taking the brunt of the damage. But Jem had hired men to renovate—and fast—and the shop had been redone to look the way he'd left it for the most part, save for some other updates. She'd researched the latest in equipment, gotten him leather tables and chairs, all of which added to the look he'd already created.

He'd loved it. She'd watched him just walk around the shop for a while, touching the guns and the chairs and the pictures, as though he was making sure it was all real.

And then he'd finally done the same to her. It was only the two of them in here tonight—he'd booked a private session, he'd told her. But instead of drawing and getting stencils ready, he was sliding a hand under her tank top, kissing her neck, picking her up and placing her on the table so he was standing between her legs.

"I thought you were tattooing me?" she asked, but she was far from complaining.

"Got to prepare. Relax. Make sure every inch of your skin's ready for me," Gunner murmured. He licked at her collarbone, nipped at her skin and she carded her hands through his dark hair.

They'd both gone through what seemed like complete transformation the past months. Somehow she'd never felt more like herself. She was complete, and she was done running.

Gunner was on the same page. If he hadn't told her—which he had—she'd know it by his kisses, each one a promise. He was tugging down her sweats, pulling off her tank top.

"Because you have to take it off for the session anyway," he said seriously.

"And my pants?"

"All for your comfort," he assured her as he dropped them to the floor and dragged a finger gently along her wet sex. She gasped at the jolt of pleasure. "See? Better already?"

"Yes," she agreed, because stopping now might kill her. Between the danger and her wounds, just being with him like this hadn't happened frequently enough. Since the first time she'd let him see her scars, before Landon was caught, the sex had been during stolen, frantic moments.

His finger slid inside her as his thumb played along her clit. She pulled his head to her, kissed him, tongue sliding along his.

A second finger slid into her, and her hips rose to meet the touch. He always made her feel like this—aching with need and so completely wanted.

She moaned into his mouth as they kissed for a while. Then he kissed his way down to her breasts, laved her nipples until they were swollen and tender with arousal, until she was so wet and needful, she clawed at him for more.

She helped yank his pants down impatiently. Stroked his cock as he groaned. Guided him inside her, then pushed against him so he was forced to enter her quickly. She was on her back and he was standing over her, holding her thighs up, watching her face as he thrust.

"Fuck yeah, Avery. So tight and wet."

"Yes."

"For me."

"Only. All for you." Pleasure strummed every inch of her body as her climax built, started with the intense tightening in her belly and spread until her orgasm took away any coherent thoughts. Gunner rocked into her as she contracted around him until he came too, with a shout that sounded like her name. And then he half collapsed onto her as they recovered. And then he began to draw. While he was still on top of her.

"Should I be offended?" she asked.

"Did you come?"

"I think you know the answer to that." She felt boneless. He smiled, slid off her, covered most of her with a towel. When she looked down, she noted that he'd kept one of her scars exposed. He ran his finger across it, the way she did sometimes. It was only slightly raised and pretty thin, considering how ragged the cut had been.

"Drea did a good job," she said, tried to keep the sadness out of her voice, and he nodded. "I promised her I'd fix it further."

"I wish we could fix her," she whispered.

"Me too." He pressed his lips to one of the scars. "But this is your night. She'd want this."

Although Avery couldn't claim to know Drea well, she did know her well enough to recognize the truth in Gunner's words. She knew he would cover the scars so well that the first thing she saw when she looked in the mirror would be his work, not Donal's.

She also knew that when Gunner looked at her, he didn't see any scars at all. This was all for her. "Make it beautiful," she told him.

"Can't improve on perfection," he teased, and she giggled. Giggled. It had been so long since she felt free.

There were still more tests coming at them— she knew that there might be problems from what they'd done to Landon—problems from whatever they decided to do in the future as S8.

But they'd handle them together. "I love you, Gunner."

She'd said it to him so many times in the past month. Loved saying it as much as she loved him.

"Love you, *chère*." He traced a finger over her skin. "Ready?"

"Yes."

She'd seen him do something similar to cover scars. The first night she'd met him, he'd been tattooing over the breasts of a mastectomy patient, making her look and feel beautiful. And now he was going to make his mark on her, turn something horrible into something beautiful.

He was so good at that.

The buzz of the needle was like a drug to her. She let herself drift in and out, confident that Gunner would keep all his promises.

He didn't finish it all that night, but he covered the large one on her upper torso and he repaired the very first tattoo he'd given her in painstaking detail.

"You can't even tell anything happened," she said. "But it did. And you made it okay."

"I'm always going to make it okay," he told her fiercely. "Always."

She believed him.

Epilogue

All she could remember was Danny. He helped her. Saved her from her family and now the handsome, dark-haired man was refusing to let her see him.

He looked so grim when he told her for what had to be the hundredth time, "That's right, Drea—I won't let you be with Danny."

"Why?"

"Maybe one day, you'll know the answer to that."

He'd told her the real answer, a few times, that she was broken up with Danny, that she was a doctor. That Danny had hurt her. That she'd run from him. That she'd asked Jem for help and now he was helping her.

Sometimes she felt as if she was going crazy. After two weeks, she still couldn't remember anything he'd told her. He'd even gone so far as to show her a picture of herself on the FBI's database.

A wanted woman. Because of Danny.

So although she might believe it somewhere deep inside, because she knew that Danny was the head of a motorcycle club that sold drugs and could believe he'd get her in trouble, she remembered how bad it had been at home. How much better it had been with Danny.

You're a doctor.

You're strong as hell.

You'll remember everything soon.

Jem told her that. A doctor did too.

"So basically, I'm in hiding from the FBI?" she asked. They were in a rental house, he'd told her earlier, and it was cozy and furnished and very comfortable, but she was going stir-crazy staying inside. There was only so much TV she could watch, and she'd read so much her eyes were strained.

Nothing could take her mind off the fact that she had no memory and that she was a fugitive, supposed to give testimony against a man she thought she loved. A man who had used her.

"Yes. And I'm not turning you over to them. Not when you're like this. Not ever." He'd paused. "We can talk about it when you get your memory back."

"Okay."

He looked troubled. "Drea, look, I've got to go away for a little while, for work. And I've asked a friend of mine if you can stay with her. She's cool. I know you'll like her."

As he spoke, the doorbell rang. He went to grab it and when he came back, he was with a woman who wore a black pantsuit, her white hair swept back into an elegant chignon, and she had a serious look on her face. She made Drea feel completely underdressed and intimidated in her tank top and she tried to shrink into herself, wrapped her arms around herself.

"Drea, this is Carolina," Jem said. "I was just telling Drea that you're going to make sure she's okay."

"I will," Carolina said in her cool, dulcet tones. Her voice was calming and Drea felt better hearing it. "I'll keep everything under control."

"What if I never remember?" Drea blurted out suddenly, and Jem and Carolina turned to look at her. God, she hated feeling so out of control and lost, but she had a feeling she'd been like that for a lot of her life.

Carolina gave her a small smile. "I'll tell you what I always used to tell Jeremiah. We'll deal with everything when and as it comes, not before."

"Okay. Yes. I can do that," Drea told them both, and for once, she truly believed it.

Acknowledgments

Writing a book is never a solitary process, so I have the usual suspects to thank.

For Danielle Perez, my fantastically patient and most enthusiastic editor. For Kara Welsh and Claire Zion for the overall support, for the art department who always comes through with one cover that's more amazing than the next and for everyone at New American Library who helps with all aspects of my books.

For my readers and writer friends who keep me going with their support.

And always, to my family, because I could never do this without them.

Don't miss the first novel
in the Section 8 series,

SURRENDER

Now available from Signet Eclipse.

Prologue

Zaire, twenty years earlier

The explosion threw him forward hard, the heat searing his body, debris cutting into his back as he covered his face and stayed down. Darius didn't need to look back to know what had happened—the bridge had exploded. Simon had purposely cut off their last means of escape. It would force their hands, Darius's especially.

"Darius, you all right?" Simon shook him, yanked him to his feet and held him upright. His ears would continue to ring for months.

"How much ammo do you have?" he called over the din. Couldn't see the rebels yet, but he knew they were coming toward them through the jungle.

"Stop wasting time. You go." Simon jerked his head toward the LZ and the waiting chopper about thirty feet away, crammed full of important rescued American officials and the like. Already precariously over capacity. "Go now and I'll hold them off."

Simon had always had a sense of bravado and a temper no one wanted to deal with, but one against twenty-plus? Those odds were not in the man's favor. Darius shook his head hard, and it was already spinning from the explosion.

"You are no fucking help to me," Simon told him. "I can't watch your back this time, Darius."

"Fuck you."

"Leave. Me. Here."

"If I do that, I'll come back to just a body."

"You're never coming back here." Simon's teeth were bared, ready for battle—with the rebels, with Darius, if necessary.

"If we both fight, we've got a better shot," Darius told him.

"You would tell me to leave if things were reversed, Master Chief, sir."

Simon stood straight and tall, hand to his forehead, and Darius growled, "Don't you dare salute me, son." Their old routine. Simon managed a small smile, one that was as rare as peace in this part of the world.

"Don't take this from me, Darius. Let me save your goddamned life. You have your son to think about—I won't take you away from Dare."

Dare was in middle school—his mother had already left them both, and pain shot through

Darius at the thought of leaving his son without a parent.

Simon knew he had him, pressed on. "The team will always need you, and me—well, you can always find someone who can fight."

"Not like you."

"No, not like me," he echoed. "You go and you don't ever return."

Darius didn't say anything, and for a long moment they were silent, listening to the rustling that was still a couple of miles away. The blood was running down his side, and if he stayed in this wet jungle much longer with a wound like that . . .

"There's one spot left for a ride home." Simon told him what he already knew. "That seat is yours."

"I'm half-dead already."

"You think I'm not?" Simon asked, and Darius flashed back to a younger version of the operative in front of him, walking along a dusty road two miles from Leavenworth.

Darius had gone from being a Navy SEAL, fresh from capture in an underground cell where he'd been held for twenty-two days, to a medical discharge, to a phone call inviting him to join a very different kind of team. The CIA was creating a group—Section 8. For operatives like him. They'd have a handler and all the resources they'd need. Their only rule: Complete the mission. The how, when and where were up to them.

He was maybe the sanest of the group, and that was saying something. Simon always had the look of a predator, occasionally replaced by a childlike wonder, usually when Adele was around. If you looked at the team members' old files, you'd see everything from disobeying orders to failing psych exams to setting fires.

But if you knew S8, you'd see the mastermind. The wetwork expert. The demolitions expert, the one who could handle escape and extractions with ease. They could lie and steal and hack. They could find any kind of transport, anytime, anywhere, anyhow, that could get them the hell out of Dodge.

In the beginning, they'd been nothing more than angry wild animals, circling, furious with one another and their circumstances. But once the trust grew, it was never broken.

Separately, they were good. Together, they were great.

And now, three years later, two S8 operatives stood near the wreckage of a bridge in Zaire and they were both about to die.

"If you could save fifteen people . . . or just one . . . ," Simon prodded.

"Don't you pull that trolley problem shit on me—I've been to more shrinks than you and I'm not leaving you behind like this," Darius said, his voice slightly vicious. But they both knew he'd relent. He'd done everything Simon had asked of him, and this was for the good of the rest of the team.

"They'll never recover without you," Simon told him. "You're the goddamned heart of the team."

"And you're my best goddamned friend," Darius growled. Simon's expression softened, just for a second.

"Just remember the promise," Simon warned. *We don't try to find out who's behind S8. No matter what.*

Neither Darius nor Simon believed what happened today was a screwup their handler could've known about. But their promise referenced him specifically. They knew they'd been brought together by the CIA, but their handler picked the jobs, gave them orders and anything else they needed. Once they started distrusting him, it was all over.

"I'll remember," Darius told him now.

"Good. Go." This time, Simon's words were punctuated with a push. Darius barely caught himself, and when he turned, Simon was already running in the direction of the rebels, the crazy fucker confusing them with his contrary tactics. Because who the hell ran toward the bad guys?

Darius made his choice—he was a liability, so he made his way to the helo, pulled himself on board and shoved himself into the pilot's seat. Within minutes, the steel bird was grinding gears, rising above the heavy cover of jungle. As the chopper blades cut the air smoothly with their *whoompa-whoompa-tink*, Darius turned the helo and stared down at the man who'd left himself behind as Darius took the rescued civilians— aid workers, a diplomatic attaché and other Americans who'd been working in the area— away. He'd never take credit for the glory on this one, though. Simon could've sat in this pilot seat as easily as Darius did.

There was a chance Simon could fight them off. There was always a chance. And as he watched for that brief moment, he hoped beyond hope that Simon could win, fight his way out of the mass of humanity that was trying to kill him simply because he was American.

One last glance afforded Darius the view he didn't want—the mob surrounding Simon. It was like watching his friend—his teammate— sink into a manhole as they swarmed over him.

Section 8 had ended at that moment, at least for him. He'd later learn that their handler had agreed, and the group of seven men and one woman who'd been thrown together to work black ops missions around the globe with no su- pervision and very few, if any, rules, had been officially disbanded, the surviving members given large sums of money to buy their silence and thank them for their service.

He would have to explain to the team why he'd left Simon behind, although they'd know. They'd get it. They all prepared for that eventuality every single time they went out. It was part of the thrill.

There was no thrill now as he watched his best friend die. And he didn't turn away, stared at the spot until he couldn't see anything anymore, and knew he'd never get that image out of his mind.

Chapter One

Twenty years later

Dare O'Rourke believed in ghosts because they visited him regularly.

He woke, covered in sweat, shaking, and immediately glanced at the clock. He'd slept for fifteen minutes straight before the nightmare. A record.

The screams—both those in the dream and those that tore from his own throat whenever he allowed himself the luxury of sleep—would stay with him as long as he lived, wrapping around his soul and squeezing until he wished he'd died that terrible night.

A part of him had, but what was left wasn't a phoenix rising from the ashes. No, Dare was broken bones and not of sound mind. Might never be again, according to the Navy docs, who said the trauma Dare had faced was too severe, that he wasn't fit for duty. He had no doubt those doctors were right, wasn't sure what kind of man he'd be if he *had* been able to go the business-as-usual route.

He'd never be the same.

The CIA felt differently. *You'll survive. You'll recover. You're needed.*

And even though he knew the world needed rough men like him, no matter how fiercely the government would deny his existence if it came down to brass tacks, he told them all to fuck off and went to live in the woods. He was no longer a SEAL, the thing that had defined him, the job he'd loved for ten years.

Dare had prayed for many things that night in the jungle, including death, but none had been answered. And so he'd stopped praying and holed up alone and just tried to sleep through the night.

Three hundred sixty-three days and counting and not an unbroken sleep among them.

Three hundred sixty-four was a couple of hours away, the day giving way to the dusk, and the car coming up the private road couldn't mean anything but trouble.

Three hundred sixty-three days and no visitors. He saw people only when he went into the small town monthly for supplies. Beyond that, he remained on his property. It was quiet. He could think, whether he wanted to or not.

As for healing . . . that would all be in the eye of the beholder.

He rolled out of bed, flexed the ache from his

hands before pulling on jeans and a flannel shirt he left unbuttoned. Barefoot, he went out to greet his guest.

He met the car with his weapon drawn, put it away when the car got close enough for him to see the driver.

Adele. A member of the original Section 8—a black ops group of seven men and one woman recruited from various military branches and the CIA. All loose cannons, none of them taking command well. All of them the best at what they did. A real-life A-Team, except the reality wasn't anything like it was portrayed on television.

Dare's father—Darius—had been a member, was MIA and presumed KIA on a mission last year. At least that's what Adele had told Dare.

All Dare knew was that S8 had officially disbanded when he was thirteen, and for years, its members worked black ops missions on their own steam. Until they'd gotten a call—that call—the remaining six members and one last job. Back into the jungle they'd sworn not to go back into. *A mistake to go*, Darius told him. *We're too old.* But they were still strong, with plenty of experience. And they went anyway.

Four men never returned. Adele and Darius did, but they were never the same. Refused to talk about it and went off on more unreachable missions until they'd both disappeared more than a year ago.

Dare had wanted to assume that the secrets of the group were all dead and buried with them.

Fucking assumptions would get him every time. He knew better. His father and Adele had come back from the dead more than once.

Adele took her time getting out of the car. She was stately looking, at one time considered more handsome than pretty, with short hair and kind blue eyes, a thin frame that belied her strength. It was hard to believe she was as deadly as the men she'd worked with.

"I have a job for you," she said when she reached the porch he refused to leave. No preamble, all business. The only thing contradicting her deadliness was the frail frame she now carried.

She was sick—he could see it in her pale coloring, the darkness shading the skin under her eyes. His heart went out to her; she'd been the closest thing to a mother he'd ever had, even though she'd been far more like a mother wolf than a nurturer.

But it had been enough. "I can't."

"You're not broken, Dare." Adele sounded so damned sure, but why he wanted her reassurance, he had no idea.

He jerked his gaze to her and saw her own quiet pain that she carried, kept so close to the vest all these years. "It was all a setup."

Adele neither confirmed nor denied, but the truth of his own words haunted him.

It was a setup . . . and you were supposed to die.

A Ranger had received a dishonorable discharge for rescuing him against a direct order. Dare would never forget the soldier's face, and he doubted the soldier would ever stop seeing his.

Two men, bound by pain.

He closed his eyes briefly, thought about the way he'd been found, nearly hanging from his arms, up on a platform so he could watch the entire scene being played out in front of him.

The villagers. His guides. American peacekeepers. His team. All slaughtered in front of him.

The fire came closer now . . . and he welcomed it. Had prayed for it, even as his captors laughed at his predicament, spat in his face. Cut him with knives and ripped his nails off one by one. There was nothing he could offer them, nothing they would take from him.

He'd offered himself multiple times. They refused. He must've passed out—from pain, hunger, it didn't matter. He clawed at the wood, his wrists, forearms, fingers, all broken from trying so hard to escape chains not meant for humans to fight against. It hadn't stopped him—he'd been nearly off the platform, ripping the wood out piece by piece, when the worst of the rape happened in front of him.

It would've been too late.

Could've closed your eyes. Blocked it out. Let yourself pass out.

But if they were going to be tortured, the least he could do was not look away. And he hadn't, not even when they'd nailed his hands to the boards, not for twenty-four hours, until everyone was dead, the village was razed, the acrid smell of smoke burning his nose, his lungs. The sounds of the chopper brought him no relief, because he knew they'd save him before the fire reached him.

The group of Army Rangers had been going to another mission, stumbled on the destruction by way of the fire. They'd come in without permission, the Ranger who'd saved him taking the brunt of the blame, or so Dare had heard later.

Dare hadn't gone to the hearing for that soldier who'd saved him. It wouldn't have helped either of them. In the next months, Dare was sure the soldier would be found dead under mysterious circumstances, another in a long line of men who'd interfered in something S8 related.

He turned his attention back to Adele, who waited with a carefully cultivated pretense of patience. "Why come now?"

She hadn't seen him since right before that last mission. Hadn't come to the hospital. Hadn't called or written. And while he'd told himself it didn't bother him, it had.

"Your sister's in trouble."

Half sister. One he'd never met before out of both necessity and her mother's insistence. He didn't even know if Avery Welsh knew he existed. "I thought she was well hidden."

"We did too."

"Where is she?"

"On her way to the federal penitentiary in New York—or a cemetery—if you don't hurry."

"Are you fucking shitting me?"

She twisted her mouth wryly. "I assure you, I'm not."

"What did she do?"

"She killed two men," Adele said calmly. "The police are coming for her—she's about forty-eight hours away from being sent to jail for life. Of course, there are other men after her too, and they make the police look like the better option."

So the men who were after her had tipped off the police. "She's what—twenty-two?" A goddamned baby.

Adele nodded. "You'll have a small window of opportunity to grab her in the morning at the apartment where she's been hiding."

"You want me to . . ." He stopped, turned, ran his hands through his hair and laughed in disbelief. Spoke to the sky. "She wants me to help a killer."

"Your sister," she corrected. "Is that a problem?"

He laughed again, a sound that was rusty from severe underuse.

Avery had been secreted away with her mother before she'd been born, the relationship between her mother and Darius brief once she found out what Darius's livelihood was. But after that last mission, everything S8 related seemed to die down. Until Darius went missing. Until Dare was almost killed.

Until Adele showed up on his doorstep, dragging the past with her like an anchor.

"She's a known fugitive and I'm supposed to hide her?" he asked now.

"She's family—and she needs your protection."

He turned swiftly, fighting the urge to pin her against a column of the porch with an arm across her neck. The animal inside him was always there, lurking barely below the surface, the wildness never easily contained. "What the hell is that supposed to mean?"

Adele hadn't moved. "Don't make me spell everything out for you, Dare. You know you're still wanted. Why wouldn't she be?"

"I can't do this. Find—"

"Someone else?" she finished, smiled wanly. "There's no one but me and you, and I'm about to buy the farm, as they say. Cancer. The doctors give me a month at best."

"I'm sorry, Adele, but—"

"I know what happened to you. But we protect our own."

"I didn't choose to be a part of your group."

"No, you were lucky enough to be born into it," she said calmly.

"Yeah, that's me. Lucky."

"You're alive, aren't you?"

He wanted to mutter, *Barely,* but didn't. "Where's my father, Adele?"

She simply shrugged. "He's gone."

"Yeah, gone." Darius had been doing that since Dare was six years old.

"They're all gone—the men, *their families.* All *gone* over the course of the last six years. Do you understand?"

He had known. Dare had kept an eye on the families left behind by S8 operatives. Even though Darius had growled at him to stay the hell out of it, he'd found a line of accidents and unexplained deaths. They were all spaced widely enough apart and made enough sense not to look suspicious to the average eye.

But he wasn't the average eye. This was an S8 clean-house order, an expunging, and Dare knew he was still on that list and there was no escaping it.

For Avery, he would have to come out of hiding.

"Hiding won't stop your connection with Section 8," Adele said, as if reading his mind.

"I'm not hiding," he ground out.

"Then go to Avery—show her this from Darius."

She handed him a CD—the cover was a photograph of Avery. He glanced at the picture of the woman, and yeah, she resembled her father—the same arctic frost blue eyes—but her hair was light, not dark. She was really pretty. Too innocent looking to have committed murder, but he'd learned over the years that looks could never be trusted. "And then what? I'm no good for this."

"You're better than you think."

"Bullshit—I'm just the only one you've got."

She smiled, but it didn't reach her eyes.

He looked at the picture stuck into the clear CD case again, and something deep inside him ached for his lost childhood. He hoped Avery had had one. "I'll think about it."

With that, she walked away, turned to him when she was halfway to her car and stood stock-still in the driveway. The back of his neck prickled. "Best think fast, Dare."

It was part instinct, part the way Adele paused as if posing. She gave a small smile, a nod, her shoulders squared.

He sprang into action, yelled, "No!" as he leaped toward her, Sig drawn, but it was too late.

The gunshot rang out and he jumped back to the safety of the house, cutting his losses. Adele collapsed to the ground, motionless. A clean kill. Sniper.

She'd made the ultimate sacrifice—going out like a warrior to force him to get off his ass and into action ending a life that was almost over anyway. His father would've done the same.

Now there was nothing to be done here but get away and live. A hot extract involving just himself.

He shot off several warning rounds of his own to buy himself time. He took a quick picture of Adele with his cell phone camera and then went inside, grabbed his go bag and the guitar, then ignited the explosives he'd set up for a just-in-case scenario because, as a kid of a Section 8er, he was always a target.

That entire process took less than a minute, and then he took off in the old truck down the back road, the CD still in his hand.

Adele was too good not to know she'd been followed. She'd trapped him by bringing the trouble literally to his front door.

He cursed her, his father and everyone in that damned group as he motored down the highway, even as another part of his brain, hardwired for danger, made lists of what he'd need.

New wheels.

Guns.

New safe house with a wanted woman.

He threw the CD on the seat next to him and fingered the silver guitar pick he wore on a chain around his neck.

Goddammit, there was no escaping the past.